Jayne Ann Krentz is the critically acclaimed creator of the Arcane Society world, Dark Legacy, Ladies of Lantern Street and Rainshadow Island series. She also writes as **Amanda Quick** and **Jayne Castle**. Jayne has written more than fifty *New York Times* bestsellers under various pseudonyms and more than thirty-five million copies of her books are currently in print. She lives in the Pacific Northwest.

www.jayneannkrentz.com
www.facebook.com/JayneAnnKrentz
@JayneAnnKrentz

* Not published by Piatkus

JAYNE ANN KRENTZ

LIGHTNING IN A MIRROR

PIATKUS

PIATKUS

First published in the United States in 2022 by Berkley,
an imprint of Penguin Random House LLC
First published in Great Britain in 2022 by Piatkus

13 5 7 9 10 8 6 4 2

A CIP catalogue record for this book
is available from the British Library.

ISBN 978-0-349-43221-2

Printed and bound in Great Britain by Clays Ltd, Elcograf S.p.A.

Papers used by Piatkus are from well-managed forests
and other responsible sources.

Piatkus
An imprint of
Little, Brown Book Group
Carmelite House
50 Victoria Embankment
London EC4Y 0DZ

An Hachette UK Company
www.hachette.co.uk

www.littlebrown.co.uk

For Frank, as always, with love

LIGHTNING IN
A MIRROR

PROLOGUE

Five years earlier . . .

Harlan Rancourt stood in the shadows of the night-darkened alley and watched the medics carry his father's body out of the wreckage. The explosion had demolished an entire corner of the building. Shards of glass and slivers of metal littered the street. No one who was in the second-floor lab could have survived.

If it hadn't been for the heated quarrel that had taken place a few hours earlier, he would have died with Stenson Rancourt.

On the other side of the street the two men responsible for the explosion stood talking to the police. Harlan could not hear what they were saying but he knew they were lying, spinning a story that would portray them as innocent near-victims.

But Victor Arganbright and Lucas Pine were anything but innocent. The blast had accomplished what they had intended. It left them in control of the Foundation—the powerful, secretive organization that had been in the hands of the Rancourt family for two generations. Stenson Rancourt had intended to hand off control to a third generation.

To me, Harlan thought.

The medics loaded the body bag into the ambulance and closed the doors. Harlan turned and went deeper into the alley. He was confident no one had seen him. He was very, very good at blending into the background.

His talent for going unnoticed was the one thing that might keep him alive. Once Arganbright and Pine realized his body was not inside the demolished lab, they would start hunting for him. They would be able to throw the considerable weight of the Foundation's security apparatus behind the task.

He had tried to walk away from his inheritance, but that was no longer an option. Revenge required total commitment.

CHAPTER 1

Olivia LeClair was halfway across the parking garage and thinking about getting a cat when she realized the man coming toward her intended to murder her.

"Hi, remember me?" the killer said. "Brian. Brian Gatewood. We met at that speed date event last week. I didn't realize you lived in this apartment building. What a coincidence. I just moved in. I'm on the tenth floor."

As if she didn't have enough to deal with, given the new wave of nightmares that had been robbing her of sleep lately. The dream images came in whispers and ghostly fragments: A voice she almost recognized told her to run. A cobalt blue mirror stood in the way. Unseen monsters chased her. And now she was about to confront a very real killer. She needed a vacation.

Brian Gatewood was good-looking in an open, Mr. Nice Guy way, and he was smiling, a friendly, ever-so-slightly flirtatious smile. The misty Seattle night had dampened his jacket. His running shoes were leaving footprints on the concrete floor. He had a grocery bag cradled in one arm and a key fob in his hand. A baseball cap was angled low over his eyes.

"I remember you," she said. "Welcome to the building. I think you'll like it here. The amenities are terrific."

She accompanied the warm words with a dazzling smile. In the months since she and Catalina had opened Lark & LeClair, she had discovered she possessed a talent for acting. It came in handy in the private investigation business.

"That's why I signed the rental agreement," Brian enthused. "The amenities. What floor are you on?"

Killers were often excellent actors, too. The problem for Brian was that no matter how smooth and polished his performance, he could not disguise the faint, almost invisible wavelengths that sparked in his aura. To a woman who could read energy fields as easily as she read books, the shafts of pale radiance spelled one word: *blank*. It was the paranormal community's slang for *sociopath*.

That information, while chilling, was not what signaled Brian's intention to attack—not all sociopaths were violent. A lot of them were content to lead relatively quiet lives as con artists and fraudsters. They broke people's hearts and ripped off their money, but they didn't slice open jugulars.

But there was the other kind, the sort that fed on people's fear, pain and, in some cases, blood. Brian Gatewood was one of those. The warning blazed in his aura in the form of hot currents of bloodred energy.

"I'm on the ninth floor," she said. "You'll love the gym. It's on the top floor."

"Looking forward to trying out the equipment," Brian said.

She calculated the distance back to the relative safety of her car and then estimated how many steps she was from the locked doors of the elevator lobby. It didn't take a mathematician to know she was trapped. She didn't stand a chance of escape in either direction. Even if she could outrun Brian—doubtful, given that she was in heels—he would have no problem overtaking her while she was in the process of trying to unlock either the car door or the lobby entrance.

She stopped, careful to keep smiling. "Lucky me. I'm so glad you're here. I just remembered I left my key fob on the kitchen counter. You can let me into the lobby. I won't have to call the concierge desk and ask someone to rescue me."

Brian hesitated for a split second, just long enough to confirm her suspicion that the fob in his hand wouldn't open the lobby doors. Things were not going quite the way he had planned.

He recovered quickly. "Sure. Hang on." He glanced at the vintage camera hanging from a leather cord around her neck. "That looks like an antique."

"It is," Olivia said. "Mid-twentieth century."

"Do you collect old cameras?"

"Just this one."

He lost interest in the camera and went toward the door. The path he was following would bring him very close to her. She stepped aside as if to get out of his way. He altered course ever so slightly, just enough to ensure he closed the distance between them.

She took another step back and let her handbag slide off her shoulder onto the concrete floor.

"Damn," she said. "I just bought that bag. Now it's going to have garage dirt on it. That stuff never comes off."

She bent down, trying to appear as if she was intent on retrieving the handbag.

"I'll get it," Brian said. "So, what did you think about the speed date event? Any luck?"

He slipped the key fob into the pocket of his jacket. When his hand reappeared, she saw that his fingers were closed around a knife. He started toward her, moving fast.

"Nope, no luck," she said.

She straightened, raised the camera and peered through the viewfinder. Senses kicked up, she focused a crushing wave of energy on

Brian's aura and pressed the crystal button that, in a real camera, would have released the shutter.

Paranormal energy flared around Brian. For those with the psychic senses required to view the scene, it looked as if he was about to become the victim of spontaneous human combustion. But instead of going up in flames, he convulsed. For a few frozen seconds he stared at her in disbelief. His mouth opened on a cry of panic and rage.

"Fuck you, bitch. What are you doing to me?"

The grocery sack fell from his hand, the contents scattering across the concrete floor. Brian's eyes rolled up in his head. He collapsed with a thud that echoed in the shadows.

Olivia was stunned. She watched the unconscious man as if he were a snake. Her pulse skittered. She started to shake. Great. The last thing she needed was a panic attack.

She forced herself to concentrate on what to do next. A faint but fairly steady aura still glowed around Brian. Okay, so he wasn't dead. There was no way to know how long he would remain unconscious. Maybe minutes. Maybe forever.

She had discovered the camera in Swan Antiques a few days ago. She knew almost nothing about it—just that she had some sort of intuitive connection to it. She had become obsessed, never letting it out of her sight. She carried it everywhere. Slept with it beside her bed. Sure, that was not normal, but *not normal* was pretty much the definition of an obsession.

The realization that the old camera might be a psychic weapon had come over her slowly but surely. Tonight she had been forced to put the suspicion to the test. Now she was certain she could have killed Brian if she had generated a little more heat through the crystal lens.

She got her senses and the incipient panic attack under control with an effort of will and studied the items that had tumbled out of the grocery bag—a roll of duct tape, a wig and a syringe.

She drew one more deep breath, took out her phone and called a familiar number. Roger Gossard, the head of Gossard Consulting, a cutting-edge psychological forensics agency, answered on the first ring.

"Olivia," he said, his voice sharp with concern. "What's wrong? Are you all right?"

She looked at the unconscious man and the items that had fallen out of the grocery sack.

"Gatewood was waiting for me inside the garage," she said.

"*Inside?* Shit. I don't know how he got past us. Where are you? Are you safe?"

"I'm all right. I'm in the garage near the elevator lobby. Gatewood is unconscious." She paused, swallowed hard. "I think he suffered a seizure."

"A seizure?"

She put one hand on the camera and looked at the fallen man. "Maybe a brain aneurysm. How should I know? I'm not a doctor."

"I'm on my way in with the team," Roger said. "We'll be there in a couple of minutes. We'll take charge. Are you sure you're okay?"

"Yes. Remember, you promised to keep Lark and LeClair out of this. I'm supposed to be working undercover. If the media finds out our firm was involved in the investigation, they'll run with it. Catalina and I are still trying to live down the rumor that we're running a psychic investigation agency. We don't want to attract any more clients who think we read palms and tell fortunes."

"Don't worry. Gossard Consulting doesn't want the wrong publicity, either. Any hint of the paranormal would hurt our credibility. Got to protect the brand."

"Speaking of your brand, you'll be thrilled to know your psychological profile was right about one thing. The Speed Date Killer really does look like Mr. Nice Guy."

CHAPTER 2

T hought you were dead," Victor Arganbright said.

"You mean you hoped I was dead." Harlan Rancourt contemplated one of the hundreds of pictures that cluttered Victor's large paneled office. "You never really believed I was permanently out of the way, did you? That's why you spent the past five years looking for me."

Five years. He had been on the run for five very long years, hiding not just from the Foundation but from the past. In the end he had been forced to acknowledge that, although he could probably evade Arganbright's security people indefinitely, he could never outrun the past. It was always there, one step behind him. He was so damned tired of running.

"You did a good job of hiding," Lucas Pine said.

"Coming from you, that is a compliment," Harlan said.

He studied the painting a moment longer. The oil was a mediocre nineteenth-century picture of the oracle of Delphi. It wasn't much to look at. The oracle was shown in her classic pose, seated on a three-legged stool that straddled the crack in the floor of a vast cavern. The figure, draped in a hood and flowing robes, delivered her prophecy as she inhaled the mysterious fumes that seeped up through the opening in the rock. Those who had paid handsomely for her pronouncements waited nearby, anxious to hear her cryptic warnings and advice.

It was, of course, up to the customer to interpret the meaning of the prophecy. You paid your money and you took your chances.

The pictures hanging on the walls and stacked on the floor of the office varied in quality, artistic style and value. Some were hundreds of years old. Others were modern. But they all had the same theme. Arganbright was obsessed with the subject of oracles.

So am I, Harlan thought.

He turned away from the painting and regarded the two men he was confronting. He was well aware he was taking a risk, but it was a carefully calculated risk. That was the only kind he took, and he was very good at the business. He was a grand master–level chess player when it came to judging the odds and predicting the outcomes. But even for him this was a major move. If he was wrong it could cost him his life, or worse. He might end up in a locked ward at Halcyon Manor, the psychiatric hospital where the Foundation confined the real monsters.

It was late afternoon. Arganbright and Pine had been working in the office when he had called Victor's private number to inform them that he was standing thirty floors below their penthouse at the front door of the Foundation tower. After ending the call he had been met by two armed guards and escorted upstairs in a private elevator.

Victor was seated behind a massive desk. Lucas lounged on the corner, one elegantly shod foot braced on the floor, arms casually crossed. They had dismissed the security team, but Harlan was sure both men were armed. They watched him as if he was one of the psychic monsters the Foundation hunted down and housed in Halcyon.

Monsters like Larissa Whittier.

They all had good reason to be wary of each other. It was no secret his father had viewed him as the heir apparent to what had become the Rancourt family business—or criminal mob, depending on
your point of view—the Foundation. He knew that as long as he was
alive, he represented a threat to the men who were now at the top—
Arganbright and Pine.

They made an intriguing couple. Pine, silver-haired and polished,
had the looks and stage-trained voice of an actor. It would have
been easy to assume he was just another retired Las Vegas show
personality—a former lounge singer or a magician, perhaps. He was
retired, all right—from the CIA.

Victor Arganbright appeared at first glance to be Pine's polar opposite. He radiated the grim, humorless demeanor of a man who was
haunted night and day by his self-imposed task of tracking down a
dangerous conspiracy.

Harlan understood. He was obsessed with the same conspiracy.
It went by the code name Vortex, and it dated from the days of the
top secret Bluestone Project. Bluestone was a clandestine government
program that had been established in the latter half of the twentieth
century to conduct research into the paranormal. At its height it had
consisted of as many as three labs, possibly more. But the entire project had been shut down decades earlier, in the last century. The order
had been given to destroy the labs and any records associated with
them.

But it was impossible to conceal a secret as big and as dangerous
as Bluestone forever. Over the years, rumors had circulated. Physical
evidence in the form of objects infused with a lot of hot energy had
surfaced. In the case of the tiny town of Fogg Lake in the Cascade
mountains in Washington State, the DNA of an entire population
had been changed, thanks to a disastrous explosion in the secret
Bluestone lab that had been built in the nearby cave system.

The paranormal gases that had been released had blanketed the community in a strange mist. The locals had slept for two days. When they woke up they discovered that things had changed; they had changed. Some began seeing auras. Others had visions or developed uncanny abilities. The paranormal energy released in the explosion had awakened latent psychic talents. The new traits had proved to be inheritable.

"How did you do it?" Lucas prompted.

"How did I stay off your to-do list?" Harlan said. He crossed the room to stand at the floor-to-ceiling windows overlooking the Las Vegas Strip. There was still some daylight in the desert sky—the real action wouldn't start until night fell—but it was always midnight inside the casinos. "I used the same technique you're using to conceal the Foundation here in Vegas. Closing down the Los Angeles operation and moving the headquarters here was a brilliant move, by the way. It's the last place anyone would think to look for a government contractor devoted to paranormal research, investigation and security."

Victor cranked back in the big leather chair. "You're telling me you've been hiding in plain sight?"

"You could say that. I've also been doing a lot of traveling."

"We sure as hell never figured you'd take a dead-end job in the federal government," Victor said.

"Good benefits," Harlan said.

Victor ignored that. "The position of director of the Agency for the Investigation of Atypical Phenomena has been empty for years. Decades, in fact."

"And no one even noticed," Lucas added dryly.

"Which was very convenient for you, wasn't it?" Harlan said. He turned away from the window and wandered across the room to study another oracle picture. The restless energy that had been driving him for days was pushing him, urging action. His intuition warned him time was running out. "Somehow the money just kept flowing. I assume that was your work, Pine?"

"Don't look at me," Lucas said. "It's not my fault the agency's budget keeps getting approved year after year. You know how it is with government spending. Once it starts, it's hard to shut off."

"Especially when the budget of said agency is top secret and off-the-books," Harlan said.

"Why are you here, Rancourt?" Victor asked.

"I just got this cool job as director of the Agency for the Investigation of Atypical Phenomena a few days ago," Harlan said. "Like any ambitious new manager, I wanted to get out into the field immediately to see how the agency's primary contractor was performing."

"The Foundation isn't the agency's primary contractor—it's the agency's *only* contractor," Lucas said. "And for the record, this is a private corporation. It doesn't take orders from the government. It has a contract with the Feds, which can be canceled at any time."

Harlan studied another painting. "The Foundation may not take orders from the agency, but it is happy to take money from it. I am now the person in charge of approving your budget."

"Are you threatening to cut off our funding?" Victor said. "If so, you're wasting your time. I'll admit the government money is useful, but we can survive without it. You'd be amazed at how many eccentric billionaires are delighted to finance paranormal research."

"Eccentric billionaires such as yourself?" Harlan said. "I know about your private hedge fund. You've done very well in the markets, haven't you? You've got a real talent for investing. Still, I doubt that you want to lose access to your government slush fund. And those government-issued security credentials your agents carry probably come in handy on occasion."

"We can handle the financial end of things and produce our own credentials if need be," Lucas said. "Tell us why you're here."

Harlan turned away from the painting. "You know why I'm here."

Victor's eyes glittered. Energy shifted in the atmosphere.

"Vortex," he said.

Harlan looked at him. "I'm sure you're aware of the chatter in the paranormal underworld."

There were a lot of myths and legends linked to the lost labs of the Bluestone Project, but not much in the way of hard facts. The secrets of the Vortex lab were the most deeply buried—literally. In the years following the shutdown of the project, everyone believed to have worked inside the Vortex lab had disappeared or died under suspicious circumstances.

For the most part, Bluestone had faded into the dusty storage drawer of the archives reserved for failed and/or potentially embarrassing government projects. Paranormal weapons? Psychic spies? Assassins who could kill without a trace? Get real. These days no sensible, ambitious politician or bureaucrat wanted to be associated with paranormal research. It was a guaranteed path to career disaster.

But if even a few of the rumors about Vortex were true, the old lab was a catastrophe waiting to happen.

Victor sat forward and folded his hands on top of the desk. He had the intent, focused vibe of a hunter who has caught the scent of prey. "The chatter has been getting louder. What's your interest in Vortex?"

"The same as yours," Harlan said. "If that lab still exists, it's extremely dangerous. We have to find it before someone else does."

"'We'?" Lucas repeated carefully.

"We," Harlan said.

Victor's eyes narrowed. "Your father and your grandfather chased the rumors of Vortex for years. And now you're after it. Why come to us?"

"I'm ninety-five percent certain I have a way to locate the lab," Harlan said. "But I'm going to need some help."

A great stillness settled on the room. For a moment no one moved.

"If you know where the lab is located, why did you come here?" Lucas asked.

"Because he doesn't know where it is," Victor said slowly. He did not take his gaze off Harlan. "He needs us to find it."

"Not you, specifically," Harlan said. "I need an oracle."

Victor's brows shot upward. "You make it sound as if there is more than one."

"The talent is not common, but yes, there is more than one. I need the right one."

Decision time. He took his phone out of the pocket of his rumpled trench coat and started toward Victor's desk. He stopped when one of the paintings caught his eye. A chill of knowing iced his blood. The hair on the back of his neck lifted. He stared at the picture, riveted.

"Where did you get this?" he asked.

For a heartbeat he thought Victor would not answer.

"I picked it up at an auction," Victor said. "It was cheap. There were no other bidders."

The painting was unique in that it was not a traditional version of the oracle theme. Instead of a cavern, the hooded figure stood in the foreground of a vintage mid-twentieth-century laboratory. The instruments and devices on the workbenches looked clunky by modern design standards. They were studded with dials and switches. There were no computer keyboards, no monitors, no bright screens.

Several of the machines appeared to have been modified. A large paper chart on the wall was labeled *Paranormal Light Spectrum*.

The handful of men and women gathered around the oracle were dressed in classic lab coats, complete with plastic pocket protectors that held pens and small spiral-bound notebooks. Everyone in the scene stared at the oracle with expressions that ran the gamut from shock and disbelief to outright horror.

The oracle's features were obscured by the hood. She was not perched on a three-legged stool. She stood, one arm raised, finger pointing at a strange structure in the middle of the room—a crystal pyramid enclosed in a glass chamber. The pyramid was large enough to hold a human figure standing upright. The door was a dark blue mirror.

The oracle's prophecy was written in flowing script across the bottom of the painting. *Here there be monsters.*

Harlan managed to wrench his gaze away from the picture. "It's the Vortex lab. It must be."

"I agree," Victor said.

"It was done by someone who was there," Harlan said.

"Or by someone who saw a photograph," Lucas suggested.

"I think the oracle was the artist," Harlan said.

"Or else she took a picture and had someone else paint it," Victor said.

"The question, of course," Lucas said, "is why go to the trouble of creating a painting of the scene? If there was a photograph, why not preserve it? You could make as many copies as you wanted. And why use the iconography of the Delphi oracle?"

"Someone wanted to leave a message that had a shot at surviving," Harlan said quietly.

"Exactly." Victor grunted with satisfaction, as if Harlan had just confirmed his own conclusion. "Photographs are fragile. In the era of the Bluestone Project you couldn't put them online. You dumped them into boxes along with hundreds of other pictures that got tossed into the trash when you died. Even if they did last, they deteriorated. A properly done oil painting, on the other hand, can last for hundreds of years."

"And people hesitate to throw away an interesting work of art," Lucas added. "The artist who did that picture was good. The subject is unusual and, therefore, intriguing. It makes the viewer ask questions. Art like that has a shot at surviving."

"That was what it was designed to do," Harlan said. "But only those who know something about Vortex would ask the right questions. I assume you examined the back of the canvas?"

"We took the frame apart," Victor assured him. "Checked everything. No hidden signature. No date. Nothing. Looked at every object in the picture with a magnifying glass. Didn't find any clues to the location of the lab."

"The oracle," Harlan said.

Victor fixed him with an intent gaze. "What about her?"

"I need the oracle who is a direct descendant of the one in that picture."

"We're aware of only one true oracle," Victor said. "Harmony, the librarian in Fogg Lake. She doesn't have any connection to Vortex. She's been predicting storms and destruction for months now. We think the prophecies are Vortex-related, but she hasn't been able to come up with anything concrete that we can use to find the old lab."

Harlan brushed that aside. "I'm not talking about the Fogg Lake oracle. I need the one in Seattle. Olivia LeClair."

Lucas and Victor exchanged bewildered glances.

Lucas shook his head. "Olivia isn't an oracle. She's an aura reader—a very good one, but that's her only talent. She's co-owner of a private investigation agency, Lark and LeClair."

"Let's hope for everyone's sake you're wrong," Harlan said. "Because if she doesn't have her grandmother's talent, we don't stand a chance of finding the Vortex lab in time."

"In time for what?" Lucas asked.

"That's the bad news," Harlan said. "I don't know exactly what will happen if we don't find Vortex. Whatever it is, it will not be good."

Victor's eyes burned. "You're in a rush because you think someone else has picked up the trail."

"And is closing in fast," Harlan said. "The chatter among the collectors, raiders and dealers who work the paranormal artifacts trade has been increasing for a year, but in the past month it has become so intense that something must have changed."

Victor sat quietly, not speaking.

Lucas glanced at the warning written on the painting. "If even some of the stories about what went on inside the Vortex lab are accurate, we have a problem."

"They were playing with forces they did not understand in that damn lab," Victor said. "Forces they could not control."

"My grandfather and my father were convinced they were trying to create enhanced talents—super soldiers and spies—that could be used for military purposes," Harlan said.

Victor sighed. "They got monsters instead."

"That's not the worst part," Harlan said. "After all, you can kill monsters."

Lucas raised silver brows. "You should know."

Harlan looked at him.

"We're getting off track here," Victor said. "All right, Rancourt, I'll bite. What's worse than having to hunt down monsters?"

"That's the rest of the bad news," Harlan said. "I don't know. You were right, the Vortex team was playing with forces they did not understand. We've learned a few things about paranormal physics since Bluestone was shut down, one of which is that paranormal energy tends to hang around for a long time. Decades. Centuries. That old lab must be very hot."

"Like the Fogg Lake lab," Lucas said.

Victor slowly shook his head. "Whatever was going on at Vortex was a lot more dangerous than what was happening at Fogg Lake. That was why they tried to erase every scrap of evidence about it when they shut it down. Whoever took charge of that project did one hell of a thorough job."

"'Thorough' is one word for it," Harlan said. "'Ruthless' is another. If any of the Vortex staff survived, they did such a good job of hiding that neither my grandfather nor my father could find them, and trust me, they both looked—hard."

"If Vortex was creating monsters, they must have been using some sort of paranormal tech," Lucas said. "If the machine was not properly deactivated when the lab was destroyed, we should assume, until proven otherwise, that the device is in working condition."

"Even if it isn't functional," Victor said, "we all know there will be no shortage of ambitious fools who think it can be made to operate again. And that means people will get killed."

Lucas's mouth tightened. "Harlan is right. We don't have any choice. We need to combine forces to find Vortex. I'll call security and get a team together—"

"No," Harlan said. "Not yet. I don't need a lot of your security people. They'll get in the way and draw too much attention. Put the team on standby. First, I have to secure the cooperation of the oracle. Everything depends on her."

Victor drummed his fingers on the desk. "What makes you think Olivia is the descendant of the woman in the painting, Rancourt?"

"I can't be absolutely certain," Harlan admitted. "But the odds are she's the granddaughter of a woman named Grace Goodwin. According to my grandfather's private files, Goodwin was identified as a researcher who may have been on the Vortex staff."

"Your grandfather's *private* files?" Victor snorted. "What the hell happened to them?"

Harlan shrugged. "Don't tell me you were naive enough to believe the files you found in my father's office were all of the Rancourt records."

Victor's mouth twisted. "We knew there was a high probability the Rancourts had hidden a few secrets."

"My grandfather began collecting the private files when he established the Foundation," Harlan said. "My father continued the practice. I inherited them."

"Where are they?" Victor growled.

"Let's talk about that some other time. Priorities." Harlan opened his phone and pulled up the photo of another painting. "I want to show you something."

He put the phone on the desk so that Victor and Lucas could both see it. They reacted very much as he had expected: Intrigued and curious at first. Then comprehension struck with the force of a bolt of lightning.

"Another oracle painting," Victor said. "Looks like it was done by the same artist who did my Vortex lab picture. Same warning. *Here there be monsters.*"

"I think that was the artist's signature," Harlan said.

Lucas looked up. "Where did you get this?"

"Long story," Harlan said. "Some other time. I need to get to Seattle."

"How do we know you didn't come here asking for our cooperation because you think you've figured out a way to regain control of the Foundation?" Victor asked.

"I'm already in charge, remember?" Harlan said. "The Foundation reports to the director of the Agency for the Investigation of Atypical Phenomena. That would be me."

"Thought we made it clear," Lucas said. "The Foundation is an independent corporation."

"With one client—my agency." Harlan picked up his phone and slipped it into his coat pocket. "For what it's worth, I don't trust you, either. But I suggest we work out the details of our association some other time. At the moment we're stuck with using each other. This is one of those 'the enemy of my enemy is my friend' situations."

"Maybe," Victor said. "Regardless, there's something we should talk about before I make that call to Olivia LeClair. Do you know a woman named Larissa Whittier?"

Harlan ignored the chill in his gut. "Skilled at making paranormal poisons. Murdered a couple of people, tried to steal some dangerous artifacts that belonged to my grandfather. Attempted to destroy two generations of the Chastain family. Motive—revenge. She's currently in a fugue state in a locked ward at Halcyon."

"I see you've read the classified report," Victor said. "I asked you if you know her."

"Never met the woman," Harlan said. "The Rancourts aren't a close family."

Victor and Lucas went very still.

"You do know who she is, then?" Lucas asked.

"Imagine my surprise a few days ago when I discovered I had a half sister," Harlan said. He glanced at his watch. "I'll take the Foundation jet to Seattle this evening. Call the oracle. Tell her I want to see her in her office first thing in the morning."

"You can fly commercial," Victor growled. "Plenty of time to get to Seattle before the meeting with Olivia."

"I don't want to waste time sitting around an airport."

"Do you have any idea what it costs to put the company plane in the air?" Victor muttered.

"As a matter of fact, I do," Harlan said. "I'm the guy who approves your budget now, remember?"

Lucas grimaced. "Who knew a Rancourt had a sense of humor?"

"I wasn't joking," Harlan said.

Victor groaned. "I'll call Olivia, explain the situation and make sure she knows the Foundation security team in Seattle will protect her as long as you're working with her."

"Make the call and tell her who I am and to expect me, but I told you, we can't risk a security team, not even the one in Seattle," Harlan said. "Pulling in security would send up red flags to anyone who is watching. We need to keep this close."

Victor pondered that briefly. "I'll try to persuade her to assist in the investigation, but I'll warn you right now, she might refuse. The Rancourts left a nasty reputation for the Foundation behind. We're still dealing with the fallout. As far as Olivia is concerned, she has no reason to trust you."

"I'll deal with Olivia."

Lucas looked skeptical. "How do you plan to do that?"

"Simple," Harlan said. "I've got something she wants, and I discovered long ago that's more than enough to gain someone's cooperation."

Lucas's eyes got very cold. "What do you have that she would want badly enough to make her willing to cooperate with a Rancourt?"

"A lead on her mother's killer," Harlan said.

CHAPTER 3

Not what I expected," Lucas said.

"No." Victor contemplated the door through which Harlan had just left. "He's not his father or his grandfather. But he is quite possibly a lot more dangerous."

"The interesting thing is that he doesn't look like much of a threat." Lucas thought about Harlan Rancourt's surprisingly normal aura. "He's definitely got some talent, but nothing special. Most of our security and research personnel are stronger. I'd say he's probably an average intuitive talent."

"If the rumors are true that he handled security for his father—not the routine enforcer stuff—Harlan tracked down the monsters. They said the bad guys never saw him coming."

"That was over five years ago," Lucas said. "We've always considered the possibility that he was there that night and that the blast was meant for us. We figured something went wrong with the timing, right? The bomb exploded prematurely? If Harlan was nearby, he might have been wounded by the blast. The shock waves could have done permanent damage to his energy field."

Victor tipped his head to one side and squinted a little. "That might explain why he is no longer a high-end talent, assuming he was in the old days. But just because he lacks some serious psychic power doesn't mean he's not dangerous."

"Granted"—Lucas exhaled—"it's easier to commit murder with a gun than it is to do it with some exotic monster talent."

"But the gun or a knife or any other weapon always leaves evidence," Victor said. "Regardless, what worries me now is that we don't know his full agenda. I'm convinced he's as desperate to locate Vortex as we are. But then what?"

"One obvious possibility comes to mind," Lucas said. "Revenge. He probably blames us for the death of his father and the fact that we are now running the Foundation. We stole his inheritance. He knows as well as we do that his job as the director of the Agency for the Investigation of Atypical Phenomena doesn't give him any real power. We could cut the Foundation free tomorrow. If, in addition to everything else, he lost his talent five years ago, he's got one hell of a motive for vengeance."

"Five years is a long time to wait to take revenge." Victor paused. "But you know what they say."

"A dish best served cold. Larissa Whittier certainly took her time about the business. Speaking of Whittier, I think Rancourt was telling the truth when he said he only recently learned that she existed and that they were related by blood. He certainly didn't seem to be interested in her."

"Maybe," Victor said. "I'm not so sure."

"Really? You picked up some nuance that I missed? You're the one who makes a point of ignoring emotions and subtle social signals."

"That's just it. There wasn't any emotion. No nuance. No subtle social signals. Nothing to ignore. But what do I know? I'm just the guy who connects the dots."

Lucas looked at the man who was his soul mate, the man he had never expected to find—the love of his life. He hadn't been looking for love when he sat down at the poker table on that long-ago night. He had intended to pick up some easy money—he was very good at poker—and then hit a certain nightclub.

The vibe of the man sitting on the other side of the table had changed his plans for the evening. By the following morning, his plans for the rest of his life had changed. He had known that even if he never saw Victor again, he would never forget him; would never *want* to forget him. Their blowout Las Vegas wedding had put a public seal on the unshakable connection between them.

"I can't believe he managed to sneak up on us the way he did," Lucas said. "Got to admit I never expected him to show up at the front door."

"Huh."

Victor got to his feet and went to stand at the bank of windows overlooking the Strip.

Lucas watched him. "What?"

Victor clasped his hands behind his back and watched a vintage pink Cadillac cruise the Strip. "Five years ago, he disappeared without a trace. The next thing we know he's not only at our front door—he's in charge of the government agency that is our one and only client. We *should* have seen him coming."

"Can't argue with that," Lucas said.

Victor snorted. "It's enough to make me wonder if the old story about him is true."

"Which story would that be?"

"The one that claims he has the ability to make himself invisible," Victor said.

"There's no such thing as a talent for invisibility."

"That we know of. There's so much about the paranormal that we haven't begun to discover. Theoretically, a talent for manipulating light waves might make some form of invisibility a possibility."

"Maybe," Lucas said. "But that would require an incredibly powerful talent, and powerful talents have powerful energy fields. Harlan Rancourt's field looked so damn normal. Low-grade psychic at best."

"That's good, I suppose. It means he won't scare the daylights out of Olivia when they meet."

"Trust me, if she walked past him on the street, she wouldn't look twice."

CHAPTER 4

If I disappeared tomorrow would you walk into hell to find me?"
Olivia asked.

She did not look up from her phone. She wasn't supposed to be
on it. The rules of the speed date event were quite specific about that.
All phones, watches and assorted tech were to be powered down for
the evening. But she had concluded the event was a waste of time, so
she had palmed her phone from her handbag. She was now holding it
under the edge of the cocktail table, where the event coordinator
could not see it.

The knee-length burnt orange wool coat she was examining was
stunning, but sadly, the color was over-the-top for Seattle. Most of
the outerwear on the city's streets came in shades of gray, black, navy
and forest green. If she were to stroll down Pine Street in a burnt
orange coat, she might as well carry a sign that shouted *tourist*.

The man who had just sat down on the other side of the small
round table did not respond to the question. With a sigh, she looked

up. It was obvious from his uncertain expression that he thought she was texting.

"I said, if I disappeared tomorrow would you walk into hell to find me?" she said.

"Excuse me?" He looked around and then leaned forward. He lowered his voice. "I think they said that we should turn off our phones."

"Sorry." She dropped the phone into her large handbag, wedging it between her turmeric-yellow wallet and the vintage camera. She took a closer look at her new date. The name tag stuck on his shirt identified him as Nathan.

"Hi, Nathan. I'm Olivia," she said, going for bright and sparkly. "I'll repeat my question. If I disappeared tomorrow would you walk into hell to find me?"

"Uh." Nathan got a deer-in-the-headlights look.

She recognized the expression. Nathan was rapidly coming to the conclusion that she was weird. Within the next thirty seconds he would do what the previous dates had done—excuse himself and take off to find the restroom, where he would hide out until the bell rang.

It was not Nathan's fault she had signed up for the Four Event Success Guaranteed package offered by the speed date agency. So far most of the people she had met had been nice. A bit boring—but nice. The experiment had been a disaster for her, however.

She had purchased the package because it was 20 percent off. The first event had been a washout, but she had told herself to be optimistic. You couldn't expect immediate success. But now she was midway through the second event and the prospects were looking even more dismal.

"I'm not sure exactly what you mean," Nathan said.

He did a quick furtive glance around the room. It didn't take any psychic talent to know he was searching for the restrooms.

She gave him another shiny smile. "The matchmaker said we are supposed to ask each other questions. That's my question."

"Oh." Nathan cleared his throat. "Well, uh, I guess it would, you know, *depend*."

At least Nathan was considering his answer, not running for the restroom. That was promising.

"What would it depend on?" she asked.

"How well I knew you. Whether or not you and I were, you know, close."

"And if we were close?" she pressed. "Then would you walk into hell to find me?"

Panic sparked in Nathan's eyes. He glanced at the table where the event coordinator sat. When he realized there was no salvation coming from that direction, he made a heroic effort to move forward.

"My turn," he said, bubbling with artificial enthusiasm. "My question is, where do you like to go on vacation?"

"Hawaii. My turn. If I went missing would you walk into—"

"I guess I'd call your friends first," Nathan said. He sat back in the booth, putting a little more distance between them. "See if they knew where you were. Then, uh, maybe call the cops. Hey, I like Hawaii, too. Do you snorkel?"

"No." She leaned forward, closing the space he had just made. "How hard would you look for me?"

"Well, uh, I'm not an expert when it comes to search-and-rescue work. Don't you need a dog for that?" Nathan shot to his feet. "Excuse me. Gotta hit the restroom. Be right back."

And another one bites the dust. No, that wasn't right, Olivia thought. *I'm the one who just bit the dust. Again.* She realized she didn't care. The speed date experiment was a failure. If she hadn't bought the Four Event Success Guaranteed package she would leave right now. But she had made an investment, and the fine print was firm—no refunds.

The event coordinator rang a bell and announced a short break.

Olivia opened her phone again. Definitely not the burnt orange coat, but maybe something similar in gray. No, she hated gray. She had way too much of it in her closet—outerwear, mostly. Underneath her jackets and coats she usually wore the rich, vivid colors she loved, but she was careful to wear them with caution, aware people would think she was from out of town. There was a Pacific Northwest look, after all. Tonight she had opted for a cobalt blue sheath but she had dialed back the impact with a cropped and fitted black jacket, black heels and a black handbag.

She gave up on the shopping, opened the page of the animal shelter and reviewed the photos of cats available for adoption. She had visited the page a number of times in the past few days, studying each new arrival with great care. None had stood out as the Right Cat.

Tonight, however, she was excited to see a new addition to the list, a gray domestic shorthair. The caption said his name was Joe. He was not the handsomest cat on the page. There was nothing particularly striking about him, except for his eyes—they seemed to be looking right at her—but she was drawn to him.

She was studying the details of his life before he arrived at the shelter—there weren't many—when the woman at the table on the other side of the booth spoke up.

"I don't think we're supposed to be on our phones," the woman said in a low voice.

"I've got the sound off," Olivia said.

"Smart. So, any luck with the dates?"

"No," Olivia said. "You?"

"A couple of possibilities. A lawyer and a guy who says he's got a hot start-up."

"Every computer engineer in Seattle says they've got a hot start-up."

"I know. My name is Elly, by the way."

"I'm Olivia."

"I'm not interested in a long-term relationship," Elly said. "I just want to find someone who's into cross-country skiing and likes to drink wine afterward."

"That shouldn't be too difficult."

"That's what I thought when I registered with this agency."

"At least your dates aren't all making excuses to head for the restroom."

"No." Elly hesitated a beat. "None of my business, but do you want some friendly advice?"

"Sure."

"I couldn't help overhearing your conversations this evening. I'm a psychologist. I feel I should tell you that you are sabotaging yourself."

"I don't understand," Olivia said.

"Your first question—the one about walking into hell—is not designed to open a dialogue."

"I don't want a dialogue, I want an answer. After I get the right answer we can start a dialogue."

"The thing is, a question like yours is pretty much guaranteed to send a prospective date running for the hills—or, in this case, the restroom," Elly said patiently. "It's not a normal opening to a conversation with a stranger. It's an unsubtle way of demanding a commitment before you even know the guy's last name."

"I'm trying to be efficient," Olivia said. "There's no point wasting time on someone who doesn't give the right answer."

"Has it occurred to you that a man who gives you the answer you think you want might turn out to be a little strange?"

"How?"

"Obsessive?" Elly suggested.

"The agency claims they run background checks on all their clients."

"Obsessive personalities are not easy to detect in a standard background check. Case in point, the Speed Date Killer. You must have seen the news. He used agencies like this one to hunt for targets."

"Way to send a few chills down my spine."

"Sorry. Just trying to make my point."

Olivia drummed her blue nails on the table while she considered the criticism. "You're right. I need to be more strategic."

"That would be my advice."

The bell chimed. There was a moment or two of noise and commotion as each man moved on to the next table. Most of the women made notes. Olivia went back to the cat adoption page and took another look at Joe while she waited for her next date.

She was reminding herself that adopting a cat was a huge responsibility when a sudden shock of awareness raised the fine hairs on the back of her neck. Adrenaline jolted through her, kicking up her pulse and her other senses. She recognized the all-too-familiar fight-or-flight response.

She caught her breath and looked up in time to watch her new date lower himself into the seat across from her. The man moved as if he was half leopard. It was both intriguing and unnerving. If she had been walking down the street and he had leaped out of a dark alley she would not have been able to move fast enough to escape.

She registered the heat and power in his aura. *Monster.* He wasn't the first one she had encountered. Her best friend and business partner, Catalina, had recently married a man with an aura that, technically speaking, qualified as a monster talent. Slater Arganbright. When you got involved with the Foundation you learned that when it came to monsters there were nuances. Serious nuances.

The dark-haired monster with the blazing aura watched her with the eyes of a man who wrestled demons on a nightly basis. Scary? Yes, under the right circumstances. But she had recently discovered she could be more than a little scary herself.

His gaze shifted to her phone. She realized he could see Joe. Hastily she turned off the tech and dropped it into her handbag. Resting one hand protectively on the bag as if trying to conceal a secret, she examined her date more closely.

His name tag read *John*.

Pity about his style, or lack thereof. John looked as if he was deliberately trying to fade into the woodwork. The dark gray suit with its white shirt and narrow, navy blue tie were so ordinary and so un-Seattle that he actually stood out in a room filled with men dressed in various versions of the Pacific Northwest gear look—a casual mash-up of jeans, sneakers, black pullovers and backpacks. His hair was cut short and neatly parted on the side. He wore a pair of black-framed glasses.

Everything about him shouted *ordinary, boring, nonthreatening.* He reminded her of the sign posted on the outskirts of her hometown, Fogg Lake: *Welcome to Fogg Lake. Nothing to See Here.* And just as with Fogg Lake, there were a lot of secrets under the surface.

Her new date was the most interesting man in the room.

She took a deep breath and lowered her talent so that she was no longer distracted by his fascinating aura. She did not want to scare off this date. She had to open a dialogue. She knew how to do this. She interviewed nervous clients every day at Lark & LeClair.

"Hi," she said, trying for flirty and charming. Nonthreatening. Her inner voice was shrieking, *Don't screw up.* "My name is Olivia and my question—"

"The answer is yes," John the monster said. "If you disappeared I would walk into hell to find you. I know the way. I've been there."

CHAPTER 5

Olivia stared at him. "Who are you?"

It was clear she was beyond startled or surprised. She was disoriented. Shaken. Stunned. What Harlan did not understand was why he was feeling some very similar sensations. Sure, it had been a long day. A long week. A long five years. Still. No excuses. He had spent a lot of time and effort learning the discipline of self-control.

He reminded himself he could not afford to lose focus. He leaned forward and lowered his voice so that he would not be overheard.

"My name isn't John," Harlan said. "I just grabbed the name tag of someone who apparently did not show up tonight. I'm Harlan Rancourt. I believe you're expecting me."

The stunned expression vanished from her amazing eyes. She pulled herself together in a heartbeat.

"Well, crap," she said.

"I get that a lot."

She slid out of the booth and reached back for her handbag and coat. "Let's go. Tonight has been a waste of time. Might as well do some work."

He rose and prepared to follow her. The woman seated in the neighboring booth gave Olivia a small knowing smile. *What the hell was that about?* he wondered.

There was no time to analyze the situation. Olivia was on her way to the front of the restaurant, moving fast. He hurried to catch up with her.

Okay, he had not expected a joyous welcome—he was well aware the Rancourt name was anathema to many of those currently connected to the Foundation. His father's old loyalists had been kicked out or otherwise sidelined, and there were probably more than a few of Stenson's enemies deeply embedded in the organization. Nevertheless, for some inexplicable reason he was jolted by Olivia LeClair's lack of warmth.

Focus, man. You've got a job to do. You're not here to get laid.

Maybe that was the problem. It had been a long time since he'd been involved in a sexual relationship. Vortex had taken over his life in the past few months. But he would be willing to allow an interruption to his monastic routine for Olivia. He had been studying her from afar for the past few weeks, researching her online, pulling what information he could from the Rancourt files.

He had discovered she had an edgy, stylish vibe and that she spent a lot of time in art galleries. Her auburn hair was cut in a sleek wedge. If he had not known she was a private investigator he would have assumed she was an artist or an interior designer. He did not possess an edgy, stylish vibe—to his knowledge he did not possess any particular vibe—and he could not remember the last time he had walked into an art gallery for the sake of the experience. If he happened to be in one it was because he was looking for a picture that involved an oracle.

At the entrance of the restaurant he shrugged into his well-traveled trench coat and retrieved his duffel bag from the seating host. He waited while Olivia slipped on a sleek dark green coat that framed her face with a high, wide collar. He did not offer to assist her. He was pretty sure she would not thank him. And, all right, he was afraid to touch her. He did not need another psychic rush like the one that had made him stop breathing a few minutes ago.

When she was ready he opened the door of the restaurant and ushered her out into the chilly Seattle night. He glanced back at the sign in the window. *Closed for a private event.*

"Does that speed date concept really work?" he asked.

"Not for me; not yet, at any rate." Olivia gripped the strap of her handbag very tightly, evidently afraid he would try to steal it. "I've been told that I'm sabotaging myself with my first question."

"The one about walking into hell? Well, I showed up, gave you the right answer, and here we are, leaving together."

Olivia shot him a withering look. "Not funny."

"Right." He adjusted his glasses. "How much are you on the hook for?"

"Too much. I've got two more speed date events to go. There's a no-refund policy." Olivia studied him intently. "Forget my dating problems. Victor Arganbright said I should expect you at the offices of Lark and LeClair first thing tomorrow morning. Why did you show up here tonight?"

"The Foundation and I are not the only ones looking for Vortex. I think we're running out of time."

"I know Victor and Lucas are obsessed with the old Vortex legend. I take it you are, too."

"'Obsessed' is a harsh way to put it."

"But accurate?"

"Yes, unfortunately." He surveyed the street. "Where did you park?"

"I didn't drive," she said. "I used an app to call a car service. I'm not keen on parking in the garage of my apartment building these days."

"Understandable. Pine filled me in on your role ih catching the serial killer who was targeting women who attended speed date events."

Olivia reached into her handbag and took out her phone. "Did he?"

"I'm surprised you decided to use a speed date agency after working undercover to catch a killer who did his stalking in speed date events."

"I studied the speed date business while I was working the job. I liked the concept. Straightforward. No games."

He nodded, thinking about it. "You're right. It does seem like an efficient strategy. Focused. Targeted. No time wasted."

"That's how it struck me, but apparently I need to improve my conversational skills."

He frowned. "Why?"

She shot him a cool, sidelong look. "I have been advised that my opening question might attract the wrong person. You know, the *obsessive* type."

"I don't think so. It's a solid question. Cuts through the social noise and gets to the bottom line."

"'The social noise'?" Olivia repeated, her voice very neutral. "As in, polite conversation?"

"Right."

"There is such a thing as being too focused, Mr. Rancourt."

"Really? I've never run into that particular issue. Speaking of that undercover job, nice work keeping your name out of the media. The credit for the arrest went to a police task force and a local forensics consulting firm."

"Both of which deserve the credit. The cops did the hard work of running down all the leads and isolating the solid clues. The consulting agency came up with a psychological profile and asked Lark and LeClair to assist in an undercover operation."

"What went wrong?"

"The killer got past the team watching my apartment building," Olivia said.

"The authorities said the perp suffered a seizure. Arganbright and Pine told me they were amazed by the timing of that seizure but they couldn't come up with any other explanation."

"It was amazing, all right."

"And convenient."

She had been about to tap her phone but she paused, wary now. "I was very lucky."

"Evidently when the killer woke up he was hallucinating. Claimed he had been attacked by an extraterrestrial who used a ray gun. He confessed to all of the killings because he is convinced he'll be safer in jail. Seems to think that if he gets out, the visitor from outer space will come after him with the weapon."

Olivia gave him a steely smile. "What's the name of your hotel? I'll need it for the driver. He can drop you off first."

It occurred to him that in his race to find her he had neglected to book a hotel. Before he could explain the situation, the lilting notes of a musical instrument drifted down the street. It also occurred to him that he had been so focused on Olivia he hadn't done a proper recon.

"Sounds like a flute," he said.

"A recorder, I think." Olivia glanced around. "One of those simple instruments that children learn to play in school."

He turned to do a quick scan of his surroundings. There was a small group of people approaching from the end of the block. Tech workers leaving the office late and heading out for a beer and some bar food. He glanced in the other direction and saw a couple coming toward where he stood with Olivia. The two people were intent on what was obviously a very private conversation.

"Harlan?" Olivia said, her voice sharp. "What's wrong?"

He ignored her to continue the sweep. On the other side of the street a man wearing a stocking cap and an ancient coat that was two sizes too big stood next to a rusty grocery cart piled high with a jumble of found objects. An unrolled sleeping bag dangled over one side of the cart.

There was no obvious threat, but Harlan had learned that it was never a good idea to ignore his intuition. It was the primary reason he was still alive.

"Are you all right?" Olivia asked, concern lacing her voice now.

He could feel energy shifting in the atmosphere and knew she was watching him with her other senses.

"I'm fine," he said. "But I don't like standing around here on the street. For one thing, it's cold. For another, I'm hungry. Do you mind if we find a restaurant where I can grab a bite to eat and maybe get a drink? We need to talk."

He didn't like the idea of sitting around in a public space like a restaurant, either, but there wasn't much choice. Her office was several blocks away and it was closed. It was too soon to suggest they go back to her apartment. At this point she had no reason to trust him beyond Arganbright's assurance that, for now at least, he was allied with the Foundation. It was highly unlikely she would invite him into her home.

Olivia considered briefly and then made a decision. "I agree. You should get something to eat."

He waited a beat. She just stood there looking at him.

"Excuse me," he said. "This is your neighborhood. How about offering a helpful suggestion?"

"Well, I could say something snarky about how your appointment with Lark and LeClair is for tomorrow morning, not tonight, and mention that I had other plans for this evening, but—"

"But?"

She sighed. "I know how important this Vortex business is to Victor and Lucas. The Foundation is a good client and it always pays its bills so, hey, my time is yours. Not like you interrupted anything that was trending in a positive direction."

"You are not in a good mood, are you?"

"Nope." She gave him an overly bright smile. "How about you?"

"I'm not in a good mood, either."

"Luckily for you, I can multitask." She started walking. "That means I can conduct business when I'm in a lousy mood. There's a good restaurant at the end of this block. When did you last eat?"

He fell into step beside her and reflected on the past forty-eight hours. He remembered a cup of coffee and an egg sandwich at the airport in DC.

"Breakfast," he said. "In another time zone."

"And before that?"

"Dinner. A sandwich at my desk. What's with the sudden concern about my food history?"

"I suppose the fact that you haven't had a good meal during the past twenty-four hours explains part of the problem."

"What problem?"

"Your aura is twitchy."

Alarm and disbelief shot through him. Just how much could she read in his energy field?

"'Twitchy'?" he repeated, careful to keep his voice level. "What the hell is that supposed to mean?"

"It indicates the obvious. You're a strong talent who has been running hot for too long. You've almost exhausted your psychic energy reserves. You need food and sleep."

"I told you I was hungry," he muttered.

He was officially worried now. Something was off here. His talent made him very, very good at looking like a low-grade, below-average psychic. Just a subnormal member of the paranormal community. Nothing special. Nothing scary. *How much could she see?*

"I'm impressed that Victor let you use the Foundation jet," Olivia said. "I'm told he always complains about how much it costs to put it in the air. It's for emergencies only."

"Vortex is an emergency."

"It certainly is to Victor and Lucas—and, evidently, to you. But no one seems to know why that lab, assuming it really exists, is suddenly a problem. If it was part of the Bluestone Project, it's been buried since the middle of the last century. People in the antiquities trade tell me there have always been rumors, but no one claims to have seen an actual artifact with a connection to that lab. Why is the Foundation so worried about Vortex now?"

"I don't have all the answers," Harlan said. "Just enough to know that I need your help."

"Victor said he wants me to assist you in your inquiries. That's a rather vague request. My partner, Catalina, and I have discovered the hard way that vague requests from Victor usually mean trouble. Why did you ask for me specifically?"

"I have reason to think you're the key to Vortex."

The faint music sounded again, closer this time.

Olivia looked around. "That's the recorder we heard earlier."

"Yes."

Harlan shook off a small chill and did another survey. The tech workers had disappeared around a corner. The couple engaged in the intense conversation were in the process of climbing into a car they had apparently summoned. The homeless man was moving away.

"What's wrong?" Olivia asked.

Harlan realized he was massaging the back of his neck. "I got that 'someone is watching you' vibe."

She shoved her hands into the pockets of her coat. "Trust me, I know the feeling."

He looked at her. "You're getting it, too?"

"Not right now, but I've had the sensation off and on for months. It's been getting worse during the past week, probably because I'm coming up on the anniversary of my mother's . . . death."

"You believe she was murdered. I think so, too."

CHAPTER 6

Olivia stopped very suddenly and turned to face him. In the light of the streetlamp her expression was stark. Her eyes were shadowed pools of mystery.

"What do you know about my mother's death?" she said, her voice quiet and cold.

"I know that she died about a year ago while hiking alone in the woods. A fall, according to the authorities."

"My friend Catalina and I believe she was murdered, but we haven't been able to prove it. Do you have some evidence?"

"Nothing concrete," he admitted. "Not yet. But there is reason to believe it was connected to Vortex."

"Is that true or are you saying that because you need my help?"

"Both. If we find Vortex, there's a high probability we'll find your mother's killer, or at least get some answers about her death."

She gave him another long look. He knew she was once again studying his aura. Whatever she saw there apparently convinced her he was telling the truth. Then again, maybe she had simply decided to take a chance on him because she had no other options.

"Deal," she said.

She walked on in silence, determination radiating from her. She was committed now. That was good, he told himself. He needed her. But he was aware of an underlying pang of disappointment. It would have been nice if she had agreed to help him because she liked him. Instead she had struck a bargain.

Rancourt, get a grip. You've got what you want, what you need— her cooperation. You're the one who offered the deal. Just be glad she grabbed it.

Olivia stopped at the end of the block.

"This is the restaurant," she said.

He did a quick check. The place had a quirky name and a warm, welcoming vibe. Through the windows he could see a cheerful fire blazing in a sleek, modern hearth. The mirrored back bar glowed. Bottles of expensive liquor sparkled on glass shelves. Best of all, there were booths that would afford a degree of privacy, and luckily one of the empty ones was positioned against the back wall, not far from the kitchen entrance.

"Looks great," he said.

"You're okay with Mediterranean fusion?"

"I'm okay with food." He pushed open the door. "I'm not particular."

The woman behind the podium smiled. "Two for dinner?"

"Please," Olivia said.

"Follow me."

The host picked up a couple of menus and headed toward a window seat. Harlan made it a practice to never sit in front of a window. He slipped a twenty-dollar bill out of the inside pocket of his jacket and transferred it to the host's hand with the ease of long practice.

"We would prefer the booth at the back," he said.

The woman stared at him, confused. "The one near the kitchen and the restrooms?"

Harlan glanced at the Emergency Exit sign over the darkened hallway.

"Yes, please," he said. "It's perfect."

The woman did not argue. She made the twenty disappear and gave him a bright smile.

"Of course," she said.

"Thanks," Harlan said.

When they reached the booth, Olivia started to sit down.

"Do you mind taking the other side?" Harlan asked.

She raised her brows but she acquiesced without comment. Harlan sat down across from her and automatically did another scan of the room. Satisfied that he had a good view of the rest of the restaurant, the bar and the front door, and that they were sitting close to an emergency exit, he allowed himself to relax a couple of degrees.

He turned back to find Olivia watching him with a trace of amusement.

"You remind me of one of those old Wild West gunslingers who always sat with their backs to the wall in case another badass shooter walked into the saloon looking for trouble," she said.

For some reason he was embarrassed. "I like to keep a low profile."

"You do realize the woman who just seated us thinks we're having an affair and that we asked for the worst booth in the restaurant because we're afraid one of our spouses might discover us having dinner together?"

"No," he said, startled. "I admit I'm paranoid these days, but I'm not that creative."

"Because you're focused on Vortex?"

"No, because I'm just not the creative type." A troubling possibility occurred to him, one he had not considered until now. "Is there a significant other in your life who might not like the idea of your having dinner with me?"

"Nope. Why do you think I signed up for the Four Event Success Guaranteed package?"

He nodded. He felt a little more cheerful for some reason. "That's good."

"Convenient, you mean." She smiled a little too sweetly. "For you."

"Well, yes. The fewer questions, the better. I don't have time for long explanations."

"You'd better make time, because I'm going to ask for a detailed explanation."

"I thought Arganbright—"

"Victor told me diddly-squat. Just that this is about Vortex and that the Foundation is paying me to assist you."

Before Harlan could say anything, the waiter appeared, hovering with an air of expectation. "Can I get you anything from the bar?"

"You certainly can," Olivia said. "I'll have a glass of the house sauvignon blanc."

"And for you, sir?" the waiter said.

It dawned on Harlan that what he wanted was a stiff shot of whiskey, but he decided to go with a glass of wine on the theory that it would make a better impression.

"The house red," he said.

It was a compromise, but it was the best he could do under the circumstances. White wine was a bridge too far.

The waiter left. Olivia studied the menu as if the decision of what to order was a matter of grave importance. He was so hungry he would have been thrilled to open a can of beans. He picked up his menu. When he was finally able to decipher the fancy font and translate it, he settled on cioppino. After about two seconds he reminded himself that high-end restaurants usually served small portions. He added a side of pasta topped with pecorino. He probably needed vegetables, too. He decided the zucchini and feta fritters would cover that issue.

He set aside the menu just as the wine arrived. A large basket of focaccia and a little dish of greenish-gold olive oil arrived with it. He seized a chunk of the bread, plunged it into the olive oil and took a large bite.

He chewed, swallowed, drank some wine and tore off another hunk of bread.

Olivia watched him work his way through the basket of focaccia. She made no comment, but he thought he caught a glint of humor in her eyes. He flushed.

"I told you I haven't eaten since breakfast," he said around a chunk of the focaccia.

She ignored that. "You didn't mention which hotel you're booked into here in Seattle. Is it nearby?"

"Right. The hotel. I don't have a room yet. I wanted to find you first."

"How *did* you find me tonight?"

"I called Lucas Pine when the plane landed. Told him I didn't want to wait until tomorrow morning to talk to you. Evidently you weren't answering your phone."

"The event coordinator made us silence our phones. I wasn't supposed to be on mine but I got bored and went online."

"Pine tried your business partner and found out she was in New Zealand."

"Catalina and her husband, Slater, were married in Las Vegas a few weeks ago, but they never got a chance to take a real honeymoon."

"Apparently that came as a surprise to Arganbright and Pine."

"Imagine that. I guess Catalina and Slater forgot that they are supposed to clear all travel plans through Foundation headquarters."

"More sarcasm, right?"

Olivia gave him a bright, totally fake smile. "You must be psychic."

"As I was saying, Pine couldn't get in touch with you or Catalina, so he called your administrative assistant."

Olivia nodded. "Daniel Naylor. He knew I was attending the

speed date event. He warned me it probably wouldn't turn out well. He'll want a full report in the morning."

Harlan got a wary feeling. "What are you going to tell him?"

Olivia flashed another too-shiny smile. "That he was right. It was a disaster."

Harlan made an executive decision. He would not pursue that line of inquiry. He had a feeling he was the disaster, as far as Olivia was concerned.

"I must say Victor and Lucas are certainly being very helpful," she continued. "Amazing, considering you're a Rancourt."

"As you pointed out, Arganbright and Pine are also obsessed with Vortex."

"What sparked your interest?" she asked. "And why the sudden urgency?"

There was no more bread in the basket, so he drank some of the wine. After a healthy swallow he lowered the glass.

"Most of the paranormal community assumes Vortex is a myth," he said. "When my grandfather and father were in charge of the Foundation, they encouraged that notion. The idea was that it would keep the competition to a minimum."

"Your father and your grandfather tried to find that lost lab?"

"Right from the start. They were obsessed with it, too. They never stopped looking for it. Growing up, I was aware of the legends about it, but I never paid a lot of attention. I assumed that if it existed it was just another lost lab—no different from the others that were part of the Bluestone Project."

"It's been decades since the Bluestone Project was shut down," Olivia said. "Have you considered the possibility that if the Rancourts and Victor and Lucas haven't been able to generate any solid leads using the resources of the Foundation, then maybe Vortex really is nothing more than a myth?"

"I used to blow off the legend, but I can't do that anymore. Things have changed in the past year. The rumors are getting hotter, spreading outside the Foundation into the wider paranormal underworld."

Olivia frowned. "Define 'wider paranormal underworld.'"

"Bluestone wasn't the first project designed to investigate the paranormal, and the Foundation is not the only organization that tries to explore, monitor and police atypical phenomena."

"I know there have always been some people with talents but I wasn't aware of other organizations dedicated to the paranormal."

"Most are frauds and cons, but yes, there are other groups that take a serious interest in the subject. Back to Vortex. A few people have died under what I consider suspicious circumstances. Rogues, raiders, a couple of dealers. And it's not true that there isn't any solid evidence of the existence of Vortex."

Olivia paused, her wineglass halfway to her mouth. "I assume Victor and Lucas know about this evidence?"

"They do now. Why do you think they asked you to cooperate with me?"

Olivia contemplated him for a long moment. He took the opportunity to drink some more wine.

"This evidence," Olivia said after a moment. "Is it connected to my mother's murder?"

"I'm sure it is. I just don't know how. Not yet. But there's a link. There has to be."

"What makes you so certain?"

"I may not be the creative type, but I'm pretty good when it comes to connecting the dots."

"Everyone I know, psychic or not, thinks they're intuitive, including me. But it turns out we all make serious errors in judgment anyway."

"Trust me, I'm aware of that."

"What is this evidence you're talking about?"

He took out his cell phone and pulled up the photo he had shown to Arganbright and Pine. He set the device on the table in front of Olivia.

She looked at the image, intrigued at first. Then she sat back, stunned.

"My grandmother painted that picture," she whispered.

"That," he said quietly, "is the theory I have been working on for the past few days."

He had spent hours examining the scene. It depicted a small, neatly laid out trailer park in the center of a clearing. A forest of pine and fir punctuated with granite outcroppings constituted the land-scape. The corner of a long white building studded with narrow windows and topped with a tile roof could be seen in the background. It looked like an old convent or monastery.

The trailers were identical, vintage mid-twentieth century, painted camouflage green. There were no vehicles in the scene, just bicycles and scooters. The artist had labeled each of the trailers. Some were tagged with names, and other tags indicated a function—café, medical clinic, grocery.

There was a hooded figure in the front of the scene. The words *Here there be monsters* were written in flowing script.

"Ever seen this picture before?" Harlan asked.

"Not this particular one." Olivia could not drag her gaze away from the picture. "But I've seen others like it. I recognize the oracle figure and the title, but it's the unique style that makes me sure it's one of my grandmother's paintings. So much fierce energy. So much incredible detail. Her pictures all have this surreal quality."

Anticipation surged through him. "Do you have more paintings like this?"

Olivia did look up then, her eyes tightening at the corners. He realized he had spoken too harshly. The last thing he wanted to do was frighten her.

Social skills.

"We had two of them," Olivia said. "My mother kept them in a closet at the Fogg Lake house. I remember being fascinated by them. I asked Mom why we didn't hang the paintings alongside her own."

"Your mother was a painter?"

"Yes. She sold her art at various craft fairs while I was growing up. It was how she paid the bills. I have several of her pictures. Most are landscapes featuring scenes from around Fogg Lake. Her style is quite different from my grandmother's."

"What did your mother say when you asked her why she didn't hang your grandmother's paintings?"

"She said Grandma asked her to keep them safe and that someday I might have to keep them safe, too. She spoke of them as if they were a family secret that had to be closely guarded. But she never told me why. Over time I mostly forgot about them. Just a couple of paintings in the back of a storage closet."

"I need to see those pictures."

"They're gone," Olivia said.

"Stolen?"

"I don't think so. There's not a lot of crime in Fogg Lake. I didn't even know they were gone until I went through the house after my mother's death. That was about a year ago. I intended to pack up her things and sell the place, but I couldn't bring myself to do it. I still can't."

"But you're sure the pictures weren't stolen?"

"Almost positive. They sat there in the back of the closet the whole time I was living at home. I doubt if anyone in town knew about them. A year ago it would have been almost impossible for a stranger to break into the house without someone noticing."

"What's different now?"

Olivia swallowed some wine and lowered her glass. "The Foundation has a lot of people in Fogg Lake these days examining the old Bluestone lab that was found in the nearby caves. There are more people coming and going now. Still, security is very, very tight. Victor and Lucas make sure of that."

"Could anyone carrying the right badge get in?"

"It's possible, I suppose, but the Foundation people all know each other and the people of Fogg Lake all know each other. Strangers stand out, believe me."

"But there was no security a year ago."

"It wasn't needed." Olivia shook her head. "For what it's worth, I really don't think my grandmother's pictures were stolen—there was no sign of a break-in."

"You're an investigator. Got any theories?"

"I do, as a matter of fact." Olivia took a deep breath and exhaled slowly. "I'm almost certain my mother took them out of the closet before her death."

"What do you think she did with them?"

"I have no idea. I can't imagine she would have sold them. She viewed those paintings as an inheritance to be protected."

The waiter returned to the table with a large tray.

"Going to need to make some room," he announced.

Harlan quickly retrieved his phone. The waiter set a dainty Nicoise salad in front of Olivia. He arranged the large bowl of cioppino, a small mountain of pasta and a pile of fritters on Harlan's side of the table.

So much for the small-servings theory.

"I'll get some more bread," the waiter said.

He vanished.

Olivia leaned forward a little, her eyes fierce. "Where's the original of that painting you just showed me?"

Harlan picked up a fork and went to work on the pasta. "In a safe place."

"Where, damn it?"

"I found it in the vault at the offices of the Agency for the Investigation of Atypical Phenomena in DC. Relax. The agency is in a forgotten underground bunker that was built during World War Two and never used. It isn't identified on any of the old blueprints. Trust me, no one knows where it is except Arganbright, Pine and me. There is one other picture, however."

"Where's the other one?"

"In Arganbright's office," Harlan said.

Olivia tightened her grip on her wineglass. "He never told me about it. That picture belongs to me."

"Don't blame Arganbright," Harlan said around a mouthful of pasta. "He didn't know the painting had any connection to you, not until I showed him this photo and told him I was certain your grandmother painted both of them."

"How did you come to that conclusion?"

"My father and grandfather kept a set of private files, most of which were related to Vortex." Harlan paused. "I . . . inherited them."

"Inherited them?"

"'Found them' would be more accurate. In the vault in that bunker I just told you about."

"These files were assembled and maintained by Crocker and Stenson Rancourt?" Olivia said, astonishment in her eyes.

"Yes."

"Don't they belong to the Foundation?"

"Technically. My official title is director of the Agency for the Investigation of Atypical Phenomena."

"Victor did mention that when he asked me to cooperate with you," Olivia said. She smiled a very cool smile. "But that's not quite the same thing as being in charge of the Foundation, is it?"

"Close enough."

Harlan tried some of the cioppino. It was amazing. He did not know whether to slurp it down or sample the fritters. He went with the fritters.

"Do Victor and Lucas know about these files?" Olivia asked.

"They do now." The fritters were good, but the pasta was calling his name.

Olivia gave him a direct look. "Let me put this another way. Do Victor and Lucas have access to these files?"

"Not at the moment."

"They would probably kill to get their hands on them."

"Let's hope not." Harlan returned to the cioppino.

Olivia apparently decided to abandon that line of questioning.

"Forget Victor and Lucas," she said. "What do the files contain that relates to my grandmother?"

"Her real name, for starters. Grace Goodwin."

"Are you sure about that? Grandma's identification was in the name of Patricia LeClair."

"I think she assumed that identity after Vortex was shut down. The name 'Goodwin' is on one of those trailers in the painting, by the way."

Olivia regarded him in silence for a moment and then evidently decided to give him the benefit of a doubt. Progress.

"Have you found any of the other people named in the picture?" she asked.

"My father and grandfather tracked down a few, but they were all dead."

"Dead?"

Harlan ate some more pasta. "Under what you might call suspicious circumstances."

"What's that supposed to mean?"

"I'm pretty sure there was an attempt to hunt down and assassinate everyone affiliated with the Vortex lab. I think a few of the people who worked there, like your grandmother, managed to disappear, at least for a while." Harlan paused. "Your grandfather didn't make it. Evidently he died in the explosion that was supposed to destroy the lab."

Olivia's eyes widened. "He worked at Vortex, too?"

"That was my grandfather's conclusion. He made a note in the files."

"I don't understand. Surely the people who worked at Vortex were evacuated before the blast was triggered."

"Crocker Rancourt—my grandfather—was certain that the explosive device detonated before the scheduled time. He didn't think it was an accident. He suspected the assassin struck early and fast, trying to get rid of as many Vortex personnel as possible in one blow. Your grandfather wasn't the only one who died."

"That is so horrible." Olivia put down her fork. "My mother told me that her father died in a climbing accident before she was born. The body was never found."

"I don't think so. Do you remember your father?"

"No. Mom told me he was in military intelligence. He died on the other side of the world when I was a baby. Sniper's bullet. After that my grandmother insisted Mom and I move to Fogg Lake."

"But your grandmother didn't move there with you. Do you know why?"

"Mom tried many times to get Grandma to come and live with us, but for some reason she refused," Olivia said. "Mom was never clear about why. She just said Grandma needed lots of alone time because she was an artist. But we often drove down the mountain and over to the coast to visit her."

"What was Grace Goodwin like?"

"I don't remember much, to be honest. She died in a house fire when I was five. She always seemed anxious when we were there. I think it made her nervous. Fearful. She was glad to see us but we never stayed long. Looking back, I think she suffered from panic attacks."

Harlan munched a bite of the fritters and mulled over the information Olivia had provided. "Anxious. Fearful. Nervous."

"Yes. She had been through a lot, if you're right about her having been involved in Vortex. If she had been in hiding for years, it's no surprise she was anxious. We're talking serious PTSD."

"True. But according to my research, feelings of anxiety are common to oracle talents."

"No surprise. In the modern world, very few people take oracles seriously. They are considered delusional or outright frauds."

"Huh." Harlan finished his wine. "You've got a point. I hadn't thought about that angle. You seem to know a lot about the subject."

"I know a real oracle talent. She doesn't sleep much and she's a little obsessive when it comes to some things, but she's not abnormally anxious or fearful or nervous."

"I'm just saying that traditionally oracle talents are considered somewhat fragile when it comes to their nerves."

Olivia ate a small bite of tuna, chewed and swallowed. "Do you really think my grandmother was an oracle talent?"

"That's what Crocker Rancourt's notes say." Harlan cleared his throat. "Evidently the talent tends to go down through the female line, occasionally skipping a generation."

Olivia stared at him, irritation sparking in her eyes. "If you're implying I might be an oracle, forget it. I told you, I know a real oracle. Trust me, I'm not one. If I were, I'm pretty sure I would have figured it out by now."

"Not necessarily. I've spent a big chunk of the last five years researching the genetics of the paranormal senses. The oracle talent usually remains latent unless it's triggered by a traumatic incident."

"There you go." Olivia waved one hand in a gesture of dismissal. "That proves I'm not an oracle. I've had a few traumatic incidents in my life. The last one happened quite recently. I was kidnapped. Doesn't get much more traumatic than that. There's been no sign of oracle talent. I'm sure I would have noticed if I'd started announcing scary prophecies."

"Oracles often resist accepting their talents," he said.

"Imagine that." Olivia gave him a steely smile. "Maybe it's because they rarely get to deliver good news, and nobody wants bad news, so they blame the messenger. Or possibly it's the fact that the utterances tend to be cryptic, frustrating and hard to decipher."

He wasn't sure how to read her smile. It did not look promising, so he pretended he hadn't noticed.

"I think another reason oracles try to suppress their talents is because they are afraid it's an indication of mental instability," he said. "It's a tough talent. It makes other people uneasy. I'm sure it would complicate personal relationships."

"No shit. Sounds like you've done some serious research on the subject."

"Yes."

"The oracle thing is clearly not a good career path," Olivia said coldly. "No job satisfaction, and probably no money in it."

"There's always been money in it if you want to go that route. It's amazing how many people are willing to throw cash at anyone who claims to have psychic powers. It's just a matter of smart marketing."

"Most people who claim to have psychic powers are frauds," she pointed out.

"That's a whole other issue. What I have learned is that the oracle talent appears to be linked to the dreamstate. Everyone knows how difficult it is to interpret dreams and visions. Oracles need interpreters, someone who can decipher the meanings in the images."

"Is that right? And just who does that kind of work?"

"Chaos talents are the best at it."

Olivia gave that some close thought and then shook her head. "I don't think I've ever met a chaos talent."

"Yes, you have. I'm certain Victor Arganbright is one, although he prefers to think of himself as highly intuitive."

"You know a lot about this so-called chaos talent, too," Olivia said.

"That's because I am one." Harlan pulled the last crab claw out of the cioppino and used both hands to crack the shell. "And I'm a lot more powerful than Victor Arganbright."

CHAPTER 7

Harlan wasn't boasting, Olivia realized. Just stating a fact.

She watched, riveted, as he extracted the crabmeat from the claw. She could not decide if she was unnerved or fascinated.

"Is my aura still twitchy?" Harlan asked around a mouthful of crabmeat.

The matter-of-fact question fractured the small spell that had come over her. She raised her senses and did a quick survey. His powerful aura looked normal—for a monster. More worrisome was the compelling, intimate sense of bone-deep recognition. It was as if something inside her had been waiting for this man.

"Nope," she said. "I can tell you're still tired, though."

He tossed the empty claw aside and wiped his hands on the damp towel the waiter had left. "Now that I've found you, I may be able to get a decent night's sleep."

"Why were you so worried about finding me? You knew Victor had made an appointment for us to meet first thing in the morning."

He took out his wallet, plucked a credit card from it and signaled the waiter. "I was afraid someone else would get to you first."

She winced. "Nice to know I'm such a valuable commodity."

He frowned. "What?"

"You make me sound like a contest prize," she explained.

The waiter scooped up the card and vanished again. Harlan turned back to her.

"Not a prize," he said, earnest now. "A key."

"Oh, well, why didn't you say that in the first place? It makes such a difference."

The waiter returned with the card. Olivia got to her feet and reached for her coat and handbag. Harlan signed the bill, shrugged into his trench coat and hoisted the duffel bag from under the table.

"Let's go," he said.

"Where will you stay tonight?"

"I'll figure it out after I make sure your apartment is secure."

"Wait. You want to check out my apartment?"

"Yes. Lucas Pine said there are some nearby hotels. I'll find one."

"You'd better be right about this Vortex case being connected to my mother's death."

He pushed open the front door and ushered her out onto the sidewalk. "I am sure it is."

She took her phone out of her pocket, intending to use her favorite ride app, but the music of a recorder snagged her attention.

"Whoever is playing that recorder is still at it," she said.

"Yes," Harlan said.

He stopped. A curious stillness came over him.

She turned her head to see what had attracted his attention. The homeless man with the shopping cart was back. He stood in the shadows at the corner. He appeared to be holding an object to his mouth. At first she thought he was lighting a cigarette. Belatedly she realized he was the one playing the recorder.

The music had a strange, piercing quality. Not pretty, but oddly compelling. Darkly thrilling. It stirred the fine hairs on the back of her neck and at the same time made her want to get closer so that she could hear it more clearly. There were answers to be found in the music. All she had to do was follow the notes to their source . . .

"*Shit*," Harlan said. "The guy with the shopping cart. I should have figured it out earlier. Guess you were right about my twitchy aura. I wasn't paying attention."

He wrapped one hand around Olivia's upper arm and hauled her down the street. His fierce urgency broke the spell of the music. She slammed into her other senses and sprinted to keep up with him. Harlan's aura was blazing. Their physical connection intensified the effect of his energy field on hers.

She managed to slip her phone into her coat pocket.

"What's going on?" she gasped.

"We're being hunted. We need shelter."

"*What?*"

Harlan did not respond. He was clearly focused on something else—finding shelter, apparently. She was running now—in high heels. It was either that or risk being dragged down the sidewalk.

There were two possibilities, she thought. Either Harlan's obsession with Vortex had driven him off the edge of the conspiracy cliff or else he was right—someone was hunting them. Given the strange compulsion of the music, her intuition urged her to go with the second possibility.

The music faded as they ran in the opposite direction, but it still tugged at her, promising secrets and amazing wonders even as it iced her blood. Someone was using the notes as a lure.

Halfway down the street Harlan yanked her into the deep shadows of a dimly lit alley. The power of the music abruptly ceased. She could still hear the notes but they no longer pulled at her senses. Whoever was playing the recorder was competent, but the tune no longer drew her the way it had a moment ago.

"The brick walls of the alley," Harlan said, whispering into her ear. "The paranormal energy waves can't travel through them."

The music ceased altogether.

"Stay here," Harlan ordered, once again speaking directly into her ear. "Do not move."

Shivering a little from the adrenaline overload and the realization that the music had very nearly put her into a hypnotic trance, she watched Harlan move to the entrance of the alley. He slipped a hand inside his trench coat and under his suit jacket.

When his hand reappeared she saw that he was holding a gun. His arm was straight at his side so that the weapon pointed at the ground. So much for Mr. Nothing-to-See-Here.

She finally remembered that she, too, had a weapon. She opened her handbag, took out the camera and slung the strap around her neck.

Aura flaring, Harlan took a look around the corner of the alley wall. Evidently satisfied, he slipped the gun inside his jacket and moved quickly back to her.

"He's gone. Let's get out of here."

He steered her toward the far end of the alley. She wrinkled her nose against the smell. The toe of her shoe struck a small, squishy object. She cringed and looked down. Fortunately it was too dark to see what she had stepped into. This was probably the end for the heels she had bought to tone down the cobalt blue dress.

"Where, exactly, are we going now?" she said.

"Your apartment. So much for maintaining a low profile. Argan-bright told me there is a small Foundation security team on the ground here in Seattle. I'll call him and tell him I want the agents to keep an eye on every entrance to the building until dawn."

"What about you?"

"Forget the hotel. I'll sleep on your couch."

She wanted to argue, if only for the sake of form. But common sense prevailed.

"You're not quite what I had in mind," she said.

"What?"

"I was thinking of getting a cat."

CHAPTER 8

The vibe of Olivia's apartment hit Harlan with such intensity he had to pause in the entryway to adjust to the effect on his senses. The place was infused with her energy, and he wanted to savor it.

"You can hang your coat in the hall closet," Olivia said. "I'll be right back. I'm just going to get out of these heels."

It wasn't exactly a make-yourself-at-home sort of welcome— more of a grudging acceptance of his presence—but when you had been living in short-term rentals and hotels for five years, it was a good enough invitation.

"Thanks," he said.

But Olivia had disappeared around the corner.

He dropped his duffel bag on the floor, peeled off the trench coat and hung it in the small closet. He hesitated a beat and then took off his government-gray suit jacket and hung it beside the trench. Then, concluding he was on a roll, he unknotted his tie and slung it around one of the hangers.

He started to unbuckle the shoulder holster—the damn thing was uncomfortable—but given what had happened a short time ago and the fact that Olivia had already seen the pistol, he opted to leave it on.

He started to roll up the sleeves of the white shirt but caught himself in time. Olivia had seen the gun but he wasn't sure how she would take the knife sheath strapped to his right wrist. He didn't want to wear out what minimal welcome he had going.

Social skills.

When he was ready he wandered into the living room and stopped again when he was hit with a blast of drama and color.

The walls were a sun-drenched gold that provided a warm backdrop for a sofa that was the same shade of blue as Olivia's dress and two ruby-red velvet chairs. A carpet patterned with an abstract design framed a black coffee table and a couple of elegant black reading lamps.

He was studying the three paintings on the walls when Olivia returned. She had changed into casual trousers and a pullover, both in a warm shade of amber. When she saw him she paused.

"Those are the paintings I told you about," she said. "The ones my mother did. Scenes around Fogg Lake."

He contemplated the neon-green foliage and the glowing fog in one of the pictures. "Is the vegetation really that incredible shade of green?"

"Yes. There's a lot of natural paranormal energy in the atmosphere. It leaks out of the caves. Probably the reason why Bluestone chose the area for one of the labs. Would you like a glass of brandy?"

"Yes," he said. "Thank you." He turned away from the painting and noticed the array of objects neatly lined up against the wall under the windows—a cat climbing tower with multiple shelves, a high-tech cat food dispenser, a stylish red litter box and an array of cat toys. All new. All unused.

"Looks like you're serious about getting a cat," he said.

"I thought I'd start with the cat stuff first. Make sure it feels right."

"Good plan." He took out his phone. "I'll call Arganbright and tell him what's going on. He can set up a security detail for us tonight."

"All right," Olivia said. She went into the kitchen and opened a cupboard. "I'll get some sheets and a blanket."

"Appreciate that." He glanced at the jewel-blue sofa. "But I won't be sleeping on that couch tonight."

Olivia froze. "What?"

"I'll take the floor. Your sofa is a work of art. I'm not going to risk getting it dirty."

Olivia visibly relaxed. "A work of art." She looked at the sofa. "Your choice."

Now what had he said? Harlan was replaying his comment about not sleeping on the sofa and wondering why Olivia had looked momentarily alarmed when Victor Arganbright answered the phone.

"What's going on?" Arganbright said.

Harlan told him. As he talked he took another look around the colorful living room and the cat stuff lined up against the wall. He could live in a place like this.

CHAPTER 9

Olivia did not expect to sleep, but at some point she finally dozed off.

The nightmare hit hard and fast.

. . . She is in the shadows of the garage. The Speed Date Killer lunges toward her, a reptilian sheen in his eyes. He has a knife in one hand. The roll of duct tape and the syringe are on the concrete floor.

She suddenly knows what the camera can do. She tries to raise it so she can focus through it. But she can't move. She is frozen. Trapped . . .

Panic flooded her veins, bringing her awake on a tide of terror. She managed, barely, to swallow a scream. *Nightmare. You've been here before. It's just a nightmare.*

But it wasn't a dream. The killer was there, in her bedroom, lunging toward her. He gripped the knife just as he had the night she had confronted him in the garage.

But now he was in her bedroom, coming at her.

She threw herself to the far side of the bed . . . and got hopelessly tangled up in the sheets and blanket. She struggled, but she knew she was doomed. She would not be able to escape, not this time.

The bedroom door slammed open. Harlan loomed, silhouetted against the glow of the night-light in the hall. He had his gun in one hand.

"What the hell?" he said. He did not take his eyes off the Speed Date Killer but he made no move to stop him. Instead he lowered the gun. "Are you okay?"

She realized he was talking to her. She realized something else as well. The killer was motionless.

"Yes," she managed. "At least I think so."

She wriggled free of the sheets and blanket and got to her feet on the far side of the bed. Her pulse was pounding. She gasped for breath.

He was wearing the trousers and the long-sleeved shirt he'd had on earlier in the evening. The shirt was unbuttoned now, revealing a monastically plain white tee underneath. Barefoot, he moved into the room.

"Well, now, isn't this interesting?" he said.

He walked slowly around the life-sized image of the Speed Date Killer. The figure hovered about a foot off the floor.

The killer was still there, still poised to kill. *But he did not move.* It was as if he existed in another dimension.

Olivia wondered if she was still dreaming. But the rug beneath her feet felt real. The bedside clock glowed, the numbers clear. Three sixteen a.m. When she dreamed, numbers never made sense. She could not use a phone or find an address or figure out a bill when she was in a dreamstate. But now she was reading the clock quite clearly.

And Harlan Rancourt was strolling around her bedroom as if he had every right to be there.

She definitely was not dreaming.

"It looks like a ghost," she said.

"Not a ghost." He sliced his hand through the image. There was no resistance. "I think it's a hologram. Do you recognize the guy with the knife?"

"Oh, yes." She went slowly around the end of the bed. "It's the Speed Date Killer. That's exactly how he looked before he had his, uh, seizure."

Harlan switched his attention to her. His eyes heated. "You must have been the one who took the picture."

"That wasn't what I thought I was doing at the time. I don't understand."

She caught a glint of silvery light and turned quickly, searching for the source. An eerie radiance came from the lens of the vintage camera.

"The camera is projecting the image," she said. "Not me."

Harlan walked toward the camera but he did not touch it. "What were you doing in the seconds before he tried to murder you?"

"I had this feeling that I could use the camera as a weapon. I aimed it, focused some energy through the lens and pressed one of the buttons."

She went to the bedside table and picked up the camera. It was warm to the touch. The vibe was unmistakable. Experimentally she pressed one of the buttons. The silvery light vanished. The hologram winked out.

"The man was about to gut you and you wanted to take a picture?" Harlan asked, his tone suspiciously neutral.

"Of course not. I told you, I reacted intuitively."

He gave her a slow, satisfied smile. It was the first time he had smiled since he had sat down at her speed date table.

"You used the artifact to ice his aura, didn't you?" he said. "Nice work. I knew the seizure story was bogus."

She winced. "I had to come up with a believable explanation for the client. Roger Gossard knows I've got a psychic vibe, but he certainly doesn't think I can do anything so . . . so *physical* with it. Neither did I. Roger would be horrified if he knew the truth. I'm pretty horrified myself."

Harlan raised a brow. "Yeah?"

"Don't get me wrong. I'm delighted to be alive, but I'm still trying to process what happened that night. The thing is, Roger and I agree that if the police and the media get hold of the real story it would be the end of Lark and LeClair. You know what would happen if it got out that we claim to solve cases with psychic powers."

"Sure. Lark and LeClair would become a joke as far as serious clients and law enforcement are concerned. You would start attracting people who want you to hold séances."

She shuddered. "Yes."

"Right. Tell me about the camera."

She sank down on the side of the bed. "I found it in a local antiques shop. The moment I saw it I recognized it."

"You'd seen it before?"

"Not in real life. It's in a painting that my mother did."

Harlan watched her intently. "Where is the painting?"

"Hanging on the wall of the Fogg Lake house. It wasn't just that the camera looked familiar—it felt familiar."

"You recognized the psychic signature."

It wasn't a question.

"Yes," she said. "It's definitely not a traditional camera from the last century. There's no way to put film in it. No way to open it without taking it apart. The lens is a crystal of some kind, not ordinary glass. The two buttons are crystals, too."

"Did you run any experiments?"

"I tried pressing the buttons a few times but nothing happened. I could feel the power locked in the camera but I did not know how to activate it."

"Until you were attacked. Then you suddenly knew how to work it."

She looked at the camera. "Like I said, intuition."

"Sounds like the intuition of an oracle," Harlan said quietly.

"I. Am. Not. An. Oracle."

She clenched her hands together in her lap and took a deep breath. There was no point losing her temper with Harlan. All he cared about was his agenda. She had other problems, one of which was that she was in her bedroom with a man she had met only a few hours earlier and she was wearing a nightgown.

"Damn," she said.

"Think of something else about the camera?" Harlan asked.

"No." She rose, marched across the small space and took the maroon terry cloth robe off the hook. She slipped into the robe and quickly tied the sash. Feeling more in control, she shoved her hands into the pockets and contemplated the camera. "Maybe."

"Go on."

"Tonight I turned on the hologram projection in my sleep."

"I thought I explained that the oracle talent is linked to the dreamstate."

"Shut up, Rancourt. I do not want any more lectures about the oracle thing. Got it?"

"I've spent a good portion of the past five years studying the dreamstate. I'm just trying—"

She held up a hand, palm out. Harlan closed his mouth. She gave him a cool, approving smile. "That's better. As I was saying, I don't know much about the camera except that my mother must have seen it at some point, because I'm sure it's the same camera as the one in the painting in our Fogg Lake house. I did not understand what the artifact could do until that night in the garage when I was able to use it as a weapon."

Harlan studied the camera. "You iced the killer's aura—"

"Temporarily," she said quickly. "He survived, remember?"

"Think you could have made it permanent?" Harlan asked, as if the answer was of purely intellectual interest.

"You mean, could I have killed him?" She closed her eyes. "Maybe." She opened her eyes. "I've been trying to avoid thinking about that. It's not exactly the sort of thing you want to discover about yourself. The ability to crush someone's aura makes me one of the monsters, doesn't it?"

When Harlan did not respond, she tore her gaze off the camera and looked at him. He watched her with haunted eyes.

"I don't know," he said finally. "Does it?"

She understood then that he had asked himself the same question. "I suppose," she said slowly, "it's no different from possessing a gun or a knife. Intent matters."

"In your case, you used the camera in self-defense. And you didn't actually kill a man."

"But I could have. I think."

"You didn't," Harlan said. "Be grateful. Killing exacts some serious psychic pain. Even with the best intentions in the world, you pay a price—unless you're a blank. That is, a true sociopath."

"Neither of us is a blank."

"No. Now, I suggest we leave the philosophical questions for another time. What we need to talk about now is that you took the holographic image of the Speed Date Killer at the same time you were intuitively trying to use the camera as a weapon."

"So?"

"The fact that you figured out how to use the camera to save your life means that if there are other holograms on the artifact, you can probably access them."

"How?"

"Go into your other senses and do what everyone does when they get a new phone. Start pressing buttons."

"I've done that a few times."

"But not with purpose," Harlan said. "You have an idea of what you're looking for now. Focus. Use your intuition."

"I'm not sure that's a good plan."

"We need information, Olivia. We don't have time to go through a rigorous analysis in a Foundation lab."

She hesitated and then decided that knowing was better than not knowing. She picked up the camera.

Harlan cleared his throat. "You might want to aim it at the doorway, not at me."

She did not dignify that comment with a response, but she was careful to point the lens toward the bedroom doorway. Cautiously she raised her senses and pressed a crystal button.

A life-sized hologram flashed into existence. Even though she had been braced for the unknown, the vision of the man lunging toward her, both hands outstretched, eyes blazing with fury and a whisper of madness, startled her so much she gasped and stumbled backward. She would have lost her balance if she hadn't come up against Harlan's chest.

Her pulse slammed into high gear. It was all she could do not to scream. But the words stormed through her, demanding release. They exploded out of her, but not in a panicky shout or an echoing cry. Instead, she spoke in a ghostly voice.

"Dead man walking in a dying garden."

She felt Harlan's fingers closing around her shoulders, steadying her.

"Anything else?" he asked.

She took a couple of shaky breaths, collected herself and lowered her senses.

"That's the man who murdered my mother," she said.

CHAPTER 10

Harlan walked slowly around the hologram, noting and cataloging details. The figure appeared to be in his forties, tall, robust and powerfully muscled. A man who had worked hard to keep himself in good shape. The feral rage in his eyes told its own story. This was a man who had killed and had no regrets. A man who would do it again without hesitation. "What makes you so sure this is your mother's killer?"

"I'm telling you, it's the man who murdered her," Olivia said.

Her eyes were fierce and her voice was tight with fury.

"I don't doubt you," he said. "I'm just asking for information."

For a beat he thought she was not going to answer.

"I heard her voice," she finally said.

"Your mother's voice?"

"Yes, but not as if she was contacting me from beyond the grave. Nothing like that. It felt like a . . . recording." Olivia pondered that for a few seconds. Then she nodded, evidently satisfied with the explanation. "Yes, a psychic recording, similar to the hologram but audio instead of visual. I think she somehow embedded the words into the image."

"She was able to take the picture but she could not ice his aura the way you did?"

Olivia shook her head. "He killed her instead. But she shouted those words with her dying breath. Like a curse or a prophecy. I can't explain it. All I can tell you is that I sensed the whole ghastly situation."

Harlan studied the image. "Whoever he is, he's dressed for a casual day hike in the woods. Boots, hat, trousers, a windbreaker, pack with a water bottle. You can see some trees and a portion of a trail behind him."

"He ambushed her on that trail and pushed her off a cliff."

"He grabbed the camera." Harlan thought about that and then nodded. "Feels right."

"But how did he know where to find her? And why would she take the camera with her in the first place?"

"He lured her," Harlan said quietly. "He knew she had the camera. Somehow he convinced her to meet him in an isolated location. Maybe he told her he would pay a fortune for it."

"No," Olivia said, very sure of herself. "She inserted the camera into one of her paintings. That means it was important. She would not have sold it."

"So why take it with her when she went to meet the killer?"

"Obviously she didn't know he was a killer," Olivia said. "She must have believed she was meeting someone she could trust."

Harlan glanced at her. "Was your mother involved in a relationship of any kind?"

"Not at the time of her death. At least, not that I know of. I'm sure she would have told me if she was seeing someone." Olivia hesitated. "I think she would have mentioned it. Now I don't know what to think."

"But you're certain you've never met this man?"

"Absolutely certain."

Harlan went back to studying the hologram. He did another turn around the image—there was nothing to see on the side away from the camera—but when he walked back to the front he caught the glint of light sparking on an object on the ground. Glass.

He took a closer look and saw a long, narrow glass tube lying next to one boot. The tube had holes of varying size in it.

"Not glass," he said. "Crystal."

"What?"

"Looks like the killer dropped a tube on the ground. If it had been glass it would have shattered. I think the tube is made of a clear, hard crystal."

"I get the impression you think it's important."

"Everything about this image is important, but that crystal tube is the most significant object in the picture."

"Why?"

"Because it's a recorder."

CHAPTER 11

Shaken by the implication of what he had said, Olivia moved closer to the hologram. She studied the recorder.

"You think this is the man who was hunting us last night, don't you?" she said.

"Can't be sure, but it's a real possibility," he said. "If I'm right, the instrument is a paranormal weapon. I've come across a small number of them during the past five years."

"Paranormal weapons?"

"Yes. Not all of them were products of the Bluestone Project."

She glanced at him, startled. "Really?"

"Bluestone wasn't the first effort to weaponize paranormal energy, Olivia."

"So?"

"So, I learned some stuff while I was ducking the Foundation. There are a few laws of paranormal physics, one of which is that firing a paranormal weapon is not easy. It requires considerable talent and a tuning process."

"I was able to use the camera as a weapon," she pointed out. "No tuning process required."

"I'm sure that's because you inherited your grandmother's psychic vibe. It was tuned to her energy field. Evidently your paranormal profile is similar to hers—close enough, at least, to let you activate the device. But even in your case, you needed a strong talent. Got a feeling you've been unconsciously resonating with the camera ever since it came into your possession, learning how to use it."

"You think the recorder player is a strong talent, not just some random sociopath who happened to find the crystal weapon."

"Right." Harlan straightened and began to prowl the small room. Everything inside him was quickening. A Venn diagram began to take shape inside his head. Interlocking circles appeared. Connections. "We know a few things about the camera now, including the fact that it's dangerous."

"And worth a fortune in the underground antiquities market," Olivia said. "It's a working paranormal weapon with a Bluestone provenance."

"It's possible a rabid collector lured your mother into the woods to steal the camera, but if that's the case the artifact would have disappeared into a private vault."

Olivia looked down at the camera in her hands. "Instead it wound up on the sales floor of a local dealer who sold it for less than a hundred dollars."

"We need to talk to the dealer who sold you the camera."

"Gwendolyn Swan. She won't be able to tell us much, though. If she had considered the camera a valuable relic she would have stored it in her basement vault. She knows paranormal artifacts."

"Do you think there are any other holographic images locked in the camera?"

"To be honest, I'm nervous about trying to find out." She shivered. "Pulling up the holograms feels like summoning ghosts."

"That's true of all photographs, if you ask me. The people in them are ghosts in another dimension. You can see them but you can't communicate with them."

"Great. I'll never be able to look at another photo without thinking about ghosts."

She concentrated. Harlan felt energy shift in the atmosphere. When she pressed a button the image of the recorder player disappeared. No new images appeared.

After a moment she looked up. "I think there are other holograms on this camera, but I can't seem to . . . wait."

Another holographic image sprang to life in the middle of the bedroom. Harlan recognized the scene immediately. He knew Olivia did, too. Stunned, they both stared at the picture of the neatly lined-up vintage trailers.

"It's the trailer park in the painting you showed me on your phone," Olivia whispered. "I can see a portion of the old monastery or convent. But there's no oracle in a hooded robe. No warning about monsters."

"This is the hologram Grace Goodwin used to paint the picture I found," Harlan said. "She created it from this photograph. I think she took the picture herself, using that camera, and did the oil painting later."

"This camera really did belong to my grandmother."

"Any other photos on it?"

Olivia heightened her energy again and pressed the second button. The first image disappeared. Another hologram took its place, an image of an island that appeared to have been taken from a small boat. The rugged landscape, rocky outcroppings and forested hillsides were familiar. The entrance of a partially flooded shoreline cavern was visible just in front of the vessel. It was obvious the craft was headed into the cave.

"Looks like an island in the San Juans here in the Pacific Northwest," Harlan said. "Same vegetation and rock formations." He walked to the far side of the hologram and smiled when he saw the iconic black-and-white markings of the large marine mammal caught in a graceful dive. "An orca. That almost guarantees this island is in the San Juans. What do you want to bet there's a dock inside that cavern?"

Olivia did not respond. He sensed energy shifting in the room again and turned to look at her.

She was gazing at the hologram, eyes heating. Her lips parted and she spoke in the same eerie dreamstate voice she had used when she identified her mother's killer.

"The invisible island with no name conceals the invisible town with no name. To stop the monsters you must quench the lightning in the mirrors."

The voice abruptly stopped. Olivia snapped out of the trance. She was visibly shaking. Her eyes were feverish.

He took her arms and eased her gently down onto the side of the bed.

"Are you all right?" he asked.

Olivia took another breath and looked at the image of the island.

"I think so," she said. "What just happened?"

"You went into a trance. You spoke. Do you remember what you said?"

She took one more deep breath and pulled herself together. "I wasn't in a trance. I was concentrating. Focusing. Of course I remember what I said. *The invisible island with no name conceals the invisible town with no name. To stop the monsters you must quench the lightning in the mirrors.*"

"Yes," Harlan said. "Was it your mother's voice?"

"No. It was my grandmother's voice this time."

"Congratulations. If I'm right, you just became a full-fledged oracle talent."

"I had a bad feeling you were going to say that."

CHAPTER 12

The leader of the Foundation security team that had kept watch on the apartment tower during the night called at five a.m. Harlan was coming down the hall, fresh from a shower, when his phone rang. He took the call.

Olivia listened while she fired up the coffee maker.

"Appreciate the report," Harlan said into the phone. "No, we won't need you today, but stand by for tonight. Thanks."

He ended the call and sat down at the dining counter. "Security said there was no sign of anyone watching this building last night."

"I suppose that would have been too easy."

"Yes."

Harlan went back to his phone. Olivia sliced some sourdough bread and dropped the slices into a toaster. She started cracking eggs. From time to time she glanced at the intimate stranger she was about to feed. She found herself remembering their conversation about photographs and ghosts.

His expression had not changed when he made the comment.

Everything about him had remained focused on the problem of Vortex. But she had sensed a current of melancholia in the atmosphere. Sorrow, perhaps. Regret. And complicating the mix had been a darker, bleaker vibe. Guilt?

What are you mourning, Harlan Rancourt? And why do you feel responsible for the loss?

She finished cracking eggs and picked up a whisk. Silence reigned in the small kitchen. When the coffee was ready she poured two cups and set one down in front of Harlan.

"You're not much of a morning conversationalist, are you?" she said.

"Beats me." Harlan swiped the screen on his phone. "There's never anyone around to talk to in the mornings."

She gave him a cool smile. He did not notice, because he was fixated on his phone.

"There's me this morning," she said.

"That's different." Harlan did not look up. "You're different."

She couldn't argue with that observation, she thought. She *was* different; probably nothing like the women he usually went home with. He certainly was different from her usual dates. She reminded herself that he wasn't a date. He was a client.

She put a couple tablespoons of butter into the pan and poured in the eggs.

So what if Harlan was obsessed with Vortex? She was pretty damn obsessed this morning herself. She hadn't uttered prophecies last night. She had repeated psychically recorded messages. Captions for the photographs. Okay, so they sounded like prophecies. That didn't mean she was an oracle. The words belonged to her grandmother and her mother—paranormal voice mail. Sure, it was disturbing to hear the voices, but that was because of the emotions involved.

She was not an oracle.

There had been no going back to sleep for either of them after she pulled up the holograms. They had taken turns in the shower and gotten dressed. She had chosen a somber gray palette—iron-gray trousers and a fog-gray sweater. It suited her grim, anxious mood. They were not her favorite colors, but damned if she was ready to start wearing a hooded robe. She was not an oracle. She was . . . something else. A private investigator with a weird camera.

She was interested to note that Harlan no longer looked like an accountant or an FBI special agent. This morning he had gone with another equally nothing-to-see-here style. He had produced a pair of black trousers and a pristine white T-shirt from the duffel bag. An Oxford blue button-down shirt was layered over the tee. The top two buttons of the shirt were undone. The black-framed glasses and a pair of running shoes finished off the look. He had not yet strapped on the shoulder holster. If you saw him on the street you could easily mistake him for an employee at one of the myriad high-tech start-ups in the Pacific Northwest.

It wasn't the subtle but effective change of image that amazed her. The astonishing thing was that Harlan had managed to tune his vibe to the look. If she didn't use her talent for aura reading, she would have bought the whole picture. Well, maybe not the whole picture— there were those incredible eyes. Sea green and filled with secrets. The glasses did nothing to reduce the impact as far as she was concerned.

The man was a human chameleon. But he could not hide from her. She wondered if he realized that or if he cared.

She dished up the eggs, added thick slices of sourdough toast and set the plates on the counter.

Harlan noticed the food immediately. It was evidently one of his priorities, unlike, say, chatting with her over a cup of coffee.

He put down his phone and picked up his fork. She made a mental note. Evidently there was at least one thing that could distract him.

She rounded the end of the counter and sat down beside him. "Any luck?"

"I've got a few leads, based on your prophecy about the invisible island with no name," he said around a mouthful of scrambled eggs.

"It wasn't a prophecy. I'm not an oracle." She was getting tired of repeating herself, but she had to keep denying the verdict, because if she didn't, she might start believing it was the truth. "My mother and grandmother somehow managed to record their voices as well as those photos on that camera. I was able to hear them because I could resonate with their psychic signatures."

"Whatever. The point is, there is a lot of information in Grace Goodwin's message. It just needs decoding."

Now he was humoring her. She tried not to grit her teeth. She could put up with a lot if the trade-off meant finding her mother's killer.

"What do an invisible island with no name and an invisible town with no name mean?" she asked.

"A secret government town set up on a secret government-owned island."

She thought about that while she munched some toast. "I get that the Bluestone Project was a clandestine government operation, but why wouldn't the island and the town have names?"

"They probably did have code names, but those identifiers would have been highly classified. It was a common strategy. In World War Two, secret government towns were built to house the people who worked on the Manhattan Project."

"How do you keep an entire town a secret?"

"You make sure it doesn't show up on a map," Harlan said. "Given that most maps are produced by various government agencies and departments, it wasn't that hard to control the information, not in those days."

"But anyone flying over the island would have noticed a community that suddenly appeared on a previously uninhabited island."

"Not necessarily," Harlan said. "Believe it or not, it was actually common to camouflage naval installations, harbors, aircraft production facilities and small towns during wartime. The techniques and technologies would have been familiar to the people who established Bluestone. And it wasn't as if they had to conceal a whole town; just a few trailers. The lab itself would have been underground or in a cave system to block as much para-radiation as possible."

"So we're looking for an island and an old trailer park that don't appear on any maps?"

"The trailers would have been demolished or sunk when the word came down to destroy all traces of the Bluestone Project. The building that looked like a convent or monastery might still be there, though. It obviously predated the trailers. And you can't get rid of an entire island."

"How do we find it?"

"We delegate. Arganbright and Pine can do the research. The old monastery is a solid clue. It indicates that at one time the island was occupied by a religious order. There will be tax records—unless those were also destroyed."

Olivia drank some coffee. "What about the last part of the recording?" She refused to call it a prophecy. *"To stop the monsters you must quench the lightning in the mirrors."*

"Beats me," Harlan said.

"What?" She looked at him. "I thought you were the hotshot chaos talent who sees all and knows all."

"I'm good, but I'm not a magician. I need data."

"I am, of course, devastated to discover that you have limitations."

"Arganbright and Pine said you are a very good aura reader."

"Yep."

"Any limitations?"

"Sure."

"Can you tell the difference between normal and not-normal auras?" he asked. He sounded as if he was feeling his way.

"I can spot a seriously unstable aura and the blanks. But

straight-up, cold-blooded evil is remarkably stable, in my experience."

"So you can't always tell the good guys from the bad guys?"

"Nope. I don't know of anyone, psychic or otherwise, who can do that. People are just too complicated, and their auras mirror those complications."

Harlan drank some coffee and set the cup on the counter with an air of careful precision. She thought he was going to return to his phone. Instead he looked at her with unreadable eyes.

"You can see my aura, can't you? All of it."

"Uh-huh."

"I thought so. Most people see only what I want them to see."

"That aura-manipulation talent of yours is . . . interesting."

"'Interesting' is one word for it," he said. "The old saying that people see what they expect to see is true, but it goes deeper—they see what they want to see, what they need to see."

She looked at him over the rim of the coffee cup. "I would think it would be a very useful talent. You make it sound like there's a downside."

"There's a downside to every talent, isn't there?"

"So they say. What's the downside to being a chameleon talent?"

His brows rose. "'Chameleon talent'?"

"That's the term that came to mind. 'Camouflage talent' would be an equally apt description, I suppose."

He drank some more coffee while he thought about that. "'Camouflage talent' is as good as any other label. Sounds better than 'illusion talent.'"

"Who called you that?"

"Someone I do odd jobs for occasionally."

"So what's the downside of your talent?"

"It's hard to explain." Harlan paused for a moment, evidently searching for words. "When you realize you can make people see you the way you want them to see you, it becomes instinctive. A reflex."

"Probably a handy skill set when it comes to getting dates."

"Among other things."

She smiled. "Such as hiding in plain sight for five years while Victor Arganbright and Lucas Pine employ the resources of the Foundation to hunt for you?"

"My ability to manipulate my aura proved useful these past five years."

"But?"

"If I walk into a restaurant without my camouflage, I raise the hair on the back of every neck in the room. People are afraid of me, but they have no idea why."

"So you stay below the radar, but that means no one ever sees the real you."

"Something like that."

"Including the people you date."

"Including them." He looked at her. "But last night you saw the real me, and you didn't run."

"I grew up in Fogg Lake and I'm a private investigator who handles cases for the Foundation. You are not the first high-level talent I've met. Takes a lot to make me run."

Harlan watched her for a long moment.

"Maybe you're not running because you've got two high-level talents yourself."

"I'm not an oracle, Harlan. I can use the camera because I resonate with my grandmother's psychic signature. That does not make me a dual talent."

She could tell he wasn't buying her explanation, but he didn't argue with her. Instead he slowly lowered his mug.

"There's a theory that having more than one strong talent leads to sensory overload," he said. "Too much stimulation. Most people don't have the power and control it takes to handle one high-level talent, let alone two. The result is usually a fragile parapsych profile."

"Whose theory is that?"

"It was formulated early on in the Bluestone Project, and the Foundation researchers are still mostly convinced it's true," Harlan said. "At the very least the experts are wary of multi-talents."

"Well, you're certainly not unstable. Nature gave you two talents and, obviously, the ability to control both."

"You're sure of that?"

She raised her brows. "Trust me, I wouldn't have let you sleep here last night if I wasn't sure of it. At the very least I would have insisted on having the security team standing guard outside my bedroom door—not down on the street."

He nodded, accepting that statement. "I'm okay with my chaos talent. It has its uses."

"How does it work?"

"Sort of like a Venn diagram. I look for the places where the circles overlap. Connections."

"But you're not okay with your ability to camouflage your aura."

"It's good for only two things," Harlan said. "Hiding in plain sight and scaring the shit out of people. It makes me one of the monsters. I'm good at hunting them because I can think like them."

CHAPTER 13

Olivia choked on her coffee. She sputtered, coughed and spewed. Harlan reached over and thumped her on the back a couple of times. She grabbed a napkin, wiped her mouth and mopped up drops of coffee on the counter.

"There you have it," she said. "Proof that I am not an oracle. I sure didn't see that coming."

Harlan winced. "I get that a lot."

Olivia swiveled around on the chair to face him. "You're serious, aren't you?"

Harlan's mouth tightened. His eyes burned. "I'm serious."

"This is . . . fascinating."

Harlan blinked. "Fascinating?"

"Intriguing? Interesting? Riveting? Did your father, Stenson Rancourt, have any unusual talents?"

"He was a strong chaos talent—like my grandfather—but he did not possess any other particular talent. Just the above-average intuition that most talents have." Harlan swallowed some coffee and lowered the mug. "Which he often ignored, especially when it came to women."

"I've heard he was notorious for his affairs."

"He loved my mother. Deeply. After she died in a car accident he—" Harlan stopped.

"Became a womanizer?"

"He devoted himself to building his legacy, the Foundation, and finding Vortex. He never took any of the women seriously."

"I see." She considered what he had said a moment earlier. "So, according to the experts, dual talents are usually unstable monsters?"

"It's a theory."

"And one of your talents gives you the ability to think like a monster. I guess that explains how you tracked me down, doesn't it?"

His brows shot together over the black frames of his glasses. "What?"

"You think I have two talents. That makes me a monster, right?"

"No, damn it, that's not what I meant."

"You can think like a monster, so you were able to find me."

Irritation flashed in Harlan's eyes. "That's not how it happened."

"Are you sure?"

"I've spent a lot of the past five years researching paranormal genetics. Turns out strong talents often appear to skip generations, but it's more likely they remain latent unless something happens that forces them to the surface. That could explain why dual talents don't show up very often."

"You're really worried about this whole monster thing, aren't you?"

Harlan looked at her. "Wouldn't you be if you just found out you had a half sister you never knew existed who is now locked up at Halcyon Manor because she's in a fugue state after murdering a few people and trying to poison others?"

Olivia stilled. "Ah. So that's it. This is about Larissa Whittier."

"You're aware of her?"

"Sure. The Foundation is a giant rumor mill, and Lark and

LeClair is tapped into it, thanks to Catalina's husband. Slater Argan-bright is one of Victor's nephews. Now I understand your concerns."

"My concerns?"

"Okay, deep down you're scared to death that you're going to end up like Larissa Whittier, right?"

"I'm not scared to death. I'm trying to be realistic."

"You're scared because you've both got Rancourt genes," Olivia said. "But you've got other genes as well. Regardless, the genetic aspect isn't important in this situation."

Harlan's eyes narrowed. "Is that right? You're an authority?"

"Yep. I thought I explained—you control your talent, it doesn't control you. Larissa Whittier is, or at least was, in full control of her talent, too. The critical factor, the only one that truly matters, is that you both had the power of choice. Whittier chose the path of revenge and took it way too far, which is a really stupid thing to do, because people—including, I'm sure, a number of real oracles—have been warning against it for centuries."

"He who walks the path of revenge should first dig two graves—one for himself."

"Exactly. See? You don't need an oracle. You can do your own prophecies."

"How do you know I'm not out for revenge?"

"Because Victor and Lucas are still alive. This has all been very interesting, but I vote we get on with the business at hand. I've got an obsession, too, remember? I want to find the person who murdered my mother."

For a couple of beats Harlan looked as if he had no idea what to do with her statement.

"You're not taking this seriously, are you?" he said.

"The monster theory? No. I've got more pressing issues. So do you."

Harlan took a breath, swallowed the last of his coffee and got to his feet.

"Time to visit Swan Antiques," he said.

"Too early. The shop won't be open yet."

"In my experience, that's the best time to catch people who have information I need. Where does Swan live?"

"Over her shop."

"Convenient."

CHAPTER 14

The rumble of the boat's engines shattered the tranquility of the island morning just as the Piper was putting the final touches on one of the topiary crypts.

He had a name, Jake Spode, but he preferred the code name the government agency had given to his father—Piper. Spode had adopted it at the start of his own career.

The boat engines slowed. Anticipation twisted with fear flashed through him. Maybe the plan had gone smoothly. Maybe they had picked up the oracle. He would not know until they docked. There was no communications technology on the island. No computers. No phones, not even landlines. The only way to make a phone call or use a computer was to take the boat to a neighboring island or a town on the mainland.

It was inconvenient, but the strict policy against any and all tech was one of the strategies that had made it possible to hide in plain sight. The island with no name was no longer invisible, thanks to GPS and other forms of modern technology, but the Piper had discovered another tactic for maintaining a cloak of invisibility—private ownership concealed under layers of shell corporations and trusts.

Spode forced himself to power down his excitement. Strong emotions were dangerous inside the maze. The hot currents of energy played havoc with them. The heavy paranormal atmosphere tended to enhance and distort spikes of fear, rage, hope and desire.

He took a few more snips and stood back to admire his artistry.

The crypt was large and architecturally detailed. He had designed and built the frame using a photograph of an elaborate stone burial vault he had admired in the Recoleta Cemetery in Buenos Aires. That had been a few years ago, when he was still powerful, still getting contracts from clandestine intelligence and security agencies around the world—back in the days when he had been able to leave the island whenever he wanted and remain away for extended periods of time.

The inspiration for the various topiaries that formed the maze had come from the grand cemeteries of the world. In addition to those in Recoleta, there were examples from Paris and New Orleans. But unlike those elegantly laid out cities of the dead, the necropolis his father and he had constructed was an intricate puzzle with a great secret at the center.

His father had begun the maze of crypts and tombs and burial vaults. Each topiary was a record of a successful mission. Memento mori taken from the targets were buried beneath the various vaults and monuments.

The tokens of the deceased were, of necessity, small. In the early years, his father, the first Piper, had possessed a penchant for jewelry. There were a number of wedding rings, bracelets and watches buried in the maze. Unlike his parent, he preferred more personal souvenirs.

At the start of his career he had gone with the traditional choice— a lock of hair preserved in a small glass box. Over time he had craved more intimate reminders of his achievements. He had settled on a finger from each target. There was more work involved, because each pinkie had to be properly preserved, but there had always been plenty of time for DIY projects between contracts.

For years there had been only his father and himself on the island, but in those days they could come and go freely. Their assignments took them all over the world. But things had started to change after the first Piper died. An unfamiliar loneliness had set in.

He had found a student who had eventually become a friend and a comrade in arms. He and Barrow had worked as a team for a decade. But a year ago things had begun to change—they had begun to change. The prospect of rapid deterioration and death had driven them to the edge of desperation. To survive they needed outside help. That meant taking huge risks. They had made the decision to bring in a small number of students who could be trained to work as assistants. Disposable assistants. The old-fashioned term was *cannon fodder.*

The Piper found the psychic dissonance produced by the juxtaposition of life and death in the maze stimulating. It disturbed the students, often to the point of panic, but it taught them control—unless it killed them, in which case they became plant food.

The paranormal heat generated by what was left of the old Vortex lab had transformed the cemetery plants in astonishing ways. The foliage grew so thick that it formed impenetrable walls. The natural poisons and toxins produced by several species had intensified over the years. Thorns that in the outside world would have delivered a minor scratch were now stiletto-sharp and just as deadly. The carpets of exotic mushrooms growing inside the crypts beckoned the unwary with dazzling colors and unpredictable radiation.

At night the garden was a paranormal carnival of the macabre made luminous with energy. Only the most advanced students were allowed to practice their skills after dark. He could not afford to lose too many. Natural talents had always been rare. Those who could handle the enhancement treatments were even more scarce.

When it came to recruitment, there was another complication as well. Potential students had to be able to effectively disappear without drawing the attention of a family or the authorities.

The throb of the boat's engines was suddenly muted. Barrow had piloted the vessel into the cavern where the small dock was located. Spode experienced another hit of desperate hope. Ruthlessly he squelched it, but not before a hallucination materialized.

For a horrifying moment he saw his father's body again, just as he had found it that day in the maze. The first Piper's face was contorted in anguish. The remains of a partially devoured mushroom lay on the ground beside him. Spode knew that his parent had not eaten the mushroom by mistake. The truth was that the first Piper had no longer been able to cope with the stress of the enhancement treatments. He had been slowly going insane, slowly dying. A prisoner on an invisible island.

In those days Spode had been filled with a sense of his own power. He was sure the treatments had made him stronger than his father, certain he was immune to the rapid deterioration that had destroyed the first Piper. He knew now that was not true.

Spode suppressed the vision, took the small, flashlight-shaped device out of his pocket and generated a little psychic energy through the crystal switch. A spear of ultraviolet light appeared. He aimed it at the ground.

The device was one of several artifacts he and his father had discovered in the old Vortex lab. It guided him through the maze to the concealed exit. In the old days he had not needed the paranormal GPS. He had been strong enough to navigate the green necropolis with his senses. But the deterioration in the past few months had become so serious he could not afford to take the risk of getting lost. Barrow would have to rescue him, and that would not be good optics. The students would realize he was weakening. The Piper had to look strong at all costs.

Another jolt of excitement shot through him just before he reached the concealed gate. He made himself pause in front of a box-wood statue of a weeping angel to clip a few errant leaves. Woodies were usually quite obedient, but as with even the most devoted students they occasionally required discipline.

Satisfied that he had himself firmly under control, he went to the concealed gate and opened it. He moved out of the maze and waited until the gate closed, leaving no visible trace of its existence. When it was back in place, the only thing that could be seen was the vine-covered brick wall that surrounded the maze.

He and Barrow were the only ones who knew of the various con-cealed exits. As far as the students were concerned there was a single point of entry and exit. It was never a good idea to let the students in on all the master's secrets. Bad for discipline. Also dangerous. There was always the risk that an ambitious apprentice, exulting in his newfound powers, might toy with the notion of taking the master's place.

Spode arrived at the entrance of the cave in time to see Barrow and the Messenger climbing the steps. His heart nearly failed him when he realized they were alone. There was no sign of the oracle. He wanted to howl his despair to the skies.

Fuck.

He had his emotions firmly in hand when the Messenger reached the top of the steps.

"I have bad news, sir," he said.

His name was Fletch. Like the other eight students currently in training, he no longer used his last name. Also like the others he was young—nineteen. When Spode had found him on the streets of Se-attle a few months ago, Fletch had possessed some minimal talent for aura reading. It was probably one of the things that had kept him alive. The enhancement process had endowed him with a second tal-ent that was still developing: the ability to fire one of the old Vortex weapons. He was not yet able to make it work properly, but he was getting there. In the meantime, he had become proficient with a regular pistol.

"Obviously the news is bad," Spode said. He was careful to keep all emotion out of his voice.

Barrow appeared at the top of the steps. He shook his head, saying nothing. The grim despair in his eyes said it all. They were both dying. The students would start dying soon, too; they just didn't know it yet. There was no point telling them. It would affect their performance. They needed to stay mission focused.

"We can talk in the gazebo," Spode said.

He led the way to the fanciful structure perched on the cliff overlooking the dark, cold waters of Puget Sound. In the distance a pod of orcas was on the move. Apex predators. The animals' high-speed leaps out of the water signaled a hunt in progress. He and Barrow had once been apex predators, too. Now they were weak and dying before their time. Just like the first Piper.

He sat down on a bench. Barrow sank down on the seat across from him. Fletch remained on his feet. He looked anxious.

"What went wrong?" Spode asked.

"We followed the oracle last night." Fletch straightened his shoulders, trying hard to look professional; trying to look like a warrior. "She went to a restaurant, alone. There was a private event going on. We waited for her, but when she left there was a man with her."

Spode frowned. "One of the people who attended the event?"

"Must have been," Fletch said. "No one else was allowed inside. Looked like a hookup. The guy didn't seem to be a problem at first. Figured he was an accountant or something. We knew we could handle him if it came to that. Ink was able to get a fix on the oracle with his recorder, but before he could do his thing the oracle and the man who had picked her up went into another restaurant. We had to wait while they ate dinner."

"Go on," Spode said.

"When they left the restaurant they started walking. There weren't many people around so Ink used the recorder again. All of a sudden the oracle and the guy with her started running. They went into an alley."

Barrow's bleak expression turned another shade of grim. He met Spode's eyes. "Sounds like they knew they were being followed."

Spode nodded and turned back to Fletch. "Do you think the oracle picked up on the recorder, or was it her companion?"

"Ink said he was sure it was the guy she hooked up with who realized what was going on," Fletch said. "Anyhow, he went back to her apartment with her. Had a duffel bag. Looked like he planned to spend the night."

"That means he's the problem," Spode said to Barrow. "We have to assume he knows that Olivia LeClair is the oracle. It's . . . unfortunate that he got to her first."

"Ink and the rest of the team are still in Seattle, keeping an eye on the oracle," Fletch said. "Ink said to tell you they will take care of the man and grab the woman first chance they get."

"We are close." Spode watched the orcas for a while. "So close."

"Yes, sir," Fletch said. "We'll get her, sir."

There was, Spode thought, nothing quite like the supreme self-confidence of youth, especially youth that had been psychically enhanced. Once upon a time he had enjoyed that glorious sensation, too.

"Go get something to eat," he said.

"Yes, sir."

Fletch took off, loping up the path to the old monastery.

Barrow watched him for a moment. "The kid needs another dose of the serum."

"So do you." Spode exhaled slowly. "We both do. But the stuff is killing us."

"It's the only thing keeping us alive."

Spode nodded.

They sat together in silence, two men who had killed together and were now facing death together. They had never been lovers, but somewhere along the line they had become closer than most lovers.

"Think the man who grabbed the oracle last night is from the Foundation?" Spode asked after a while.

"Damned if I know," Barrow said. "I think we should assume he is. For now, at any rate."

"The situation is fluid," Spode said. "There's too much at stake. I can no longer handle it from here. I need to be on the ground."

"Are you sure that's a good idea?"

"No, but we don't have any choice." Spode pushed himself to his feet. "I'll prepare another dose of the serum for both of us."

The words of the oracle he had killed nearly a year ago whispered in his head. *Dead man walking in a dying garden.*

CHAPTER 15

Disaster.

Or maybe, finally, a seriously lucky break, Gwendolyn Swan thought. Either way, the already dangerous project had become riskier by a factor of . . . who knew?

She and her sister had tried to calculate the potential downside when they arranged to put the camera into Olivia's hands, but the main concern at the time was that she would go straight to Victor Arganbright and draw the attention of the Foundation.

They had not foreseen the possibility of an outsider—a complete stranger—getting involved.

The man standing beside Olivia LeClair in front of the sales counter was an unknown quantity and, therefore, a major complication. The card he had given her read *John Reynolds, Insurance Investigator.*

Really? Olivia had brought in an insurance investigator? What the hell was this about?

Gwendolyn braced herself behind the counter and managed a polite smile. There was no need to worry about Olivia—she was a useful pawn. The risk factors linked to her were known and had been accounted for. But the insurance investigator was a new headache.

"Mr. Reynolds's company issued a policy that covered a collection of antique cameras that may have included this one," Olivia said.

"There was a break-in at the client's home a few months ago," Reynolds said. He adjusted his black-framed glasses. "Several cameras were stolen, including one that closely resembles the antique Ms. LeClair purchased in this shop."

"I see," Gwendolyn said. *Shit.*

"Our client has been keeping an eye out for the stolen items online, hoping to recover some of them," Reynolds continued. "He spotted this one when Ms. LeClair went looking for information about it."

"I was hoping to find a collector who could help me identify it," Olivia explained. "It's a very unusual camera. I'm curious about the manufacturer. There are no markings. No serial number. It may have been a prototype that never went into production."

Gwendolyn stifled a groan. This was not good. *Shit, the Sequel.*

"The client showed the photo to my boss, who asked me to run it down," Reynolds said. "There's been a dispute about the value of the collection."

"If you ask me, the insurance company is trying to avoid writing the check to cover the client's loss," Olivia said. "You know how insurance companies are."

"Due diligence," Reynolds said. "We don't pay off when we suspect the client is trying to defraud us. Bottom line is that I tracked the camera to Ms. LeClair. She agreed to help me."

Olivia got a what-can-you-do expression. "It sounded like a better option than having an insurance company accuse me of stealing the camera."

"I see," Gwendolyn said again.

She and Eloisa had anticipated that Olivia might do some online research but they had not expected an insurance investigator to take notice. She wished she could call Eloisa to discuss the problem, but there was no time. She had to make a decision.

Reynolds did not appear to be a serious threat. He seemed to be exactly what his business card said he was—an insurance investigator pursuing an investigation. If it wasn't for the fact that he was standing right in front of her, looking bored—an insurance company guy going through the paces, doing his job—it would have been easy to forget he was even in the shop.

But when you were closing in on the location of the Vortex lab and its secrets, you had to pay attention to every detail, including the sudden appearance of an insurance investigator.

There was no putting the toothpaste back into the tube. The project was going forward. All she could do was try to maintain control.

"The camera was one of several low-value objects in a box of miscellaneous collectibles that I picked up at an estate sale," she said. "If you'll give me a minute I'll check my records."

"Appreciate it," Reynolds said.

He turned and strolled across the room to a display counter that held a mid-century record player. He raised the lid of the machine and picked up the tonearm as if to take a closer look.

"Please do not touch that," Gwendolyn said, putting some acid into her voice. "It's quite delicate."

"Sorry." Reynolds lowered the tonearm and wandered off to examine a music box.

Olivia gave Gwendolyn an apologetic smile and lowered her voice. "Sorry to bother you, especially at this hour of the morning, but Mr. Reynolds practically accused me of stealing the camera. I'm trying to prove that it's not the antique he's searching for."

"I understand," Gwendolyn said. She went to her computer. "I promise you the provenance is pristine, at least from my end. Can't speak for the former owner. You know how it is with collectors. If they want an object, they don't always ask a lot of questions about how it happened to come onto the market."

Olivia glanced over her shoulder. Apparently satisfied that Reynolds was occupied with a mid-century radio at the far end of the showroom, she leaned partway over the counter.

"That's certainly true in our market," she murmured.

"Yes. Does Reynolds understand that I cater to a particular kind of collector?"

"No. As far as he's concerned, he's just chasing a stolen camera."

"All right, give me a minute here," Gwendolyn said.

She did not have to do much searching. A plan had sprung to mind. She knew exactly where she was going to send John Reynolds, insurance investigator.

"Here we go," she said. "The camera and the other items in the box that I picked up came from the estate of Blake Sefton. Classic eccentric collector, I'm told. Lived outside a small community called Cedric Valley. I think it's in the foothills of the Cascades."

"There are lots of tiny towns and communities tucked away in those mountains," Olivia said.

"True." Gwendolyn looked up from her computer. "I'm afraid that's all I can tell you."

Reynolds lost interest in the radio and came back to the counter. "You said you picked up the camera at an estate sale. Who handled the Sefton estate?"

"According to my records, Sefton left the house and the contents to a local historical society," Gwendolyn said. "The society sold off Sefton's collection of antiques and collectibles to raise cash. I don't think they were ever able to unload the house. If you think you can hold me responsible for selling stolen goods, Mr. Reynolds, you can forget it. My financial records are in perfect order. If Ms. LeClair has any complaints, I will, of course, be happy to refund her money."

"No, that's fine," Olivia said quickly. "Everyone knows you run a legitimate business. As far as I'm concerned, Mr. Reynolds is going to have to prove this camera was stolen before I hand it over to him."

"I'll let you and Mr. Reynolds sort it out," Gwendolyn said. "I do not want to get involved in anything shady. In my business, reputation is everything."

"Yeah, dealers of art and antiques tell me that all the time," Reynolds said. "You'd be amazed how many of them don't ask too many questions when it comes to their business dealings."

"Goodbye, Mr. Reynolds," Gwendolyn said.

"Appreciate the cooperation," he said.

He was already halfway to the door.

Olivia gave Gwendolyn another apologetic look.

"Sorry about this," she whispered.

"Forget it," Gwendolyn said. "I understand, believe me. There are reasons why nobody loves insurance companies."

CHAPTER 16

Gwendolyn waited until the door closed behind Olivia and John Reynolds. She went to the window and watched the pair walk the length of the alley and disappear around the corner.

The Closed sign was still in the window. She locked the door, hurried back to the sales counter and picked up her phone.

Eloisa answered on the first ring.

"Is this about the camera?" she asked, her voice sharp with anxiety.

"Yes. We've got an interesting development. Olivia LeClair walked into my shop a few minutes ago. She was not alone. She had an insurance investigator with her."

"An *insurance investigator*?"

"I know. I didn't see that coming, either. His name is John Reynolds. Said he was chasing a stolen camera that was similar to the one I sold to Olivia."

"Shit."

"That's certainly the word that came to my mind, too. He wanted the name of the previous owner."

"What did you tell him?"

"The truth, more or less. If he buys the story, he won't bother to drive to Cedric Valley to find Sefton's house. But if he does head there, we'll know he's a problem."

Eloisa was quiet for a moment. "If he insists on checking out the house, we have to assume he's not who he claims to be."

"Exactly. There's only one reason why he would want to look at the empty house of an eccentric collector who once owned an odd camera."

"He's hunting for the same thing we are looking for."

"Exactly," Gwendolyn said.

"Could you see anything in his aura?"

"It looked perfectly normal. I didn't pick up any strong vibes. But I'm just average when it comes to reading auras. It's obvious Reynolds has convinced Olivia LeClair that he's the real deal. Under the circumstances, I don't think we can afford to take any chances. If he convinces LeClair to hand over the camera on the grounds that it's stolen, we're going to have a serious problem on our hands."

"And if he's chasing what we're chasing, he's an even bigger problem. There's enough competition out there as it is."

"Either way, we need to get him out of the picture as quickly as possible."

"Getting rid of Reynolds has to look good," Eloisa said.

"I agree. But it also occurs to me that if he does go to Cedric Valley, we may have a golden opportunity to kill a couple of birds with one stone."

"*We* don't kill birds. That's a job for a professional."

"I'll make the call."

CHAPTER 17

I f you want my opinion, I don't think Swan bought our story," Olivia said. "Your camouflage trick looked good, but her aura was sparking like crazy. She was tense and agitated."

They were sitting in a coffee shop on First Avenue, drinking Americanos. Harlan had his back to the wall, positioned so that he could watch the door. The exit to the alley was only steps away. He had ordered a double shot and was on his phone again. She wondered somewhat idly how long it had been since he'd had a polite conversation with another human being.

"It doesn't matter if she bought my cover," he said. He did not look up from the phone. "That interview was all about stirring the pot. Successful dealers in the paranormal artifacts trade are tapped into the local market like no one else. They hear all the rumors. I'm sure she got on her phone the minute we walked out the door."

"Think she'll call you with more information?"

"I doubt it. But with luck she'll call someone who will call someone and get things rolling. Meanwhile I need to get a look inside Blake Sefton's house."

"What good will that do? Sefton is dead and his collection was sold off."

Harlan held up his phone. "According to the public records, the taxes on the house are being paid by the historical trust, which, interestingly, is a private charity operated by another trust. What do you want to bet that the second trust was set up by a shell company with headquarters on an offshore tax haven?"

She thought about that while she drank some coffee. Slowly she lowered the cup. "You're really good at this no-coincidences way of looking at the world, aren't you?"

"It's how I've stayed alive, Olivia."

It wasn't the words that chilled her; it was the way he spoke them. Assuming there were no coincidences was just an everyday habit for him, like wearing a seat belt.

"Obviously the technique is working for you." She tapped one finger on the side of the cup. "How did Blake Sefton die?"

Harlan smiled a slow, cold smile. It went well with the ice in his eyes. Once again he held up his phone to show her a string of search results.

"Excellent question," he said. "Sefton died of a heart attack. It was several days before the body was found. A local sheriff's deputy noticed that the curtains in the living room were pulled shut every day for a week. That was not Sefton's usual routine. The deputy decided to check and found the body."

"Hmm. Any sign of a break-in?"

"Apparently not. There's nothing in the report." Harlan dropped the phone into the pocket of his windbreaker and picked up his coffee. "Was your grandmother a collector?"

"I don't think so. She had a small house and a garden over on the coast. Mom and I visited often. But I was only five the last time we were there. I doubt if I would have noticed a paranormal vibe. If I did, I would have assumed it was normal—just part of Grandma's house."

"No sign of a gallery or a vault?"

"If she had one, it must have been hidden. I certainly don't remember it. Mom never mentioned it, either."

"But Grace Goodwin was hiding from whoever was assigned to murder the Vortex team. She must have been paranoid as hell. Every time you and your mother visited she would have been afraid that you were in danger. I think she would have had a safe room or an escape plan. Probably both. You said you were five when she died?"

"Yes." Olivia hesitated. "There was a fire. The house burned to the ground. The authorities attributed the cause of the blaze to painting chemicals stored in a closet."

"Safe rooms are almost always underground. If your grandmother had one it would not have been completely destroyed by a fire. Do you remember your last visit with Grace Goodwin?"

"No, not really." Olivia touched her handbag, aware of the camera inside. She could feel a whisper of the familiar vibe even through the leather. "Sometimes when I'm waking up from a dream, I think I remember something that happened the last time Mom and I went to the coast—something bad—but whenever I try to pin down the details, everything dissolves. I told you, I was only five."

Harlan watched her intently. "Is it the same dream every time?"

"I think so, but I can't even be sure of that much."

"When did the dreams start?"

"I've had them off and on for years, but lately they've been coming more frequently."

"Lately?"

"You want to know the truth?" She opened her handbag and took out the camera. "They've become more intense since I picked this up at Swan's. Probably because it's infused with my grandmother's and my mother's vibe. The energy is affecting my dreams. Maybe I shouldn't sleep with it beside my bed—"

Between one heartbeat and the next she plunged straight into a waking dreamstate. Her heart pounded. Her breathing got tight. She wanted to run but she could not move.

. . . She hears her grandmother's voice. "The monster is coming. I will hold him off as long as I can. Run."

There is a terrifying clang as the steel door slams shut. Crushing darkness. The thud of a heavy bolt sliding into place. Waves of light in colors that do not exist in her box of crayons.

Her mother takes her hand. "Come with me, sweetheart. We must run."

A brilliant, dark blue mirror glows on the wall. Her mother leads her through it . . .

Darkness.

Olivia felt the rush of the fever dream sweep through her. The warning roared in her head.

"No," she got out in a hoarse voice. "*No.*"

She slapped a hand across her own mouth. The need to speak was overwhelming. She fought it with everything she had. She was in a public place, a coffee shop. If she slipped into a dreamstate voice the way she had last night and started talking, everyone in the room would conclude that she was mentally unbalanced.

But the words were screaming inside her, seeking escape. She had no choice but to deliver them. She had to get them out. She kept her palm over her mouth and looked at the door. She might be able to make it outside if she made a run for it . . .

"Here," Harlan said. He pushed his phone across the table.

She glanced down and saw that he had pulled up a blank screen. The notebook feature. The little keyboard was ready and waiting. Frantically she grabbed the phone and tapped the letters. The words spilled out onto the page.

The feverish sensation receded with each keystroke. She could do this. She could control the compulsion to speak, at least to some extent.

When she was finished, the desperate need to give voice to the words evaporated as suddenly as it had come upon her. She looked down to see what she had written.

When the time comes you will know how to go through the mirror.

CHAPTER 18

Olivia pushed the phone across the table and picked up her coffee cup. She set it down immediately, because her fingers were still shivering in reaction to the adrenaline sluicing through her veins.

"I can't go on doing this," she whispered. "People will think I'm crazy. For all I know, I really am going insane."

"No," Harlan said. "You're an oracle. This is how your talent works."

He was not looking at her. He was studying what she had written on the phone.

"I find your sympathy underwhelming," she said.

"You'll get used to it."

"Your inability to project sympathy?"

"No, your talent." He closed the phone and put it back into his jacket pocket. "Any idea what triggered the vision?"

"It wasn't a vision, damn it." She paused, trying to assess what had happened. "An anxiety attack, maybe. Complete with video. It felt as if I was suddenly in the middle of a nightmare."

"Or a memory?"

She felt herself go very cold. "I don't see how that could be possible. I don't believe in repressed memories." But the dream had felt so real.

"Memories are tricky things," Harlan said, his tone surprisingly gentle. "Just ask any cop who has interviewed an eyewitness. Also, there is selective amnesia. It can occur after a traumatic event. There are any number of reasons why you don't recall a specific memory unless or until you encounter a triggering incident."

She sighed. "I know. You're right. It's just that I can't remember anything before or after the dream sequence. If it is a real memory, there should be more context."

"Maybe we can provide some." Harlan folded his arms on the table and fixed her with his raptor eyes. "It was my question about the safe room that triggered the nightmare, wasn't it?"

"Yes." She made another attempt to pick up the coffee cup. This time she succeeded. Not a drop was spilled. Empowered, she took a fortifying swallow and set down the cup. "You know, it occurs to me that I didn't have these problems until you showed up."

"You're blaming me for your talent?"

"Why not? No coincidences, remember?"

She was oddly shocked when she saw a flash of anger and something that looked a lot like hurt in his eyes and his aura. The emotions vanished in the next instant. Harlan was back in control.

"I don't have time to argue about this," he said.

"Too busy saving the world from Vortex?"

"And maybe finding your mother's killer in the process."

Olivia winced. "That's harsh but, okay, you have a point. Continue with the inquisition."

His mouth tightened but he let the comment go.

"You went into the trance or whatever you want to call it when I asked you if your grandmother had a safe room."

Olivia got another jolt of anxiety, less intense this time but enough to kick up her pulse and send a frisson of alarm across her senses. She forced herself to breathe.

Harlan watched her with a wary expression. "Are you all right?"

She gave him a flashy smile. "You bet. Never been better."

"I sense sarcasm."

"Impossible. You're immune. Let's move along. You're a client. I've got a job to do. I am determined to be mature and professional about this case."

"Good. So, what do you think triggered a trance—"

"Stop." She held up a hand, palm out. "Do not use that word around me."

"What happened to 'mature and professional'?"

"I'm serious, Harlan Rancourt. I was not in a trance."

"All right," he said in the patient tone one might use with a stubborn child. "Walk me through your nightmare."

She thought about it. "In the past I think I've had small slices of the same nightmare. I just couldn't make sense of them. I've heard someone tell me to run. This time I realized it was my grandmother's voice. She was speaking to my mother, not me. She says, 'The monster is coming. I will hold him off as long as I can. Run.'"

"Go on."

"I hear a heavy steel door close."

"A vault door?"

"I think so. I'm with my mother in the darkness. There's a weird cobalt blue mirror on the wall. It's full-sized. Like a door. Mom takes my hand and somehow leads me through the mirror. After that— nothing. Just darkness."

"And you think this happened when you were five?"

"That's the last time I saw my grandmother so, yes, I would have been five. Assuming this is a real memory."

"A lot of people can't remember anything from their childhood except snapshots. But in your case I think the explanation for your lost memory is relatively straightforward. You were a little kid. You must have been terrified. You didn't understand what was happening. You and your mother were locked in a vault that was probably infused with a heavy dose of paranormal heat. Sounds like you got another blast of some sort of energy when your mother took you through the mirror."

"Sensory overload."

"At the age of five you hadn't come into your aura-reading talent. Your brain was still developing. So were your senses. You had no way to handle what sounds like a lot of extremely intense energy and trauma. To protect you, your brain shut down for a while."

"I suppose there is some sense to that logic."

"You said your grandmother's house was destroyed in the fire. What happened to the property?"

"Mom sold it years ago. She told me she never wanted to go back. Too many memories. But after she was killed something made me want to take a look at the place."

Harlan was intrigued. "Find anything interesting?"

"The couple that bought the property built a small weekend get-away cottage, but I don't think they ever used it, at least not often. When I went to see the place there was a For Sale sign out front. Looked like it had been there for years. I couldn't get too close because there was a fence and a gate, but I didn't pick up any traces of serious heat."

"That's no surprise. The earth would absorb any energy coming from underground. If we excavate we might be able to find the original vault. No telling what your grandmother might have stashed inside."

Olivia realized she was deeply curious now. "We would have to buy the property."

"The Foundation can afford it," Harlan said. "We'll look into the matter after we conclude this case. For now, though, we have to focus on the Sefton house."

"We're going there now, I assume?"

"Yes." Harlan got to his feet. "Looks like about an hour-and-a-half drive from Seattle."

CHAPTER 19

The drive to the Sefton house turned out to be longer than Harlan had estimated, thanks to an accident on the interstate and construction on the narrow two-lane state highway that led to the small rural town of Cedric Valley. Olivia was behind the wheel because they were using her SUV.

His duffel bag was in the back of the vehicle. Olivia had given him an inquiring look when he stowed it. He had explained he never went anywhere without it. She hadn't asked any questions.

He tried to focus on the new data he had acquired that day, but he kept getting sidetracked by the woman sitting beside him. She was a key, a mystery and endlessly fascinating. She was one of only a handful of people he had met in his adult life who could really *see* him. There was something very intimate about sharing the front seat with her. He wondered if she felt the same vibe.

"What, exactly, do you plan to do once we get to the Sefton house?" Olivia asked.

"I don't know," he admitted. "Depends on what we find when we get there."

"The way I see it, there are two possibilities. Someone may be inside the house or the place will be empty."

"True."

"If there are people inside, it is highly unlikely they will invite us to take a tour of the house," she warned.

"You'd be surprised at how convincing I can be when I work at it."

"Is that right? How would you persuade complete strangers to let us prowl through their home?"

"I could tell them you and I are engaged to get married. That we drove past their house, decided it was the home of our dreams and want to make an all-cash offer to buy it."

"Married? You and me? The home of our dreams? Forget it."

He winced. She didn't have to make it sound so completely outlandish.

"In that case I'll go with my infallible standby story," he said.

"What is that?"

"I'll explain that we're scouts for one of the big subscription video on-demand companies looking for a location for a new television series. The Sefton house is perfect but we need to see the interiors. It's amazing what people will do if they think they can get their fifteen minutes of fame."

"Hmm. Might work. You've used that story before, haven't you?"

"Yes."

"Why?"

He hesitated. "Turns out it takes cash to live off the grid. I didn't spend the past five years living in a cave and foraging for my food. I had to work occasionally."

"Those odd jobs you mentioned? The ones you do for someone who calls you an illusion talent?"

"Yes. It's contract work for a private psychic investigation agency.

Lark and LeClair isn't the only firm engaged in paranormal investigations."

"I'm sure you're right. I hadn't given the matter much thought. Where is this other agency located?"

"A small town on the Northern California coast. Scargill Cove."

"What's the name of the agency?"

"Jones and Jones. Their chief client is an outfit called the Arcane Society. It's an organization devoted to paranormal research."

"No kidding? Like the Foundation?"

"Similar, but it's been around a lot longer. About three centuries."

"Why haven't I heard of it?"

"Arcane is very good at keeping a low profile."

"Like the Foundation."

"Turns out paranoia runs deep in the psychic world."

"Why?" Olivia asked.

"Why what?"

"Why did you hunt monsters for this Jones and Jones outfit?"

"I told you. Money."

"There are easier ways for a man with your talents to make money. You chose a very dangerous line of work."

"My talents aren't good for many things. Hunting bad guys is one of the few—"

"Forget it," Olivia said. "Back to our problem. What if there is no one inside the Sefton house?"

"That will certainly simplify things," he said.

"We're going to break in."

"You don't sound shocked."

"I saw that coming a mile off. And don't you dare call me an oracle."

CHAPTER 20

I don't think the dream-home story would have worked," Olivia said. "This house is one of the most depressing architectural structures I've ever seen. It's a gargoyle of a house. It would make a good location for a television series featuring a haunted mansion, though. That angle might have been effective."

She was standing on the back porch of the Sefton house watching Harlan insert a narrow length of metal into the lock that guarded the door. Her handbag, with the camera inside, was slung across her body, leaving both hands free. There had been no sign of anyone—not even another vehicle—for the last five miles of the trip, but the need to keep the artifact close was impossible to ignore.

The big house had probably been an imposing residence in its day—ominous but impressive. Three stories tall, it squatted in the center of a small clearing. The windows on the ground floor had been boarded up. Those on the upper floor were covered with ancient curtains. The surrounding forest cast the structure into permanent shadow.

"I told you, the television story always works." Harlan pushed open the door and stood quietly for a moment, gazing into the rear hall. "I feel sorry for any real estate agent who tries to market this place."

"What's wrong?" Olivia hurried forward to see what had caught his attention. The waves of disturbing energy hit her with the force of a small thunderstorm when she stepped through the doorway. "Yikes. You're right. Even people who don't have a strong psychic vibe are bound to notice this kind of heat. Everyone reacts to the feel of a house, and this one reeks of bad energy."

"There's a reason it's hard to sell properties that have a history of death, especially violent death." Harlan moved deeper into the shadowed hallway and switched on a flashlight. "Every house has a story. Let's see what this one can tell us."

Olivia mentally fortified herself against the unnerving currents of paranormal radiation, took a penlight out of her handbag and followed Harlan along the paneled hallway. The expensive wood must have glowed like fine art back in the day, but it was now cracked and brittle. Rotting floorboards creaked. The faint odor of mold hung in the atmosphere. Nature, the ultimate recycler, was at work.

Harlan led the way into a darkened living room. The space was dominated by a massive stone fireplace. An old carpet, faded and threadbare, covered part of the planked floor. None of the well-worn furniture appeared worth salvaging.

There was another hallway on the far side of the living room. It led to a formal dining room and then to the kitchen. Harlan stopped in front of what looked like a closet door and opened it.

"Here we go," he said, aiming the flashlight through the opening. "Basement stairs. Sefton's gallery would have been down there."

Olivia moved to stand beside him. There was a closed door at the bottom of the stairs. "Basement steps and the power has been turned off. I think I saw this movie. It didn't end well."

Harlan started down the stairs. "What can possibly go wrong?"

"Is that supposed to be a joke?" She followed him down the stairs. "Because I'm not laughing."

"Historically speaking, oracles have never been known for their sense of humor."

"Which only goes to prove that I'm not an oracle. I happen to possess a terrific sense of humor. Ask anyone."

"I'll take your word for it," Harlan said.

He opened the door. Waves of disorienting energy swept out of the darkness, flooding the stairwell. Olivia flattened one hand against the wall to steady herself while she worked to regain control of her sparking senses.

"Sefton must have had some very hot items in his collection," she said.

Harlan walked a few paces into the dark basement and swept the beam of his flashlight around the space. Light glittered on glass-and-steel shelving—empty shelving.

"This was his gallery, but the place has been cleaned out," he said.

Olivia reached the bottom of the stairs and stopped on the last step. She aimed her penlight into the room. The beam glared on a reflective surface on the far side of the room.

"Are those mirrors on the walls?" she asked, intrigued.

"Every wall is mirrored. So is the ceiling. Interesting. Also dangerous. The paranormal physics of mirrors are not well understood. They've got a history of being associated with energy from both ends of the spectrum."

"I know," Olivia said.

"I sure as hell would not have covered the walls of a gallery filled with hot artifacts with mirrors. What was Sefton thinking?"

"How dangerous would this gallery have been when the space was filled with paranormal relics?"

"Hard to say." Harlan began to prowl the room. "It would have depended on the type of heat in the objects."

Curious, Olivia took a couple of steps into the gallery . . .

. . . and froze when the feverish rush of energy swept through her. She fell into the dreamstate. The words came out of her mouth in the eerie voice she was learning to hate.

"*When the time comes you will know how to go through the mirror.*"

Harlan spun around, pinning her in the glare of his flashlight.

"Olivia. Get out. Now."

He lunged forward, clearly intending to propel her back through the stairwell doorway, but it was too late. She heard the sound of gears whirring deep within the basement walls. A heavy door slammed shut behind her.

Just as it had in the nightmare she had remembered earlier that day. *Run.*

But this wasn't a dream and there was nowhere to run.

She broke free of the trance and whirled to face the door. The beam of her flashlight flared on the polished sheet of heavy-gauge steel that now sealed the stairwell doorway.

Harlan came to a stop beside her.

"This is not good," he said quietly.

"No shit."

She crossed her arms very tightly around her waist in an attempt to control the shivers that were coursing through her.

"Are you all right?" Harlan asked.

She glared.

"Right," he said. "Sorry I asked. Let's see what we're dealing with here."

He went past her and flattened one hand on the vault-like door for a long moment. Slowly he moved his fingers, exploring every inch of the heavy steel plate.

When he turned around, his expression told her all she needed to know.

"There's probably a hidden escape mechanism on this side but it's not going to be easy to locate," he said.

"Why would Sefton have made it difficult to escape from his own safe room?"

"I don't think Sefton designed this room as a safe room. He intended it as a trap for intruders. The safe room, assuming he had one, is somewhere else."

Another shiver went through her, but this one was different. The chill wasn't an aftereffect of the dreamstate experience. It was caused by the raw fear of being locked inside a darkened room with only a couple of flashlights.

"I suppose Sefton's plan was to imprison the thieves and then phone the police," she said.

"I doubt he planned to call the cops."

She did not like the sound of that. It dawned on her that Harlan's flashlight was now focused on the wall behind her. Senses spiking, she turned to see what he was looking at.

Light flashed in a mirror on the opposite side of the gallery. At first she thought it was a reflection of her flashlight, or maybe Harlan's. But there was something off about it. Flashlight beams did not pulse in aurora-like waves. The color of the radiation was wrong, too. It was a strange shade of chartreuse that was growing steadily deeper and more intense.

As she watched, trying to comprehend what she was seeing, another mirror sparked with chartreuse energy. And then another.

"It's a chain reaction," Harlan said. "At this rate all of the mirrors and the ceiling will be channeling the energy. The reflected heat will get hotter and hotter. When things get too intense there will be an explosion. We're standing in the middle of a paranormal bomb."

CHAPTER 21

So much for my oracle talent," Olivia said. "Any halfway talented oracle would have shouted a warning *before* we got trapped, not when it was too late."

The green fire was spreading around the room, leaping and crowning from mirror to mirror the way wildfires do when they move through forests. The first sparks of chartreuse radiation were flaring in the ceiling now. She could feel the paranormal heat rising.

Harlan shot her a quick, knowing look. "Credit where it's due. You gave us a very big clue on how to get out of here."

A terrible sense of dread spiked with guilt settled on her. She recalled what she had said when she went into the short dreamstate. "'When the time comes you will know how to go through the mirror'? What does that tell us?"

"Going through a mirror—the right mirror—is our only way out." Harlan crossed to a pedestal display stand. "We have to move fast."

Harlan gripped the base of the display stand and smashed it into a burning mirror. The crack of shattering glass echoed across the spectrum. He struck again and again. Chartreuse fire rained down on the floor in shards of broken glass. A section of concrete wall was suddenly revealed.

Harlan moved on to the next mirror.

"Got it," Olivia said.

There was no need for the flashlights now. The interior of the gallery was illuminated in the eerie green radiation. She dropped the penlight into the pocket of her jacket, picked up a slender floor lamp and slammed the metal base into the nearest mirror. More burning shards cascaded onto the floor. More blank concrete wall was revealed. She moved to the next mirror.

"Is this about putting out the flames?" she asked, crashing the lamp into the next burning mirror. "Because I don't think it's working. We're just creating smaller fires."

"No, it's about finding Sefton's real safe room," Harlan said.

They were smashing a lot of mirrors, but the room was getting hotter. The wild waves of energy acted like frissons of electricity on all her senses. It was difficult to focus. She was getting dizzy. Her balance was off. She was suddenly afraid that she would faint. She took a deep breath, forced herself to concentrate and moved on to another mirror.

"Found it," Harlan shouted over the sound of fracturing glass. "Over here. Hurry. This room is going to blow."

She dropped the lamp and made her way through the mosaic of small burning mirrors on the floor, grateful she was wearing low-heeled boots. She reached Harlan's side just as he gripped the edge of a mirror. He exerted some pressure. The entire panel swung open on concealed hinges, revealing a darkened space.

"How did you find the right mirror?"

"Process of elimination. This one isn't hot. It's made of a different kind of glass."

Harlan swept the beam of his flashlight around the interior. "This was Sefton's vault and his safe room."

The space was the size of a large walk-in closet. Metal and glass shelves lined the walls. They were filled with a variety of vintage office paraphernalia—a black rotary dial telephone, a mid-twentieth-century typewriter, a slide rule, an old-fashioned desk calculator and a leather-bound notebook.

"Inside," he said. "We don't have much time."

She did not like the idea of moving into the dark, confined space, but given the dangerous energy in the outer room, there wasn't any choice. She stepped through the doorway.

Harlan followed her into the vault and pulled the heavy steel door shut. Olivia heard a bolt slide into place. *Just as it had in the night-mare.* For a few seconds memory and reality blended together. She thought she heard her grandmother's voice whispering in the shadows. *"Run."*

She did not know she had said the single word aloud until Harlan spoke behind her.

"That's the plan," Harlan said. "Sefton spent years in hiding. That means there will be an emergency exit."

"You seem very sure of that."

"Yes."

"Can I assume your certainty is based on personal experience?"

"You can." He looked around the space, flashlight slashing across the display cases. "No mirrors on the walls. That's a good sign."

"This room is very hot," she said.

Harlan touched the leather-bound notebook. "Vortex heat."

"Shouldn't we focus on getting out of here? If the main gallery does explode, it will bring down the whole house. We could get trapped."

"Right." Harlan scooped up the notebook and handed it to her. "Take this. I'll find the exit."

She dropped the notebook into her handbag and watched him flatten one hand against a wall. He worked his way quickly around the chamber and stopped when a section of shelving blocked his path. He shot her a sharp, searching look.

"Stop that," she said.

"What?"

"Stop looking at me as if you're expecting me to say something weird and creepy every time I open my mouth."

"Your last weird, creepy saying saved our lives."

"Not yet. We're still trapped in a vault, in case you haven't noticed."

"Not any longer."

He eased the shelving aside and opened a hinged wall panel. Dank, musty air flowed out of a dark passage.

"Go," he said.

She slipped through the opening. The beam of her flashlight revealed a low-ceilinged tunnel. The claustrophobia closed in fast.

"Shit," she whispered.

Harlan followed her and stopped long enough to slam shut the door to the old office.

"Run," he ordered.

She ran.

CHAPTER 22

The muffled roar of the explosion shattered the murmurs and whispers of the forest. Harlan stood at the entrance of the cave and listened to the reverberations shuddering through the trees. The ground trembled.

"That was the house, wasn't it?" Olivia said.

He glanced at her. She still had her handbag and she was not panicking. Impressive.

"Yes," he said. "I can see some smoke."

She patted her handbag. "If the notebook really is from the Vortex lab it is literally priceless. People would kill for it."

"I think everything in that vault was from Vortex. It had a unique vibe."

"The energy was different from the artifacts that have been recovered from the Fogg Lake lab. Different from what I've seen in Swan's shop." Olivia hesitated. "It felt like the vibe in my camera, didn't it?"

"Yes."

"No wonder Sefton protected it with that firestorm trap in the main gallery. If even a single pen or a coffee mug infused with Vortex heat hit the underground market, collectors and thieves would go wild."

"To say nothing of Victor Arganbright and Lucas Pine."

"Blake Sefton was one of the survivors of the Vortex lab, wasn't he?" Olivia said.

"I think that's a logical assumption."

"Like my grandmother, except that the assassin got to her eventually."

Harlan said nothing.

"And then someone murdered my mother."

He waited for her to make the next connection.

"I'm next, aren't I?" she said quietly.

He dug deep, searching for something reassuring. "I think whoever is after you needs you. I don't think anyone wants to kill you, at least not right away."

"Your bedside manner leaves a lot to be desired."

Well, he'd tried.

"I'm not a doctor," he said, unaccountably offended. "And I'm not Mr. Sunshine."

"I noticed."

"I'd like to say something cheery and optimistic, but I've got nothing," he said. "This situation has been smoldering for a while and now it's one very hot fire. Our only option is to keep moving forward."

"I agree. But if whoever is after us doesn't want me dead yet, that must mean the explosion in the gallery wasn't intended for us."

"The trap was installed years ago. It was intended for anyone who wandered into the gallery uninvited. But I don't think it was intended to bring down the whole house."

"That does seem a little extreme, doesn't it?"

"Yes."

"So what happened?" Olivia said.

"Catastrophic system failure, probably. It happens when any kind of tech gets old. I think Sefton installed those mirrors to protect his gallery and, more importantly, the items in his vault. But he put the system in place in the latter half of the last century. Paranormal energy hangs around for a long time, but the crystals used in that kind of technology are sensitive. They require tuning from time to time. It's like rebooting a computer or a cell phone."

"So over time the crystals got out of sync?"

"Theoretically they could have been rebooted before they failed, but that would require engineering skills and talent that Sefton may not have been able to maintain as the years went by. Add in the fact that there was so much energy in that basement, and you've got a disaster waiting to happen."

"We got lucky, didn't we?"

"Luck had nothing to do with it. Let's go see if your vehicle survived. If it didn't, we've got a long walk ahead of us."

"That is not a happy thought."

They made their way through the woods, following the smell of smoke. There were no sirens yet, but Harlan heard the rumble of rapidly accelerating automobile engines.

"Someone is rushing to the scene," he said. "This may be interesting."

"People are always curious about explosions and fires."

"Yes, but the people driving those vehicles seem to know exactly where they are going."

"How can you tell?"

He looked at her, saying nothing.

"Oh, right," she said. "Chaos theory and no coincidences."

"It's what I do, Olivia."

"One of the things you do," she said. "You didn't mention a downside to your chaos talent. Is there one?"

"Turns out chaos talents don't come across as the romantic type. We tend to have poor social skills."

"Give me a break. You're talking to the woman who couldn't get a date to talk to her for ten minutes at a speed date event. Don't expect me to feel sorry for you."

"No sympathy for the devil?"

"You're not the—"

The squeal of brakes and the noise of big vehicles slamming to a stop on a gravel road interrupted her. Car doors slammed.

"Ash, Trev, check the back of the house. Ox and I will take this side," a man yelled.

Harlan caught Olivia's arm and tugged her behind the cover of a jumble of moss-covered boulders. He put his mouth to her ear.

"Stay here," he said. "I'll take a look."

She hesitated as if she thought that was a bad idea, but she didn't offer any prophetic warnings.

"Be careful," she whispered.

It occurred to him that the last thing they needed was for her to go into oracle mode. Her dream voice would carry in the woods. He gestured toward the pocket of her jacket. She took out her phone and held it up to show him a blank notepad screen and the keyboard. She was prepared to input any inconvenient prophecies. Of course, by the time he was able to interpret the words, it might be too late, but he would have to take the risk. There was no other way to make sure she didn't accidentally draw the attention of whoever was in the clearing.

He made it to the cover of a large fir and studied what he could see through the trees. Two badass SUVs were parked in the driveway of the demolished house. Four armed men were moving around in a random manner, evidently not sure how to conduct a search in the nearby woods. They were dressed in black from caps to boots and wearing gear belts. At first glance they could have been mistaken for members of an official SWAT team, but there were a lot of subtle signs that marked them as private security.

"Forget it, Ink," one man shouted. "No one got out of that house alive."

"Trev is right," his companion said. "Their vehicle is still here. They didn't make it out. Shit, what the hell happened?"

"Fuck if I know," Ink said. "The Piper told us we would be able to grab them here."

Harlan took out his phone and started snapping photos. Faces. License plates. The logo on the uniforms. All male. All surprisingly young—late teens, early twenties—including Ink, the one who appeared to be in charge.

"Now what?" one of the men said. "The Piper isn't going to be happy about this. He says we need the woman. When he finds out she's dead—"

He sounded on the verge of panic.

"Shut up, Ash," Ink said. He loped down the drive to Olivia's SUV. "We don't know for certain that either of them is dead. We're dealing with a couple of talents. We need to assume they made it out of the house."

Ink was saying the right words, Harlan decided, but he sounded scared, too.

The other three men regarded the remains of the house. The flames were no longer flaring, but the heat was still intense.

"Gonna be a while before anyone can search for bodies," the one who had to be Ox said. "We can't hang around. We gotta get out of here before the cops or the fire trucks get here."

"Give me a minute." Ink opened the driver's side door of Olivia's SUV and looked inside. "This explosion is too fucking convenient."

"How do you figure that?" Trev asked.

"This guy comes out of nowhere and suddenly has possession of the woman?" Ink said. "Doesn't make sense. Maybe the house didn't blow by accident. Pretty clean way to fake a couple of deaths, if you ask me. Or maybe he planned to take us out."

Smart kid, Harlan thought.

The other three men exchanged glances. Harlan grabbed a few more photos.

Sirens sounded in the distance.

Ink pulled himself out of the car and slammed the door closed. "Get in the vehicles."

He took a small object out of the pocket of his black cargo trousers, leaned down and stuck it inside a wheel well. Straightening, he raced back to one of the black SUVs and leaped into the passenger seat. The man who answered to Ash was already behind the wheel, cranking the engine. He sent the big vehicle hurtling back down the drive to the main road. The other two followed close behind in the second SUV.

The wail of the sirens grew louder.

"Olivia," Harlan called. "We're done here."

He raced through the trees and into the clearing. Circling the burning house, he went to Olivia's SUV, crouched beside the rear right tire and felt for the tracking device. When his fingers brushed against it, he pulled it free and tossed it aside.

He was in the driver's seat when Olivia burst out of the trees. She saw that he was already behind the wheel and yanked open the passenger side door.

"Keys," he said.

She tossed the fob to him and slammed the door shut. He got the SUV in gear and stomped on the accelerator. The tires spit gravel.

When he reached the main road he stopped long enough to listen for the sirens. They were coming from the right. The men in the SUVs had gone in that direction.

He turned left and hit the accelerator again. Hard.

Olivia glanced back at what was left of the Sefton house. "Our dream home?"

"Guess not."

"Where are we going?" Olivia said.

Her air of cool control rattled him. Shock, he decided. That would account for her unnatural calm. The panic attack would come later. He made a mental note to be prepared for it.

"We've got to get off the grid for a while," he said. "I need time to do some research. These mountains are your backyard. Got any suggestions?"

"Fogg Lake," Olivia said. "The Foundation has a team on-site mapping the old Bluestone lab that was recently discovered there. Plenty of security. Most tech, including cell phones, won't work in the area because of the high level of paranormal radiation leaking out of the caves, but there are landline phones, so you can still make and receive phone calls."

"Sounds like a plan."

"There's one problem with it." Olivia checked the time. "It's getting late in the day. We might not be able to get to Fogg Lake before the fog rolls in. You can't drive through that stuff. It shuts down all traffic on the old highway every evening like clockwork. If we get caught in it we'll have to spend the night in the car on the side of the road."

"It's that bad?"

"It's not normal fog. It's infused with the paranormal radiation from the lake and the caves."

"But the worst-case scenario is that we end up sleeping in the car?"

"Yes."

"Not the end of the world."

She raised her brows. "You haven't experienced that kind of fog, have you? It's not the end of the world, but it is . . . disturbing."

"Understood. Can you handle it if necessary?"

"Yes," she said. "I can handle it."

She sounded as if she were speaking through gritted teeth.

Everything she was saying sounded logical and sensible. But her lack of emotional reaction to the near-death experience they had both gone through in the past few minutes worried him. Oracles were notoriously delicate. Fragile. The nature of their talent made them acutely sensitive to psychic trauma. He wondered if Olivia was in some sort of fugue state. The paranormal radiation in the burning mirrors had been very strong. Maybe it had affected her senses.

He gunned the engine coming out of a curve and shot Olivia a quick look, trying to get a fix on what was happening to her. He had to know what he was dealing with. The last thing he needed was to lose his oracle to a psychic crisis. She looked okay, as far as he could tell. In control. But no one knew better than he did that looks were deceiving.

"Stop that," she said. Frost coated each word. "This is not my first rodeo. I'm not going to fall apart on you. Not until it's over, at any rate."

"Good. That's good." He hesitated. "What do you mean when you say that what happened back there was not your first rodeo?"

"When I was in my teens my friend Catalina and I witnessed a murder. And I told you, a while back I was kidnapped. The other night I took down a serial killer using a paranormal artifact that looks a lot like a camera."

"Oh. Right."

"Today I survived an explosion created by a bunch of paranormal mirrors. I am now on the run with a man I barely know, a monster talent who carries a gun."

He clenched the steering wheel. "I see what you mean."

"I know you think I'm an oracle and that my ability makes me a wild card. Unpredictable. You're afraid I'm at the mercy of my talent rather than in control of it."

"It's just that, historically speaking, oracles have had a reputation for being . . . fragile."

"Let's get something straight. In real life I'm a private investigator who happens to be a very good aura reader. I came into possession of a camera that has paranormal properties and I am learning how to use it. I'm working this case with you because I'm hoping it will help me find the person who murdered my mother. I'm doing my job. Stop fretting."

"I'm not fretting."

"You're fretting."

"I just wanted to say that if you feel a little upset it would be a natural reaction."

"Yes, it would." She gave him a wintry smile. "What about you? How are you doing? You've been under a lot of stress, not just recently but for the past five years. This afternoon you nearly got fried by hot mirrors. That sort of thing takes a heavy toll on the psychic senses. Do you need to talk about what just happened?"

"All right, you've made your point. Moving along, we seem to have what looks like a plan. We're going to Fogg Lake. But first we've got to find a place with a good cell signal. I want to get the photos I took of those fake security dudes and their vehicles to Las Vegas as soon as possible so that Arganbright and Pine can analyze them. I need data."

"What about the Sefton house? It's a smoking ruin, but there will be plenty of paranormal energy left. The artifacts in the vault are buried under the rubble but they may have survived. Some of them are probably dangerous. They're all priceless."

"We'll let Arganbright handle that problem. He can send some of the Seattle team up here or have the Fogg Lake security people take charge."

"At least we made it out with a logbook," Olivia said. She reached into her handbag, removed the leather-bound volume and opened it. "Harlan, listen to this. 'A Record of Paranormal Experiments Conducted at the Vortex Laboratory under the Direction of Dr. Alexander Winston.'"

A rush of knowing hit Harlan. "I remember that name. It's in the Rancourt files. My grandfather was certain Winston was the head of the lab for a while."

"Do you think Blake Sefton was really Dr. Winston?"

"No. According to the file, Winston died in a lab accident before Vortex was shut down. Someone else took over as director."

"Who?"

"His wife, Aurora Winston. She was evidently the one in charge at the time Bluestone was terminated. She would have overseen the destruction of Vortex."

"Did she make it out?"

"There's a note that says she disappeared immediately after the labs were closed and is believed to be dead, but who knows?"

"Any children?"

"Good question. There's no information on offspring in the file."

Olivia was silent for a moment. She did not take her eyes off the logbook.

"I know someone who might be able to help both of us," she said. "Her name is Harmony. She lives in Fogg Lake. You'll like her. She's a real oracle."

CHAPTER 23

Olivia was behind the wheel when the first wisps of fog began to seep through the trees. The mist was infused with a faint green energy thanks to the paranormal radiation in the lake and the caves. She knew the illumination would brighten and become more intense as night tightened its grip on the mountains. The visions and hallucinations would start soon. Initially they would appear to be a trick of the light, small shadows dancing at the corner of the eye. But they would grow stronger and more disturbing until the faint energy of dawn drove them back.

"This is not good," she said, slowing for a tight curve. "It's coming in earlier than usual. This is going to be a bad night. Looks like we'll be spending it in the car."

Harlan studied the fog as if he could make it vanish with the sheer force of his willpower. "It's not bad. Not yet."

"Trust me, I know this road. More to the point, I know this fog. It gets thick very quickly. It won't be long before we won't be able to see a foot in front of the car. And then we'll start seeing . . . things."

"Hallucinations?"

"Yes. You're a strong talent, so you'll know you're seeing things that aren't there, but that doesn't make the experience any less disorienting. We need to find a safe place to get off the road. Once in a while someone panics and tries to drive through the fog. If your vehicle is sitting in the middle of the pavement it can end up getting pushed over a cliff into the river."

"With us inside. Got it. All right, you're the expert here. Where do we park for the night?"

At least he wasn't going to argue. That was a relief.

"There are a couple of old logging roads that make good emergency campsites," she said. "We're close to one of them. We should be able to make it."

"Your call," Harlan said. He sounded grim but resigned.

"It's clear you are not a happy camper, but look on the bright side."

"There's a bright side?"

"At least we've got food. I picked up a few things at that convenience store while you were talking to Victor and Lucas. But wait, it gets better. I always carry blankets in this vehicle. The back seat folds down, so we'll have room to stretch out."

The instant the last sentence left her lips she gave herself a mental head-slap. The reminder that they would be sleeping in close proximity sent a tide of heat through her veins. She could only hope that Harlan was still his usual socially oblivious self and had missed what some men might view as a not-so-subtle innuendo. Maybe even an invitation.

She needn't have worried. Harlan ignored the comment. As far as she could tell it hadn't even ruffled his hair as it went past. She told herself she had absolutely no business feeling disappointed. Their association was of a professional nature. Full stop.

He glanced at her. "Sounds like you've been caught in the fog on this road before."

"Pretty sure everyone who lives in Fogg Lake has had the experience at one time or another. No matter how careful you are, you can never be certain the mist won't roll in unexpectedly early. One minute the road is clear. Then you come out of a curve and there's a fog bank waiting for you. The locals say it's been getting more unpredictable lately. One theory is that it's linked to global warming."

"Or maybe something has been stirred up by the Foundation researchers who are investigating what's left of that old lab."

"Yep, that's the other theory."

"Who came up with that one?"

"Take a wild guess."

"Victor Arganbright."

"Right the first time." She smiled. "You two do tend to think alike, don't you?"

CHAPTER 24

Why that one question?" Harlan asked.

Olivia turned on her side and tugged the blanket up over her shoulder. She hadn't expected to get any real sleep, not after the adrenaline jag she had been on most of the day. She and Harlan had nearly died in the explosion at the Sefton house and now they were on the run from a bunch of scary people who wore a lot of black—not her favorite fashion color. On top of that, they were camped out in the creepy fog-bound mountains.

So, no, she would not get any real rest. She had, however, expected Harlan to fall asleep immediately. Any man who could manipulate his own aura had to possess astonishing powers of self-control.

She had been wrong. He was awake. Probably because he wanted to be awake, she decided, not because of the unsettling sense of intimacy that had descended when they locked the doors and lowered the back seat.

He was on his back beside her, inches away, one arm folded behind his head. She was intensely aware of his body heat and his scent, an elemental mix of his unique essence and dried sweat. It made for a compellingly masculine combination that sent thrilling little frissons of awareness through her.

A short time ago he had removed his glasses, tucked them into a case and put the case on top of the duffel bag. In the paranormal radiance of the fog that swirled around the SUV, Harlan appeared to be contemplating the secrets of the universe through the skylight in the vehicle's roof. *Alchemist*, she thought.

"What question?" she asked, mystified.

"The one you asked each of the men who sat down at your table at the speed date event. 'If I disappeared tomorrow would you walk into hell to find me?'"

"Oh. That question. I was trying to be efficient."

He turned his head to look at her. In the acid-green shadows his eyes burned. She heightened her senses and took a peek at his aura. Raw power and the control required to wield it blazed in the confines of the SUV. She was so close to him she was partially enveloped in his energy field. It felt good. Weirdly intimate, but good. Exciting. Enthralling.

Not for the first time she reminded herself she should be wary around Harlan Rancourt. Not for the first time she acknowledged she did not give a damn about being cautious. He was fascinating and intriguing, not unnerving or frightening.

"I get that you wanted to be efficient, but you must have realized your question was scaring off potential dates," he said.

"That was pointed out to me by the woman sitting in the next booth. Like I said, I was just trying to save time."

"Time you used to search for a cat online."

"I did a little shopping, too," she said, feeling unaccountably defensive. "Then I decided to take another look at Joe."

"The cat."

"He'll probably be gone by the time we're finished with this case. I just hope whoever adopts him will give him his forever home."

"I don't think Joe is going to get adopted anytime soon," Harlan said.

"Why not?"

"He looked tough. A junkyard cat."

"He's had a rough life, but he's still young. I'm sure he'll be willing to give some human a chance."

"You could tell all that from an online photo?"

"Something about his eyes."

"And maybe wishful thinking on your part?"

"Joe is an excellent cat," she said. "He deserves a good home."

"If you say so. About your question—"

She levered herself up on her elbow and looked down at him. "Okay, here's the story behind my speed date question. Not long ago I thought I was falling in love with a very nice man who checked most of the boxes. We enjoyed each other's company. Had a lot in common. He has a good job and a stable, healthy aura. The kidnappers grabbed me as I was on my way to meet him for a date. He was cooking dinner."

"He cooks, too?"

"Oh, yes. And he's an expert on wines. That night I was going to tell him about my aura-reading talent and see how he handled the news that I have a psychic vibe. A lot of men have a problem with a woman who claims to be able to read auras."

"Got news for you. A lot of women have problems with a man who claims to have paranormal senses."

"I don't doubt it. Anyhow, at the time, the question of whether or not a potential significant other could accept my psychic side was my litmus test. If he had been able to accept the real me, our relationship could have moved on to the next level. But I never got the opportunity to run the experiment."

"Because you got kidnapped."

"Yes. My friend Catalina and her new husband, Slater Arganbright, risked their lives to look for me."

"Can I assume your date that evening did not?"

"No. He later explained that at first he thought he'd been stood up. Then when he was told I had vanished he didn't think he had the skill set to search for me. It was a job for the police, he said."

"All of which was probably true."

"Doesn't matter. The bottom line as far as I was concerned was that he did not look for me."

"So after you were rescued you dumped him."

"In hindsight it's clear that our relationship was doomed," she admitted. "The kidnapping episode just accelerated the timeline."

"You don't think he could have handled your psychic vibe?"

"No. At best he would probably have suggested I see a psychiatrist and then he would have run for the nearest exit."

"Probably," Harlan agreed.

"Sounds like you've been there."

"Not recently, but in the past, yes. In my experience there are five basic reactions when you come out with the truth about your vibe. Number one, people think you're delusional and need psychiatric treatment. Two, people conclude you're a fraud or a con artist. Three, people who actually believe in the paranormal want to run experiments on you. Four, people develop an unhealthy fascination with you and decide you are the cult leader they've been searching for online. Five, people decide you're possessed by demons."

"I'm impressed," she said. "You've obviously given the problem considerable thought and subjected it to keen analysis. Did you come up with a solution?"

"Find someone who is also psychic, someone who won't think you're weird. Turns out that's easier said than done."

"Tell me about it. Next time I'm going to go to Vegas."

"Las Vegas?" Harlan glanced at her. "Why?"

"I heard that a woman who is connected to the Foundation, Sierra Raines, is planning to open up a psychic dating service there. Evidently she's got a talent for matchmaking."

"Interesting." Harlan was silent for a beat. "Hypothetically speaking, if you and I had met under other circumstances and I had invited you out on a date, do you think you might have said yes?"

"Hypothetically speaking, when was the last time you went out on a real date?"

"It's been a while," he admitted. "I've been a little busy lately. You didn't answer my hypothetical."

"Yes," she said. "I would go out on a date with you."

"Why?"

"Because you gave me the right answer when I asked you if you would walk into hell to search for me. I know you had ulterior motives, but you did come up with the correct answer, so yes, I would have risked a date on those grounds. In fact, some would say we've already had our first date."

"Dinner at that restaurant last night counts?"

"Don't forget the sleepover."

"Are you flirting with me?" Harlan asked. "Just checking. I have poor social skills, so I want to make sure I'm interpreting the signals correctly."

"Yes, I do believe I'm flirting. It is an exceedingly reckless thing to do under the circumstances and I'm sure I will regret it, but you and I went through a lot together today and we saved each other. That seems to have created a certain resonance between our auras. Probably one of those two-people-in-the-same-foxhole things."

"Probably."

"Or maybe just the influence of all that paranormal fog outside."

"Maybe."

"We should also factor in the natural biochemical effects generated by a near-death experience. They say it can act like an aphrodisiac."

"I've heard that," Harlan said.

"Something about the adrenaline overload eliciting the urge to affirm life in the most elemental way possible. In other circumstances we would probably get drunk and go to bed together. But we forgot the booze and I'm not sure the back of my SUV qualifies as a real bed."

"We could improvise."

"We could do that, yes."

"Do you always talk this much at times like this?"

"I don't know," she said. "I've never spent a night with a man I barely know after going through a near-death experience with said man. You could say I never saw this coming. Yet more proof that I am not a true oracle talent."

He unfolded his arm, reached up and caught her face between his palms. "Got news for you. I saw this coming before I sat down at your table at the speed date event."

"Really? Including the part where we nearly got killed by a bunch of mirrors?"

"No, not the boring part. This. Me wanting you and hoping you might want me, too."

She did not need to read his aura to know he was telling the truth. She could feel it in the urgent tension of his body. Everything about him was taut, hard, energized. There was a lot of sensual heat in his eyes and enough energy inside the SUV to start a wildfire.

This was probably nothing more than intense sexual attraction—lust—but it was the most intriguing, compelling, *thrilling* version of desire she had ever experienced. She wanted to explore it, and at that moment she could not see any reason why she shouldn't do exactly that. She might have some regrets tomorrow, but one thing was certain: Whatever happened tonight would be memorable. Unforgettable. Worth the risk.

She lowered her head and kissed him, a light, experimental kiss. Sampling the promise of the thrills ahead before she got on board the roller coaster.

"Olivia."

With a groan that came from the depths of his chest and reverberated with a senses-stirring mix of hunger, desire and need, Harlan rolled her onto her back and transformed the kiss. Sampling time was over. She was on board and starting the climb to the top. She gripped Harlan's shoulders, sinking her fingers into the fabric of his shirt to savor the strength and power of his sleek muscles. Her senses slammed into overdrive.

His kiss was the kiss of a man who had just found something very valuable, something he had needed for a long time. She understood because she was experiencing the same exultant excitement. She had been longing for this dazzling, incredibly intimate connection, too.

Higher, higher; almost at the top of the roller coaster . . .

What the hell am I doing . . . ?

No more time to think. Harlan shifted his weight and slid one leg between her thighs. They were both fully clothed but she was aware of his heavy erection pressing intimately against her lower body. She could feel herself growing damp. When his hand moved to cover one breast she shivered in anticipation and twined her leg around his, trapping him, urging him closer.

He reached down, tugged the gray pullover free of her trousers and flattened his warm palm on her bare skin. He moved his mouth to her throat.

"So soft." His voice was an aching whisper. "Hot."

She struggled to undo the buttons of his shirt, got the garment open and was about to explore further when she heard the low rumble of a car engine moving slowly on the mountain road. Shocked, she went very still.

"I don't believe it," she said. "No one tries to drive that road at night."

Harlan rolled free of the embrace and sat up. "You said sometimes some fool tries to power through."

"And ends up in the river."

They both listened as the vehicle stopped. The muffled noise of a second car echoed in the fog. It, too, came to a halt. Both engines went quiet.

Car doors slammed. She heard men's voices. They were too far away to make out what was being said, but the tension in the exchanges was unmistakable.

The music started a moment later. The ominous notes rode the paranormal currents of energy that laced the fog, seeking her, summoning her. Drawing her.

"The recorder player," she said.

CHAPTER 25

They followed us," Harlan said. He listened to the music that was slithering through the night, searching for its prey. "How the hell did they navigate that road in this fog?"

"I don't know," Olivia said. "Talk about taking an incredible risk."

"The real question is, how did they know where to stop? I got rid of the tracking device before we left the Sefton house."

"Tracking devices don't work in these mountains anyway, not this far from the main highway."

"Huh."

"What?"

"They're using the recorder."

"I noticed," Olivia said. "So?"

"Why not use it to follow us up this old side road? Why stop down there on the highway?"

"Risking the highway at night is dangerous enough. Trying to drive up this road would be impossible. It's not even paved."

"What does that have to do with it?"

"The pavement suppresses some of the energy infused in the ground," Olivia said. "The heat on an unpaved road like this one is more intense."

"They managed to follow us this far but now they're stuck down there?"

"I think so," Olivia said.

He looked at her, searching for any indication that she might be falling under the hypnotic spell of the recorder. In the eerie shadows it was impossible to read her eyes.

How was he going to protect her this time? There was no convenient brick wall. They were trapped in a vehicle parked on an isolated mountain road. The SUV's heavy frame provided some protection, but they had left one of the windows cracked open for fresh air. Closing it wouldn't do much good. The glass muted the effects of the music but it did not stop them.

The worst-case scenario was that he would have to forcibly restrain her. That would not be easy. If she was unable to fight the compulsion of the music, she would fight him. He really did not want to think about how that would end. He needed to be outside the SUV, hunting for the recorder player.

Olivia stared out the window as if trying to see through the heavy fog. "That's the same music we heard in Seattle, isn't it?"

Her voice was tight. Tension radiated from her. He knew she was running hot in an effort to suppress the pull of the music. If she lost control and tried to get out of the car to follow the lure, he would have to act. She might thank him later, but tonight it was going to be bad.

"Yes," he said.

"It's a hypnotic summons, right?" she said. "Tuned to my vibe?"

"Yes," he said. "I can hear it but it's not pulling me."

"You're doing it again," she said. "Stop looking at me as if I am a grenade that might explode at any second."

"How are you feeling?"

"Annoyed. With you."

"I'm serious. How bad is the pull of the music?"

"It's there. I can sense it clearly but I'm in control. I can handle it. Last night it caught me off guard. I wasn't prepared. Tonight everything is different. I know what I'm dealing with. Don't worry, I'm not going to run wildly into the fog to find the recorder player."

"You're sure?"

She shot him a quick glare. "I happen to be a very strong aura talent, remember? Pretty sure anyone with a powerful psychic profile could handle the recorder. It's a lot like pulling yourself out of a lucid dream. Once you know you're dreaming you can rewrite the script or wake up."

"Okay, that makes sense. Do you think you'd be able to resist if I wasn't here with you in the car?"

"Yes. Why?" She wrapped her arms around her knees and watched him the same way he had been watching her. Closely. "You've got a plan, don't you?"

"I don't think the recorder works as a tracking device. It feels like a bright, shiny lure."

"Meaning the piper can't use it to find me. It only works to draw me to him."

"Right."

"But you can follow the music back to the source," Olivia said. "That's what you're thinking, isn't it?"

"I would really like to get my hands on one or two of those guys in black, preferably the one playing that damned recorder. We need information."

"There are four of them, Harlan, at least that's how many there were this afternoon at the Sefton house. And they're armed. For your information, guns work just fine in these mountains, unless you go into one of the caves."

"Two vehicles. Probably the same two SUVs as at the Sefton house."

"'Probably'?"

"It's a good bet we're dealing with the crew we ran into earlier today."

"'A good bet'?" Olivia said. "Since when does a chaos theory talent talk about gambling odds?"

"I do it with every breath I take. So do you. So does everyone on the planet. The only difference between chaos talents and other people is that we're better at calculating the odds. But we screw up, too. And when we find ourselves standing in the rubble, we ask the same question."

"'How the hell did this happen?'"

"That question. Yes."

"Let's think about this, Harlan. You might be able to follow the strong currents of the music back to whoever is playing the recorder, but you're talking about navigating this road in some very serious fog. You didn't grow up in these mountains. You don't know how dangerous this stuff can be."

"I'm a pretty strong talent, too, remember?"

"Well, yes, but—"

"If you really think you'll be okay on your own, I'm going to see if I can grab that damn recorder player or one of his buddies."

"Fine." She reached for her low boots. "But I can't stay inside the vehicle. You need me."

"Why?"

"Kids that grow up in the city learn how to cross streets, buy weed in dark alleys and call nine-one-one. I grew up learning how to survive in these mountains at night. I know this road and I know this fog. Trust me, you're going to need me, and we're both going to need these."

She opened a gear box, took out two long, narrow tubes and slapped one into his hand.

He looked down at it. "Glow sticks?"

"The Fogg Lake version. The tubes are filled with some hot

crystals from the caves. When you remove the stopper, you'll see what I mean. Each crystal gives off a small amount of paranormal light and a vibe you can follow if you recognize it. Think of the rocks as bread crumbs. You drop them behind you as you walk through the woods and use them to find your way back."

"Which means I won't have to stick to the road to avoid getting lost."

She pulled a thick wool scarf out of the gear box and wrapped it around her neck. "Right."

"That is very good news."

CHAPTER 26

Y ou were right," Harlan said. He kept his voice low, barely above a whisper. "I do need you out here."

The serpentine notes of the recorder wafted through the glowing fog, a beacon that would be easy to follow so long as he kept his senses elevated. But the current of paranormal energy embedded in the notes did not tug at him the way he knew it was pulling Olivia. He could feel the tension in her as she walked beside him, but he knew that she was still in control.

They were wading through the eddying fog as if it were a shallow river. The air temperature was cold but nothing their jackets couldn't handle. They did not need flashlights, because the glowing mist provided enough illumination to reveal nearby objects and the rutted, unpaved road.

The energy infused in the fog was the real problem, just as Olivia had warned. The visions, shadows and apparitions that swirled in the mist had been minor distractions when viewed from inside the vehicle. But out in the open they were stronger. It required more effort to keep them at bay.

He understood now why Olivia had insisted they spend the night in the car. It was possible to walk through the stuff provided you moved cautiously, but driving would have been a nightmarish experience. The glowing mist ebbed and flowed in a seemingly random pattern, occasionally clearing enough to allow him to make out rocks and trees a yard or two away. At other times the stuff closed in without warning, reducing visibility to inches.

The recorder music was growing louder and sharper. He glanced at Olivia, who was so close beside him their arms frequently brushed against each other. It wasn't a gesture of intimacy, despite what had happened in the back of the SUV. It was common sense. Physical proximity enhanced the ability to deal with heavy energy. Two auras combined were stronger than each individually. In the unearthly light of the fog he could tell she was concentrating intently. Focused.

"How are you doing?" he asked.

"I'm fine. Stop talking or they'll hear you."

"Right."

He reminded himself that they were in her territory. She was the one with on-the-ground knowledge.

The closer they got to the main road, the more unpleasant the music sounded, at least to his ears. There was a piercing quality to the notes. He sensed the tension that was shivering through Olivia and knew she was having to pull a lot of energy in order to stay in control. He reminded himself that she had already been through a lot that day. How much could she handle?

He'd been through the same shit. How much could *he* handle?

Halfway around a bend in the narrow road Olivia reached out and clamped her fingers around his upper arm. The glare of fog-shrouded headlights could be seen from where they stood. He touched her hand to let her know he got the warning and put his mouth close to her ear.

"Stay here," he said.

She nodded.

He went forward carefully, using the cover of an outcropping of boulders. When he was in a position to view the scene on the far side of the bend in the road, he could see the looming shapes of two SUVs parked one behind the other on the pavement. Four figures moved in the mist, keeping very close to the vehicles. One of them held an object to his mouth. The recorder player.

"This is a waste of time," one of them announced. "We don't even know if the woman is within hearing distance."

Trev, Harlan decided.

The recorder player lowered the instrument. "This damned fog closed in fast. They can't drive through this stuff—not without the nav device. This is where the signal got lost in the noise. They must be nearby."

Ink was the one playing the paranormal recorder.

"Where? Can't see anything in this shit."

The speaker was the one who had been called Ox that afternoon.

"There must be a turnoff or a side road somewhere nearby," Ink insisted. "We can't see it because of the background noise. The Piper was right. These mountains are fucking hot after dark."

"Maybe they decided to make a run for it, in which case they probably went off the edge of a cliff," Ash muttered. "For all we know they're in the river. That explains why we lost the signal."

"You'd better hope she's still alive," Ink said. "You heard the Piper. If the oracle is dead, we are, too."

He raised the recorder and released another string of needle-sharp notes. Ash clapped his hands over his ears.

"Fuck it," he said. "That damn recorder is giving me a headache. I'll wait in the vehicle."

He left the small group standing near the first SUV and walked back to the second vehicle. He did not dawdle. Harlan understood. When Ash left the others he left behind the protection of their combined auras. That meant he was more vulnerable to the senses-disturbing power of the fog.

When Ash reached the second SUV he jerked open the door and jumped inside. He slammed the door shut, but the vehicle did not shield him completely from the music. He put his hands over his ears and rocked back and forth.

Harlan went back around the bend. Olivia was waiting. He put his mouth to her ear again.

"I've got my target. Not the recorder player, but this guy will have answers, too. I'll be right back."

Olivia turned her head and spoke directly into his ear. "You need a distraction. I can give you one."

He stilled and then shook his head. "Too risky."

"Trust me," she said. "I know what I'm doing. I've had a lot of practice at this kind of thing."

He wanted to ask her what the hell that was supposed to mean, but there was no time to get into an extended discussion. He had to make a decision.

He inclined his head once. She took a step back and unfolded the long scarf. It became a shawl. She draped it over her head.

In the fog the transformation was startling. She could have walked straight out of one of her grandmother's oracle paintings.

He was starting to worry that he had made a terrible mistake in agreeing to her plan but she did not give him a chance to change his mind. Without a word she turned and walked around the bend in the road.

"He who dares to summon the oracle must be prepared to pay the price."

The words, intoned in a louder version of her dreamstate voice, echoed ominously in the fog. The voice of an oracle. The currents of energy in the atmosphere enhanced the chilling effect.

The recorder abruptly fell silent.

"It's her," Trev shouted. "She's here. Somewhere."

"Shut up," Ink said. "Watch out for Rancourt. He's probably got a gun."

The operation was underway, Harlan thought. Olivia had created a distraction. He had to make good use of it.

He took the stopper off the tube and shook out one of the crystals. It fit easily into his hand and gave off a luminous energy, as promised. He made his way through the dripping trees, using the glare of the headlights as a guide. Every yard or two he dropped one of the hot crystals.

The damp ground absorbed most of the sound of his footsteps. But even if he had been stumbling through the undergrowth, snapping twigs and tripping on small rocks, he doubted that the men down on the pavement would have noticed. All of their attention was focused on Olivia.

"All who dare the fog to summon the oracle this night will be lost in nightmares."

The promise of doom shuddered through the words. Harlan realized he could not tell if she was acting or uttering a for-real prophecy. Ash, huddled in the front seat of the second SUV, was as stunned as the others. He cracked open the front door in order to hear more clearly.

"Shit," Ox snarled. "Grab her. And use the duct tape to make her shut up. She's giving me the fucking creeps."

"She just predicted we're going to die tonight," Trev said. "Are you listening? *She's an oracle and she just said we're dead men.*"

"No," Ink said. "She said we will be lost in nightmares."

"Same thing," Trev said. "The Piper told us that once the visions start, we're dead."

"We will die for sure if we don't get her," Ink said. "Hang on—I'll reel her in a little closer. Get the stun gun ready."

He put the recorder to his lips and blew a violent cascade of energy-infused notes. The terrible music once again pierced the night.

In response, Olivia spoke again in a voice that seemed to emanate from another dimension.

"He who summons the oracle tonight summons his own doom."

"Fucking oracle," Trev said. "Can't wait to gag her."

"The recorder isn't working," Ox complained. "She's not coming closer. If she runs again we'll lose her."

Ash was half in and half out of the vehicle. He gripped the wheel with one hand and stared through the windshield, transfixed.

Harlan pulled the door all the way open. Ash almost fell out of the front seat. He gasped and clung to the steering wheel to stop his downward descent.

That was when he saw the gun in Harlan's hand. He gazed at it, shocked.

"One word and you won't be any use to me," Harlan said softly. "Out. Fast. Hands in the air."

Ash sucked in some oxygen. His head jerked up and down to indicate he understood. Harlan took a step back.

Ash, moving awkwardly, scrambled out of the front seat. *Not trying to stall for time,* Harlan decided. The kid was flat-out terrified. Shivering. The combination of the disturbing fog, Olivia's ominous words and the fact that he had a gun pointed at him was too much. He was going into shock.

Harlan took the pistol out of Ash's gear belt.

Olivia, draped in the shawl, appeared briefly in the glowing mist. *"Mirrors. Fire. Dead men walking through a dying garden."*

Ink lowered the instrument. "Get her."

Trev and Ox moved warily into the fog.

Harlan fought back a wave of near panic but Olivia vanished into the glowing mist. He allowed himself to breathe again.

He was about to order Ash to move into the trees when he glimpsed a thin beam of energy inside the SUV. He took a closer look and saw that the light was emanating from a clunky-looking device on the dashboard. Artifact.

"Get it," he said to Ash.

"Huh?" Ash looked confused.

"Get that gadget on the dashboard."

Ash obeyed. He reached into the vehicle and grabbed the object.

"Move," Harlan said. "Into the trees. Whatever you do, don't drop that thing."

Ash was appalled at the notion of going into the fog-bound woods. He clutched the gadget as though it were a talisman.

"It's useless," Ox shouted. "No way we can find her, not in this stuff. She's gone."

Harlan steered Ash toward the glowing crystal that marked the path into the woods.

"Find her," Ink shouted.

He started into the fog, moving warily, but hastily retreated to the relative safety of the vehicle.

"Fuck," he said. "That stuff is impossible."

"Worse than the maze," Ox said.

"We can't lose her." Ink raised the recorder.

Ash abruptly stumbled and went down hard on his knees. The thud was audible.

"Rancourt," Ink yelled. "He's over there somewhere."

"Ash is gone," Trev shouted.

"Rancourt must have grabbed him," Ox said.

Shots rang out. Harlan knew he and Ash were invisible in the trees, but that would not protect them from a random bullet. He grabbed Ash by one arm and hauled him toward the next crystal.

More shots thundered in the night.

"Forget Rancourt," Ink yelled. "You'll never be able to find him in this stuff. It's the woman we want."

"What about Ash?" Trev said.

"He's a dead man," Ink said. "There's nothing we can do."

"It's like the oracle said." Ox's voice rose. "We summoned her, so we're all doomed."

"Shut up," Ink said. "Get in the vehicles. Trev, you take the second car."

"Forget it," Trev shouted. "The nav is gone."

"What the fuck?" Ink said. "Shit. Rancourt must have grabbed it when he took Ash. Everyone. Car one. Move."

Doors slammed, echoing in the night. The first vehicle rumbled to life. The SUV made a cautious three-point turn on the narrow road and drove slowly back down the mountain.

Ash whimpered. "Please. There are things out here. Nightmares. Just like she said."

"Yes." Harlan managed to keep the kid from stumbling into a tree. "And unless you want to deal with those nightmares on your own, you'll shut up and do exactly what I tell you."

Ash was trembling. Not from the cold, Harlan decided, and not only because of the gun. The guy definitely had some talent but evidently he lacked an intuitive understanding of how to suppress the hallucinations. Or maybe he was too frightened to focus.

A short distance away a crystal sparked in the fog. And then another.

A few minutes later Harlan and his captive emerged on the old logging road. Olivia appeared, a ghostly figure in the fog.

Ash froze. "No, please, no."

Olivia glanced at him. "Calm down. I'm not going to hurt you." She turned back to Harlan. "Are you okay? I heard shots."

"I'm good. You?"

"Fine. They got away in one of the cars. I can't believe it. I've never heard of anyone who was able to drive that road at night."

"They had a little help from some sort of paranormal navigation device," Harlan said. "Ash here had one in his vehicle, too. That's what he's carrying."

Olivia looked at the square metal object Ash was holding. "An artifact. And a pretty amazing one if it can navigate through this fog."

"Let's get inside the car," Harlan said. "We can take a closer look later."

They walked back toward Olivia's SUV. Ash had stopped whimpering. Harlan suspected he had moved beyond shock and was now numb.

"He's not in good shape," Olivia said. "His aura is wobbly."

"Damn. He can't die on me. I need answers."

"Your empathy is heartwarming."

"This bastard tried to kidnap you, Olivia."

"I know. But he's just a kid and he's terrified."

"The terrified part is good. I can work with that."

When they reached the vehicle, Harlan went through the pockets of Ash's cargo trousers, confiscating some long zip ties, a stun gun and a small kit containing a loaded syringe.

"Probably a dose of some tranquilizer they planned to use on me," Olivia said. "They are really determined to grab me, aren't they?"

"Yes," Harlan said, "they are."

He wanted to comfort and reassure her, but that wouldn't do her any good. There was nothing he could add that would make the situation sound any less dangerous, so he didn't say anything else.

"Thanks," Olivia said.

He concentrated on using one of Ash's zip ties to secure the young man's wrists behind his back. "For what?"

"Not trying to tell me I've got nothing to worry about."

"Anytime."

She eyed him. "That wasn't an attempt at a joke, was it?"

"No."

"What are we going to do with him?" Olivia asked.

"Get him into the vehicle and ask him a few questions."

He opened the cargo bay door and maneuvered Ash into the compartment. There was no resistance. Ash sat quietly, back propped against the side of the vehicle, and stared at something only he could see.

Olivia watched him for a moment. Harlan felt her energy stir again in the atmosphere.

He gripped the door, preparing to close it, but he paused.

"What is it?" he asked.

"There's something off in his aura," Olivia said. "It's unstable."

"You said it was wobbly. He's not handling the fog well. I think he's in shock."

"Maybe." She sounded bewildered. Uncertain.

Harlan glanced at the captive. Like most people with talent, he could perceive auras, but he wasn't a particularly strong reader. When he heightened his senses all he saw was an energy field that appeared fairly strong.

"What do you see?" he asked.

"There's a disturbance in some of the bands that I associate with the dreamstate. And there's something else going on as well. Ask him a question."

Harlan looked at Ash, who sat motionless.

"What's your name?" Harlan asked.

"Ash."

His voice was a monotone. There was no trace of emotion in it.

"What's your last name, Ash?" Harlan continued.

"I don't have a last name now."

"What was your last name before you lost it?"

"I don't remember."

"How did you find out my name?" Harlan asked.

"The Piper knows."

"Who are you working for, Ash?" Harlan asked.

The question evidently confused Ash. "I don't have a job. I have a mission."

"What do you do to earn money?" Harlan said.

"I don't need money."

"Why not?"

"I'm a student," Ash said.

"What are you studying?"

"I study the skills that will enable me to master my talent."

"Who is your teacher?"

"The Piper."

"Does the Piper have a last name?"

"No."

"Where is the Piper?"

"On the island."

Harlan leaned into the compartment. "What is the name of the island?"

"It doesn't have a name."

"How do you get to the island with no name?"

"I don't know," Ash said.

He slumped to one side, eyes closed. Unconscious.

Harlan grasped his shoulder and gave him a shake. There was no response.

"I think he's in the grip of a powerful hypnotic suggestion," Olivia said. "Asking questions about the island must have triggered it."

"What about the instability in his aura?" Harlan asked.

"It's still there. Sparking. Looks like a broken neon sign."

"Think he'll wake up anytime soon?"

"I don't know," Olivia said. "Maybe someone on the Foundation team in Fogg Lake will be able to bring him out of the trance. But there's more going on than a hypnotic suggestion. I think he's ill. I wonder if we should use the auto-injector you found on him."

"We don't know what's in it. Might be some kind of suicide drug that he's supposed to use if he falls into the wrong hands."

"He didn't attempt to use it," Olivia pointed out.

"Maybe that's because he went into shock and then into a trance."

"I really don't like the look of his aura. I think we should give him the injection."

Harlan eyed her. "Is that the oracle talking?"

"No, it's me, the psychic investigator who has met some people who keep emergency auto-injectors on hand for, you know, emergencies."

"We don't know if this is an emergency."

"Trust me, given the vibe in his aura, it's safe to say Ash is deteriorating rapidly. Something is very wrong."

She was right. Everything about the kid's energy felt off.

"All right," Harlan said.

He worked one of Ash's arms free of the black jacket, rolled up the sleeve of the shirt and administered the injection. Ash did not stir, but after a couple of minutes his energy felt cooler.

Harlan looked at Olivia. "Well?"

"Better. Not stable, but calmer. I wonder what was in that auto-injector."

"I don't know, but I'll save it for analysis." Harlan tucked the empty device into the leather kit and set it aside. "Why isn't he waking up?"

"I think he's still under the influence of the hypnotic suggestion. He may not wake up until we figure out how to bring him out of the trance."

Harlan clamped down on the fierce sense of urgency that was threatening to take control. He had to think. One thing was clear—at the moment Ash was useless.

Harlan picked up the artifact, moved out of the cargo bay and slammed the door shut. He started toward the passenger side door.

"You drive," he said. "I'll see if we can figure out how to use this thing to navigate the road to Fogg Lake tonight."

"Personally, I think that would be a really dumbass experiment."

"It's worth a try."

"It's not worth our lives," Olivia said. "That thing may have gotten those guys this far, but they couldn't use it to find the logging road, remember? You heard what one of them said. There's too much noise in the vicinity. He's right. What's more, that noise only gets worse as we get closer to town."

"Let me just see if I can activate it."

She opened the driver's door and got behind the wheel. She didn't say anything. She didn't have to. It didn't require any psychic talent to read her mind.

"Okay, I get it," he said. He climbed into the passenger seat and closed the door. "Dumbass?"

"I didn't say you were a dumbass. I said it would be a dumbass experiment. A subtle but clear distinction."

"Subtle. Right." He exhaled slowly and studied the device, feeling for the vibe. "You have to admit it's an interesting artifact."

"Yes, it is."

"Huh. I wonder what this button does." He pulsed a little energy through the crystal.

"Uh, Harlan, I don't think—"

A small window illuminated and displayed a murky, ghostly green image of a tiny section of the logging road directly in front of the SUV.

"Looks like an old-fashioned radar screen," he said.

"Let me see." Olivia leaned over to look at the window. "That's the logging road," she said. "It's showing us the view of what is directly in front of us. Just a few feet, though."

"We'd have to move slowly, but—"

"Dumbass idea."

As they watched, the vague outline of the road wavered wildly and briefly vanished altogether. A few seconds later it reappeared, but the image faded in and out. When it was visible it was distorted, as if they were looking at it through heavy currents of water. A few seconds later it disappeared again.

"It's not strong enough to hold a clear image in this fog," Harlan said. "But the fact that it works at all is amazing. The Foundation lab people are going to love this gadget. If the mechanism can be replicated, they may be able to fine-tune it—"

"What's that?" Olivia said.

Alarmed, she pointed to a flashing green dot in the lower corner of the screen. He took a closer look.

"Interesting," he said.

Olivia sat back quickly. "Maybe it's going to explode. You'd better toss it out the window."

"I don't think it's volatile. It feels like it's reacting to a signal of some kind."

Experimentally he turned the device in various directions. The dot continued to flash.

"I've got an idea," he said. "I'll be right back."

"Where are you going?"

"To check out a theory."

"This is no time to be testing theories."

"Don't worry."

He opened the door and climbed out of the vehicle. Slowly he walked around the SUV. When he reached the cargo bay door the green dot brightened.

He crouched and waved the artifact under the fender. A faint buzz of energy whispered across his senses. He groped for the object that was sending the signal, found it, pulled it free.

Olivia hopped out of the front seat and came to the back of the car to see what was going on.

"What is it?" she asked.

He held up the small disc to show her the green crystal glowing inside.

"You're right," he said. "I am a dumbass. This is some kind of paranormal tracking device. They must have put it on your vehicle back in Seattle. I saw Ink stick a conventional tracker in the wheel well at the Sefton house. I got rid of it, but it must have been intended as a backup. This one was on the car the whole time."

She examined it uneasily. "What are you going to do with it?"

"Hand it over to the Foundation team in Fogg Lake. They'll be thrilled. Old Bluestone tech always makes the researchers happy."

"But that device tells the bad guys where we are."

"So what? They already know we're headed for Fogg Lake."

"I guess that's true," she said. "For the record, I never called you a dumbass."

"Yes, you did."

"No, I didn't."

"The implication was crystal clear."

"Let's get back in the car," Olivia said. "It's cold out here."

CHAPTER 27

Something I've been wondering about," Harlan said. "Earlier to-night, when you scared the hell out of those guys by warning them they would end up in nightmares, et cetera, et cetera, was that the real thing?"

Olivia was lounging in the driver's seat, the wool scarf bundled around her neck and shoulders for warmth, her hands shoved into the deep pockets of her jacket. She turned her head to look at Harlan, who was cranked back a few degrees in the passenger seat. His eyes were closed, but she had known before he spoke that he was wide awake. Alert.

"The real thing?" she repeated, wanting to make certain she understood the question.

"You know what I mean," he said. "Was that the oracle talking? Asking for a friend."

"It was an act, Harlan. Nothing more. Don't tell me you fell for it. You're supposed to be the smartest guy in the room, remember?"

"We've already ascertained that upon occasion I am a dumbass."

"Yes, it was an act. I faked the voice and I had the fog for cover. My audience was primed because they were already nervous. Stress and the atmosphere of these mountains after dark will do that to people. It wasn't hard to fake the oracle thing. You said it yourself. People see what they expect to see."

"You've had experience scaring people?"

Olivia smiled. "Halloween is a very competitive event in Fogg Lake."

"I'll bet. Can't imagine kids doing the trick-or-treat thing in this fog."

"Builds character."

Harlan smiled. It wasn't a big smile, but it was a smile.

"Growing up as the son and heir apparent of Stenson Rancourt must have made for an interesting childhood," she said. "Did you ever go trick-or-treating?"

"I have a few memories of Halloween, but that was before my mother died. After she was gone the old man shipped me off to boarding school."

"That had to be tough."

"Looking back, I think he did it because every time he looked at me he saw my mom. He loved her passionately. He wasn't the same after she died. He used sex and empire building to dull the pain."

"And forgot that you were in pain, too?"

"Maybe." Harlan opened his eyes and looked out the window into the fog. "But things changed again when he became obsessed with making sure the Foundation remained the family business. He wanted me to show more interest in his legacy. He also wanted me to become as fixated on Vortex as he was."

"I gather you weren't keen on either idea?"

"I never wanted to take over the Foundation. I never gave a damn about Vortex. Not in those days. I had . . . other interests."

"What other interests?"

"I've always been curious about the history of the study of the paranormal. People have been messing around with it since the dawn of civilization. Every culture has traditions, legends, stories. Over the centuries there have been many attempts to explore and experiment. There's so much to learn."

"Guess that career path didn't work for you," she said. "Because here you are—in charge of the Foundation and obsessed with Vortex."

"Don't remind me. It's enough to make a man believe in fate."

"And oracles?"

He surprised her with another faint smile. "I've believed in oracles for quite a while now."

She thought about that and then decided to take the plunge and ask the one question she wasn't sure she wanted answered.

"Where were you the night your father died in that lab explosion?" she said.

Harlan was silent for a moment. Probably deciding how much to tell her. She didn't think he would bother to lie.

"Dad and I quarreled earlier that evening," he said finally. "It was the usual fight. He was determined to make me take over the Foundation. He called it my inheritance, but it was actually his legacy. I reminded him that I wanted to pursue another career. He reminded me, as usual, that I was a grave disappointment to him. Things ended the way they always did: I stormed out. Later he texted me to say that Arganbright and Pine had insisted on a meeting at headquarters. He wanted me present. He said the future of the Foundation would be decided that night. He needed backup."

"He was afraid of Victor and Lucas?"

"'Afraid' isn't the right word," Harlan said. "It would be more accurate to say he viewed them as enemies and competitors. He was convinced they were plotting to take over the Foundation. He was right. I returned to headquarters for the meeting. The explosion had already taken place. By the time I got there the medics were carrying out my father's body."

She shuddered. "How awful. I'm so sorry."

"Victor and Lucas were there, too. I saw them talking to the authorities."

"You assumed they had murdered your father and figured you were probably next on their target list. You went on the run."

"Something like that."

"And then you became obsessed with revenge."

"That was definitely my goal when I left the scene that night."

"You had failed to protect your father. You felt responsible."

"Yep."

"So why didn't you go after Victor and Lucas?"

Harlan turned his head to look at her. "Why do you think I didn't go after them?"

A frisson of knowing sent a small shock of electricity down her spine. "You found out they didn't murder your father."

"You're good. You should consider the oracle business."

"Don't start," she warned. "Who was responsible for your father's death?"

"His name was Samuel Pitney. He worked in one of the Foundation labs. His wife was having an affair with Dad. Pitney went mad with jealousy. In the end, my father didn't die because of a violent confrontation with the two men who wanted to take control of the Foundation. He died because he got involved in a classic love triangle. But there was no love involved. Dad didn't care about Pitney's wife. She was just another casual fling as far as he was concerned. Pitney's wife was ambitious. She wanted to marry the director of the Foundation. Pitney was insane with jealousy and rage."

"Pitney set the explosion that killed your father?"

"Yes."

"What happened to Pitney?"

"Dead," Harlan said. "He put a bullet in his head after he murdered his wife."

"How did you discover that? I'm sure Victor and Lucas don't know what happened."

"I told you, I'm a pretty good chaos talent. To be fair, I had more data than Arganbright and Pine did, because I knew my father. I went looking for the truth, expecting to prove that Arganbright and Pine had murdered Dad. The trail led me to Pitney instead."

"So much for revenge."

"What do you mean?"

"Got news for you, Harlan. Searching for the truth is not an act of vengeance."

"What would you call it?"

"A search for answers. A quest for justice. That requires a very different moral compass than the one Larissa Whittier used. You could not avenge your father, and you had failed him because you had walked away from your inheritance. You must have been in a very bad place."

Harlan folded his arms. "It definitely wasn't a good place."

"You threw yourself into an exploration of paranormal phenomena around the world and financed the project with those occasional odd jobs for that investigation agency you mentioned. Jones and Jones. That's what you've been doing all this time."

"Until I picked up the chatter about Vortex this past year," Harlan said.

"Which is a problem, because the secrets of Vortex might be extremely dangerous. But you aren't interested in controlling those secrets. You're worried about the damage they might cause."

"Arganbright and Pine are more than a little worried, too," Harlan said.

"I know. My point is, once again, you chose a different path than the one Larissa Whittier took. If she had known about Vortex she would have gone after it in order to acquire those secrets for herself. You and Victor and Lucas are just trying to protect people."

Harlan was silent for a while. "The stories about my father and my grandfather are all true. They really did run the Foundation as if it were a mob organization. Their obsession with power kept them from focusing on the important things, like research and dealing with the fallout from Bluestone. Arganbright and Pine took that on as their mission, and they are good at it."

"But the Foundation was your inheritance."

"I never wanted it, Olivia."

"I believe you." She reflected for a moment. "And you felt guilty about that, as well. You failed your father because you didn't accept and honor his legacy, and in the end you weren't able to save his life."

"That pretty much says it all."

"Those so-called consulting jobs for Jones and Jones were an attempt at atonement, weren't they? You tried to find answers and justice for other people because you wanted to atone for what you saw as your failures and, I think, to make up for your father's and grandfather's crimes. That's what this obsession with Vortex is about, too. Finding it and neutralizing the danger, whatever that is, is an act of penance."

"You think you have me figured out, don't you?"

"Not entirely, but yes, I think I'm getting to know you. One thing is for sure—you are not anything like your half sister. What will you do with your life after we take care of Vortex? Got a plan for the next five years?"

"I'll worry about that when the time comes," Harlan said.

"You're not much in the way of a long-range planner, are you?"

"No."

The finality in the single word told her that she had pushed him too far. The moment of intimacy and communication was over. Harlan had just shut down.

She looked around the edge of the seat. Ash was still profoundly asleep. His aura wasn't normal, but at least it wasn't deteriorating. Yet.

"I wonder how often he needs to take that medication that was in the auto-injector," she said.

Harlan frowned. "Good question. How does his energy field look?"

"Okay for now. But he's deeply asleep. I keep thinking about how young he is."

"I keep thinking about how he called himself a student. That his teacher is the Piper, who lives on an island with no name."

"So many questions," Olivia said.

Harlan unfolded his arms and scrubbed his face with one hand. "So little time."

CHAPTER 28

Olivia was squirming around in the seat, trying to find a more comfortable position, when she noticed she could see the trees at the edge of the road. She yawned, straightened and pressed the lever to bring her partially reclined seat into the upright position.

"The fog is lifting," she said. "It will be safe to start driving soon if we take it slow."

"Good." Harlan raised his seat. "The sooner we get out of here, the better. Ash's buddies may decide to return. You drive. You know the road. I'll keep an eye on Sleeping Beauty."

"Sounds like a plan."

She cranked up the engine and put the SUV into reverse.

"Hang on," Harlan said. "Are you going to back down this road?"

"There's not enough room to turn around," she explained. "Feel free to get out and walk point if my driving makes you nervous."

His brows rose. "You've done this before?"

She smiled. "Not everyone gets trapped out here at night by

accident. This particular logging road is Fogg Lake's version of Lover's Lane."

Harlan startled her with a quick, wicked grin. "I don't think I'll ask any more questions about how you came by your knowledge of local geography."

"A wise decision."

She used the mirrors and reversed slowly back to the old highway. The hardest part was the bend in the road where the rutted track met the pavement. She tried not to gloat as she negotiated it with finesse.

Harlan looked at her as she got the SUV safely onto the highway and pointed in the right direction.

"You're good," he said.

"Gosh, thanks."

He ignored the fake gratitude and contemplated the abandoned SUV sitting in the middle of the road.

"There may be some useful evidence in it," he said. He opened the passenger side door. "With luck the key fob is inside. If so, I'll transfer Ash to that vehicle and follow you into town."

She glanced back at the unconscious man and kicked up her senses. "He's still in a deep sleep. I think you can leave him with me. He's not going to be a problem, not for a while. Maybe indefinitely."

"You're sure?"

"I'm sure," she said. "Reading auras is what I do, remember?"

"All right. Stop immediately if you see any indication that he's waking up."

"You've secured his wrists and his ankles, Harlan. He's not going anywhere."

Harlan hesitated and then, with a curt not, got out of the vehicle. He walked back to the other SUV, did a brief inspection and then raised a hand to signal that he would follow her into town.

She put the car in gear and started driving toward home and memories.

_____

The last of the morning mist had retreated by the time the familiar roadside sign appeared.

WELCOME TO FOGG LAKE.
NOTHING TO SEE HERE.

CHAPTER 29

Olivia drove into town and stopped in front of the trailer that served as the Foundation's office in Fogg Lake. Dexter Rose, the head of the on-site security team, came out to greet them. Olivia made the introductions and then watched, amused, as Rose and the others on the team studied Harlan with open curiosity and speculation.

"Lucas Pine called," Dexter said. "Told us you two were on the way. Got a little worried when you didn't show up late yesterday. Figured you had to spend the night on the road. Welcome to Fogg Lake, Mr. Rancourt."

"Thanks," Harlan said. "I need to call Vegas."

"Your cell won't work in these mountains," Dexter said. He jerked a thumb at a trailer that sat near the general store. "We've got a landline in the office that you can use."

Olivia stood next to her parked SUV and chatted with some of the people who had turned out to examine the new arrivals. With the exception of some of the Foundation staff, she knew everyone in the vicinity. She was well aware Harlan was the main attraction. Word had spread that Stenson Rancourt's son had returned from the dead and was now working with the Foundation. The news that Harlan was chasing the Vortex rumors and that Olivia was helping him was a source of fascination.

"Before I make the call I need to know how soon you can arrange to transport a suspect to Seattle and get him on a Foundation plane to Vegas," Harlan said.

"I can put a convoy together in a few minutes," Dexter said. "It's about a three-and-a-half-hour drive to the airport."

"Sounds good," Harlan said. "I'll make sure Arganbright and Pine have the jet waiting on the ground in Seattle."

Dexter's brows rose but he did not question Harlan's authority. "The kid doesn't look like he's in great shape. What happened to him?"

"We're not sure," Olivia said. "There some instability in his aura. I think he's in a hypnotic trance. He was carrying medication. We gave it to him last night. It's working, but I don't know for how long. Do you have anyone on your staff who knows how to deal with a trance?"

"Not at the moment," Dexter said. "He needs the doctors at Halcyon."

"If he suddenly snaps out of the trance he may go rogue," Olivia warned.

"Don't worry," Dexter said. "The team will make sure he's locked down at all times." He turned back to Harlan. "Never thought I'd see the day when Arganbright and Pine would work with Stenson Rancourt's son."

"They know how to set priorities," Harlan said. "And right now the priority is Vortex."

"Understood." Dexter's eyes tightened. "So the rumors about that old lab are true, then. That's probably not good news. If the stories about what was going on there are close to accurate, Vortex was shut down and destroyed for some damn good reasons."

"Yes." Harlan started toward the trailer.

Dexter looked at Olivia. "You two got quarters lined up for tonight? This town is full. The Foundation rented every available cabin and spare bedroom. We can always find space for a couple of sleeping bags, though."

"Thanks, but that won't be necessary," Olivia said. "I didn't rent out my mother's house, because I haven't had time to pack up her things. There's plenty of room. Harlan and I can stay there tonight."

Something in her voice evidently snagged Harlan's attention. He paused and turned around, frowning. She thought she saw a question in his eyes, but in the end he did not comment.

"Where will I find you after I talk to Arganbright and Pine?" he said instead.

"The library. I want to talk to a real oracle."

CHAPTER 30

Harmony chuckled as she poured tea into two mugs. "I would love to have seen the expressions on Victor's and Lucas's faces when Harlan Rancourt showed up at their front door."

Olivia wrapped both hands around one of the mugs. The warmth felt good. They were in Harmony's private quarters on the second floor of the Fogg Lake Library. It was a cozy space complete with a pleasant fire on the hearth and a cat stretched out on the window seat. Harmony had introduced the cat as Agnes.

Harmony was the town librarian. Traditionally the apartment went with the job. Among other responsibilities, she was in charge of the local ancestry and historical archives.

She was also a true oracle.

"I'm sure Victor and Lucas were stunned," Olivia said. "But it certainly didn't take long for them to decide they were willing to do a deal with the son of Stenson Rancourt if it gave them a shot at finding Vortex."

"They think they're using him?"

"And he thinks he's using them," Olivia said. "For now, at least, they all seem to view it as a win-win. It's going to be very interesting to see what happens if and when we locate that old lab."

Harmony set the pot down and took a seat on the other side of the scarred wooden table. She was a formidable presence—nearly six feet tall with a long sweep of silver hair and the eyes of an Old Soul. She favored knee-high leather boots; long, dramatic cloaks; and metal accessories. Olivia would not have been surprised to see her buckle on a sword belt. She made the outfit look good.

Nobody knew much about Harmony. She had arrived in Fogg Lake one day a few years earlier. The librarian-oracle who had been in charge of the library at the time had announced that she was turning the job over to Harmony. She had packed her bags and left that day.

No one had disputed the change of librarians. Ever since the explosion in the nearby caves had released the paranormal gases that had changed the town forever, the librarian of Fogg Lake had always been an oracle. Each outgoing librarian had named their replacement.

"Victor and Lucas and Harlan Rancourt may be trying to manipulate each other," Harmony said. "But all of them are using you, Olivia."

"You've got it backward." Olivia drank some tea and lowered the mug. "I'm using them."

"Really?" Harmony looked intrigued. "Don't try to tell me it's the money, although the Foundation does pay its bills."

"Harlan has convinced me that if we find Vortex I might discover the identity of the man who murdered my mother. I believe him. He doesn't always tell me the whole truth, but he hasn't lied to me."

"Ah." Harmony sat back in the chair on the opposite side of the table. "That certainly explains a few things."

A short silence descended. Agnes the cat rose, stretched and bounded down to the floor from the window seat. She padded across the kitchen, sat down close to Olivia's chair and looked up with enigmatic cat eyes.

"I didn't know there was a cat living here in the library," Olivia said.

"Agnes wandered in a few weeks ago and made it clear she was taking up residence," Harmony said.

Olivia smiled, reached down and stroked the cat. "Hey, Agnes. Nice to meet you. I've been thinking about getting a cat. His name is Joe."

Agnes stared at her for a moment longer and then, apparently satisfied, butted her head against Olivia's leg. Finished with the conversation, she went back to the window seat and leaped lightly up onto the cushion.

Olivia turned back to Harmony. "I've got something to show you." She reached into her handbag and took out the camera. She set the artifact on the table.

Harmony's eyes heated a little. "That's lost lab energy, isn't it?"

"Yes," Olivia said. "And if Harlan and I are right, it has a Vortex vibe."

"In which case, you're walking around with an artifact that a lot of people would be willing to kill to acquire. Where did you get it?"

"An antiques shop in Seattle. It was just sitting on the sales floor. The dealer told me no one had shown any interest in it."

Harmony gave her an unreadable look. "Until you came along?"

"It has a psychic signature. Harmony, this camera belonged to my grandmother. My mother had it, too, although I never saw it while I was growing up. There are some photos locked inside. Not regular pictures. Psychic holograms. I'll show you one."

She picked up the camera, pressed one of the crystal buttons and focused a little energy through it.

The hologram of the camouflaged trailer park flashed into existence in the middle of the kitchen. Harmony took a quick, startled breath. Then her expression changed to recognition.

"A Bluestone operation?" she asked. "The trailers are the right era."

"Harlan thinks it's the community that was established for the

Vortex staff. There's another image that indicates it's on an island in the San Juans."

"The landscape certainly looks like the San Juans. Which island?"

"An invisible island with no name, according to my grandmother."

"Your grandmother?"

"I can somehow hear her voice in some of the images."

Harmony rose slowly and walked around the hologram. "I recognize some of the names on the trailers. They're in the ancestry records. All filed under 'Deceased or Disappeared. No Known Descendants.'"

"Harlan says my grandmother's real name was Goodwin. Grace Goodwin. That name is on one of those trailers."

"I'll see what I can find in the files later. Did your grandmother leave any other message?"

"Yes," Olivia said. "One of which is *Here there be monsters.* There's also something about stopping said monsters by quenching the lightning in the mirrors."

Harmony's eyes blazed with a strange energy. "Your grandmother was the Vortex oracle."

"That's what Harlan thinks."

"Well, well, well."

Olivia closed her eyes and slumped in her chair. "Don't say it."

"We know very little about the talent, but there are indications that it tends to go down through the female line."

Olivia opened her eyes. "Harlan mentioned that. He's convinced I've got my grandmother's talent—assuming Grace Goodwin really is my grandmother. But I don't believe I'm an oracle."

Harmony sat down. There was an understanding, sympathetic look in her brilliant eyes. "You mean you don't want to believe it."

"That, too."

"I don't blame you. It's a calling, though, not a career choice. If you are an oracle you're stuck with the talent, like it or not. The worst thing about it is that the visions are more emotional than informative.

You feel them, you sense them, you know they are real, but they are extremely difficult to translate in a way that is helpful."

Olivia swallowed more tea and set the mug on the table. "Harlan claims he can interpret my weird statements."

"Is that so? He's a chaos talent?"

"Among other things. How did you know?"

"As I said, there hasn't been much research done on the oracle talent, mostly because it is so rare. One thing we know for sure—it's not magic. It's a true paranormal talent. There is a theory that strong chaos talents can pick up the clues in a prophecy and put them together so that they make sense. But even the most powerful talent requires sufficient data to make the connections possible, let alone probable. Otherwise it's just guesswork."

"In other words, a chaos talent can't pull the interpretation out of thin air?" Olivia asked.

"Or out of his ass," Harlan said from the top of the stairs. He stopped in the doorway. "Sadly. That ability would certainly be useful right now."

"On the other hand, it's nice to know there are some limitations on your skills," Olivia said. "Harmony, meet Harlan Rancourt. Harlan, this is Harmony—a real oracle."

"A pleasure to meet you," Harlan said. "I appreciate—"

Harmony stiffened. She shot to her feet. Her eyes glittered with energy. The atmosphere around her was suddenly charged. She spoke. The words rolled through the kitchen, thunder in advance of a great storm.

"Past and present must unite to stop the storm that creates monsters."

Olivia shuddered. Harlan watched Harmony with acute attention.

"Anything else?" he asked when she fell silent.

"Nope, that's all I've got for now." Harmony fell back into her normal voice and smiled. "Tea?"

"Tea sounds like a great idea," Harlan said. "Thank you."

Olivia looked at him. "Well? Aren't you going to interpret Harmony's pronouncement?"

"Sounds pretty straightforward to me. You represent the present. I'm the past. We need to work together. Nothing new. The prophecy just confirms the theories and data I've compiled so far."

Olivia sighed. "In other words, I'm just a data point?"

Harlan looked bewildered by the question. Before he could figure out a response, Harmony put a mug down in front of him.

"What makes you so sure that locating Vortex will help you identify the man you believe murdered Olivia's mother?" she asked.

Harlan looked at Olivia. "You tell her."

"Harlan doesn't think the person who killed my mother was a random murderous collector," Olivia said. "I'm inclined to agree. The fact that the killer targeted a direct descendant of the woman who was probably the legendary Vortex oracle feels like more than a coincidence. He knew about the camera. He thought it was the key to Vortex and he was willing to kill to get it."

"Is that your intuition talking?" Harmony asked gently.

"Maybe," Olivia admitted. "But I think Harlan is right. There are too many connections in this thing."

"Not to mention the rumors in the paranormal artifacts market," Harlan added. "I'm a big believer in that kind of data."

"My mother managed to capture a hologram of her killer," Olivia said. "It's on the camera. I'll show you."

She concentrated. The image of the monster caught in the act of reaching for her mother flashed into existence. Harmony flinched and drew a sharp breath. She stared at the hologram.

"That is . . . amazing," she whispered.

"My mother left a message embedded in the hologram," Olivia said. *"Dead man walking in a dying garden."*

Harmony regarded the hologram for a long moment and then shook her head.

"I don't recognize him," she said. "I'll make some notes, but I don't see anything obvious that I can use. No jewelry. Nothing unusual about his attire."

"What about the recorder?" Harlan asked. "It's on the ground near one of his boots. Looks like he dropped it."

Harmony crouched to take a closer look. "Now, that is interesting. It didn't shatter."

"I think it's made out of some hard crystal," Harlan said. "One of the four men who chased us up the mountain last night used a similar recorder to try to summon Olivia."

Harmony straightened and studied Olivia. "What happens when the recorder is played?"

"I can feel a compulsion to follow the music," Olivia said. "But I'm able to resist it now that I recognize it."

Harmony nodded. "That makes sense. You're a powerful talent. Do you have any more information?"

"Just that Ash, the kid Harlan grabbed last night, calls himself a student. His mentor is the Piper, who lives on the island with no name. He doesn't seem to know how to get to the island."

"Do you think the Piper is the man in the hologram?" Harmony said sharply.

"That is a real possibility," Harlan said.

Olivia stopped focusing on the hologram. It winked out of existence. She felt a sense of relief when it vanished. Harmony relaxed, too.

"Unnerving, to put it mildly," she said. "Any other images on the camera besides the trailer community and your mother's killer?"

"There's one showing a view of an island taken from a boat and the one I took of the Speed Date Killer who tried to murder me," Olivia said.

"I know what happened when Brian Gatewood tracked you down and tried to murder you in your garage. When I heard about his seizure I knew you must have used some sort of paranormal energy in self-defense." Harmony's expression sharpened. "You were able to use the camera as a weapon?"

"I almost killed Gatewood with it," Olivia said quietly. "When I focused the crystal in the lens at him, he suffered some sort of seizure. He was unconscious for a time. When he recovered he was eager to confess."

"Fascinating."

"In addition to that image and another one of the island, I think there's one more locked in the camera," Olivia said. "But I haven't been able to pull it up." She looked at Harlan. "Any news from Las Vegas?"

"A few things," Harlan said. He took out a small notepad and glanced at what was written on it. "First, the license plates on the two SUVs that chased us are registered to a small private security firm. Address is a storefront in a dying strip mall outside of Seattle. Lucas Pine said it looks like the firm has only one client, a shell corporation that lists an address on an island—"

Excitement sparked through Olivia. "In the San Juans?"

"No, that would have been too easy," Harlan said. "The corporation is located on an island in the Caribbean."

"And yet it employs a security firm that has a small office here in the Pacific Northwest," Harmony mused.

"Exactly." Harlan went back to his notes. "Arganbright also told me the Foundation team based in Seattle has secured the Sefton house but that it's going to take a while to dig through the ruins to see what survived."

"What about the no-name island that you think might be the site of the Vortex lab?" Olivia asked.

"Lucas is still checking that angle. No luck so far."

"You can't make an entire island vanish," Harmony said.

"In the days of the Bluestone Project you could do just that," Harlan said, "if you had government connections. The question is, why hasn't it been found in recent decades? It's not as if no one has been looking for it."

"People, including a lot of raiders, have been searching for Vortex," Harmony pointed out. "But they had no way of knowing that it might be located on an island."

"True," Harlan said. "Until I found Olivia and her camera, I didn't realize I was looking for an island. I had some sense that the lab might have been located in the Pacific Northwest, but that's it."

"There are not an unlimited number of islands in the San Juans," Harmony said. "About a hundred and seventy or so if you count every reef and chunk of rock. But a lot of those wouldn't be large enough to support a secret government lab. If necessary the Foundation can search each island."

"That would take too much time," Harlan said. "We need to narrow the possibilities as quickly as we can. Arganbright and Pine are working that angle."

Harmony leaned back in her chair. "It's just hard to believe Vortex has been right in our backyard all these years. Hiding in plain sight."

Olivia looked at Harlan. "You told me it's not that difficult to hide in plain sight if someone knows what he's doing and has a certain talent for the business."

Harlan's eyes tightened at the corners. "Meaning?"

"It seems likely that someone probably would have stumbled across the remains of an abandoned government lab located on an island in the San Juans by now—unless the lab was never actually abandoned. What if the island wasn't owned by the government? What if someone has been living there all these years? A private island. Maybe a home to some eccentric billionaire who is obsessed with privacy?"

Harlan and Harmony both focused on her, expectation in their vibes.

"Don't look at me like that," she said. "It wasn't an oracle prophecy. Just a passing thought."

"A very interesting one," Harlan said. "There are some private islands in the San Juans. Pine is looking for a government property, but if the one we're searching for has been in private hands or a trust from the very beginning, it might have been possible to keep the lab hidden indefinitely, especially if someone has been there all along, guarding it."

"Did Victor and Lucas have any information about the recorder player?" Olivia asked.

Harlan glanced at his notes. "Lucas said that back in the day when he was in the CIA there were rumors of an off-the-books contractor who used the code name Piper. No one knew how he worked, but his kills were always attributed to natural causes. Heart attacks and strokes. It was assumed he used poison but no one knew how he managed to get so close to his victims."

"He used the recorder," Olivia said. "Maybe it does more than lure the target. Maybe it can be used to stop the heart."

Harmony looked thoughtful. "That particular talent rings a bell. I'll start the research right away."

"Did Lucas indicate the Piper is still doing off-the-books work?" Olivia asked.

"Pine says the Piper was already a legend when he was a young agent. If the assassin is still alive, he'd be very old. Hard to imagine he's still in the same line of work."

"Even contract killers can have children," Harmony said.

Harlan and Olivia looked at her.

"Who might have the talent required to inherit the family business," she concluded. She got to her feet. "I'll see what I can find in the ancestry files."

"I'll help you," Olivia said. "I can take notes."

"I have some research of my own to do," Harlan said. He pulled the notebook out of his pack. "I'm going to spend the afternoon with Alexander Winston's logbook."

CHAPTER 31

Gwendolyn Swan wrapped a leather-gloved hand around each of the dead man's ankles. "I've got the legs. You take the arms."

Eloisa grimaced but she leaned down and got a grip on the raider's wrists.

"On the count of three," Gwendolyn said. "One, two, *three.*"

They hoisted the body and half dragged, half carried it to the open door of the vault.

"This part of the business must get old after a while," Eloisa said.

"No shit." Gwendolyn maneuvered the lower half of the dead raider through the entrance. "There have always been the occasional rats who were dumb enough to try to rip me off, but most of the locals know it's a bad idea. Thanks to your drug, my shop has developed a certain reputation."

"You might be able to get in but you won't be able to get out?"

"Something like that. Lately, however, I seem to have become a target for an out-of-town crowd. They've heard I'm a single woman who has a fortune in relics with a psychic provenance stashed in my vault. They decide to try their luck and think they've hit the lottery when they discover the tunnel entrance in the alley."

"Bait in your rat trap."

"That's the general idea," Gwendolyn said.

She glanced toward the clockwork doll dressed in a vintage nurse's uniform—white cap, white dress, white shoes—standing on the far side of the basement. The figure was about four feet tall. It held what appeared to be a toy syringe in one upraised hand. But the syringe was very real, as anyone who crept into the room via the old tunnel soon discovered.

The mechanism was triggered when the intruder stepped on the board that concealed the sensors in front of the nurse. At that point the hand holding the syringe moved in an arc designed to deliver a lethal injection in whatever part of the body it struck. The needle was big enough and strong enough to pierce heavy clothing. Raiders never took the mechanical nurse seriously until it was too late.

She pulled a wallet out of the raider's jacket and flipped it open. "Just as I thought, he's from out of town. Phoenix, to be precise. The rumors about Vortex are getting hotter. They're drawing outsiders now."

Eloisa released her hold on the dead man's wrists, used the toe of her shoe to nudge a stray arm over the vault's threshold and straightened. "We've got to move fast. If the Foundation gets to Vortex ahead of us, we'll never be able to find Aurora Winston's last logbook."

"You know, I could do without the helpful advice. I'm the one who has been doing all the hard work on this project. I decrypted the code Grandmother used in her journal. I got the camera into Olivia LeClair's hands. I've been keeping the Foundation agents pointed in another direction. Do you realize how many dealings I've had with the Las Vegas crowd lately?"

"I know," Eloisa said. "I'm just worried. We're so close—"

The muffled sound of impatient pounding on the front door of the shop interrupted her.

"I thought you put the Closed sign in the window," she hissed.

"I did, but collectors are a very demanding clientele." Gwendolyn untied her leather apron and slipped it off over her head. "Don't worry, I'll take care of it. Stay down here. Serious collectors get nervous around people they don't know well."

"So do I, these days." Eloisa glanced at the clockwork nurse. "The syringe is empty. I'll refill it for you."

"Thanks." Gwendolyn started toward the stairs. "There's a vial on the top shelf in the vault. That's the last dose. I've been going through a lot of it lately."

"I'll make up another batch as soon as I get back to my lab."

Cold satisfaction tingled through Gwendolyn. "If we get Aurora's last logbook I won't need any more of the drug and you won't be returning to the lab. We're going to disappear to someplace where it doesn't rain all the time."

"*If* we get the logbook."

"Think positive."

Gwendolyn hurried up the stairs. When she reached the top she unlocked the door, stepped into the back room of the shop, relocked the door to the basement and hurried across the sales floor.

She twitched the window shade aside and peeked out into the alley. It was raining. Again. It wasn't just the rain that got to her these days. It was the seemingly endless cloud cover. It was late spring, but you'd never know it by the dull, gray skies.

She stifled a groan when she saw the figure in the doorway, let the shade fall back into place and opened the door.

"Come in, but hurry," she said. "I'm supposed to be closed."

Jake Spode moved into the shop, rain dripping off his parka. Her first thought was that he looked even more ill than he had the first time she had met with him. That had been a few weeks ago. It was obvious that he had once been tall and broad-shouldered, but now he was thin to the point of being gaunt. His face was hollow under his cheekbones. There was a lot of energy in the atmosphere around him, but Gwendolyn thought it felt off.

"Why the Closed sign?" Spode asked.

"Caught another rat." Gwendolyn checked the alley, making sure no one lurked in the shadows before closing the door. She turned to face Spode. "Your turn. What are you doing here? I thought we agreed you shouldn't take the risk of being seen in my shop."

"Things went wrong at the Sefton house yesterday. Harlan Rancourt got away with the oracle."

"*Rancourt?*" Stunned, Gwendolyn frantically tried to reassemble the facts. "Are you talking about that insurance investigator? How do you know he's Rancourt?"

"I got a feeling about him when my team reported that he didn't look like much of a problem. He obviously is a problem. I checked in with an old source who has a connection in the artifacts department at the Foundation. There's a rumor that Harlan Rancourt showed up out of the blue and met with Arganbright and Pine. He's looking for Vortex."

"So he's alive," Gwendolyn said. "I've always wondered."

"He managed to evade my team multiple times, first outside the restaurant and then yesterday at Sefton's." A savage light flashed in Spode's eyes. "I think he may be a fucking illusion talent."

"I've never heard of such a talent."

"There were rumors about Harlan Rancourt in the days when his father ran the Foundation. They said you never saw him coming until it was too late."

"He certainly looked like a fucking insurance agent to me. But now his cover is blown."

"Don't you get it?" Spode snarled. "He's a *Rancourt*. He managed to hide from Arganbright and Pine these past five years, and now he's got the oracle. We need to take him seriously."

"I agree," Gwendolyn said, trying to speak in a more soothing tone. It wasn't easy. She hated to waste time managing Spode, but she had no choice. Everything was riding on the outcome of the Vortex project, and for now they needed him, creepy vibe and all. "Do you have anything remotely resembling a plan?"

Spode's eyes sparked with rage. She knew the surge of anger was aimed at her. He had made it clear from the start that he considered himself the one in charge.

"They're in Fogg Lake," he said. "My team tracked them. Almost got them last night, but they missed again. Had to turn around because of the fog."

"You won't be able to grab the oracle as long as she's in Fogg Lake," Gwendolyn said. "That town is a Foundation fortress these days. You'll have to lure her out."

Spode smiled. Icy frissons of charged energy arced across the back of Gwendolyn's neck. Her intuition was screaming at her to run, but that was not possible. She and Eloisa needed him.

"Rancourt is a complication," Spode said, "but not for long. All I have to do is get him out of the way."

"How are you going to separate Rancourt from the oracle?"

"Bait."

Spode crossed the room, opened the door and went out into the alley. He disappeared into the rain.

Gwendolyn locked up, took a couple of deep breaths to deal with the edgy panic that was eating at her nerves and went into the storage room. She opened the door to the basement stairs. The energy wafting up from the artifacts displayed below restored a sense of calm. Eloisa appeared at the foot of the stairs. Her face was stark with anxiety.

"A customer?" she asked.

"No. Spode."

"What did he want?" Eloisa demanded in a tight voice.

"He said the man who came into the shop with LeClair isn't an insurance investigator. He's Harlan Rancourt."

"Rancourt? So he really is alive? Shit. And Arganbright and Pine are working with him? That is almost unbelievable."

"We're working with Spode. Some would say that's unbelievable, too."

Eloisa shuddered. "Don't remind me."

"Spode said the effort to grab the oracle at Sefton's house failed. The team screwed up again when they made another attempt on the way to Fogg Lake. It was after dark. The fog had rolled in."

"Rancourt and LeClair are in Fogg Lake?"

"For now. They can't stay there indefinitely, not if they want to find Vortex. It's obvious Rancourt is in a hurry."

"We have to get LeClair."

Gwendolyn gripped the handrail. "Spode seems to think he can lure Rancourt out of Fogg Lake and grab LeClair."

"You do realize Spode is fucking insane?"

"We've known that from the start."

CHAPTER 32

Harlan read aloud from Alexander Winston's logbook . . .

"There's been a breakthrough at last. I had begun to give up hope, but this afternoon the tests provided proof of Aurora's theory. We have overcome the biggest hurdle involved in focusing para-energy that is powerful enough to make a functioning weapon feasible. As is often the case, the solution is astonishingly obvious—music.

"My wife and I have long suspected that currents of music transmit energy across the spectrum. It was always obvious that music is capable of exerting a powerful effect on the human sensory system. It impacts mood, emotions, thought processes. It was the knowledge that it can also affect sleep that led us to the conclusion it can alter the dreamstate in such a way as to allow for a hypnotic suggestion to be implanted . . .

". . . I never doubted music could be used to generate not only a hypnotic state but also a weapon. All three rats died . . .

". . . I have turned my attention to the design of a prototype weapon. It is clear now the device must incorporate the new crystal that Aurora and her team developed . . .

". . . The simple recorders are ideal in many ways, not the least of which is that they do not appear to be weapons and therefore will not arouse suspicion. Unlike more sophisticated forms of the flute, they are easily mastered. From a technical point of view the crystal allows for very sharp, clear notes to be played. The purity of the sound is of critical importance when it comes to the hypnotic effects . . ."

Harmony looked up from the files she had spread out on the long workbench. She peered at Harlan over the frames of her reading glasses. "Well, now, that provides a few answers."

"Yes, it does," Olivia said. She was on the opposite side of the table, a notebook open in front of her. "So the legend is true. Vortex managed to produce paranormal weapons in the form of flutes, and we know for a fact that the man who murdered my mother possessed one. So does Ink, the young man who was trying to lure me last night."

"Maybe this person named Ink is the son of the original Piper," Harmony suggested. "Or someone with a similar talent. The real question is, why do they need an oracle? Whoever is behind the attempt to kidnap you, Olivia, must be desperate to take the risk of attracting the attention of the Foundation."

"Very desperate," Harlan said. "There's a more personal entry in the logbook that you might find interesting."

He read it aloud.

"Aurora suspects I am involved in another affair with a lab techni-cian. She has not confronted me this time, however. Perhaps she has finally accepted the fact that these relationships are not matters of the heart. She is a scientist, after all. I'm sure she understands

that my efforts to impregnate some of the lab personnel are experiments that will provide valuable information about the genetics of paranormal abilities. My talent is extraordinary. I owe it to science to produce as many offspring as possible . . ."

"Hah." Olivia shook her head. "Alexander Winston was not much of a psychic, if you ask me. If he couldn't see disaster coming in that situation, he had no business bragging about his paranormal talents."

Harlan looked up. "Disaster did, indeed, strike. Listen to this." He read the final entry in the logbook.

"I am dying. That bitch Aurora has murdered me. I saw it in her eyes. I know now the accident in the lab yesterday was her doing. I have only hours left. I am growing so weak I can barely lift this pen. I cannot believe she would destroy me merely because I conducted some scientific experiments with a couple of lab techs. Unbelievable. My life's work, ruined. And now she will get the credit for the development of the weapons . . ."

"Well," Harmony said, "no one ever claimed that possessing some paranormal talent keeps people from doing dumb shit."

"That was recently pointed out to me," Harlan said.

Olivia glared. "I did not say you were a dumbass."

Harmony looked at her with an expression of acute interest. "You called Harlan Rancourt a dumbass?"

"Mr. Rancourt has chosen to take my words out of context," Olivia said. "I have tried to correct the record. However, if he continues to give the wrong impression, I will be happy to let his interpretation of my statement stand, because he will have proven that his version is, indeed, accurate."

"I see," Harmony said. She closed a file and glanced at her watch. "This is a fascinating conversation, but it's getting late. Time for dinner. Your house is ready, Olivia. I turned on the power and stocked the refrigerator. Don't worry, I didn't touch anything else. I know how you feel about the place."

Harlan got a ping, the same ping he had experienced that morning when Dexter Rose had asked her about sleeping accommodations. Something was off. He looked at Olivia. She was smiling politely at Harmony, but the smile did not reach her eyes.

"Thanks," she said. "I appreciate it."

"Do you need to borrow any clothes?" Harmony asked. "I noticed Harlan has a duffel bag, but you didn't bring anything with you."

"I left some of my clothes in my bedroom at the house. I'll be fine."

"Good," Harmony said. "There's a pot of cheddar-and-broccoli soup and some polenta cakes in the refrigerator. All you need to do is warm them up. Oh, and I left a bottle of wine on the kitchen counter. Figured the two of you might need it tonight."

"Proof positive that you are a genuine oracle," Olivia said.

CHAPTER 33

Harlan poured wine into two glasses. "Got to hand it to Harmony. In addition to being a fine librarian and archivist, she was right when she predicted we would need a drink tonight."

"Definitely." Olivia picked up one of the glasses and walked to a window. "You now have some new information. Think it will be enough to work with?"

Harlan watched her, trying to get a read on her emotional state. Looking back at what had been a very long day, it struck him that the strange mood, whatever it was, had been apparent almost immediately after they had arrived in town. He had first noticed it when Dexter Rose had asked her where she planned to spend the night. But the vibe had taken on weight and substance when she had unlocked the door of the house she had grown up in.

She didn't seem to be depressed, not exactly. Not wistful, either. Edgy, maybe. Restless. She was gazing out into the foggy night as if searching for omens and portents. Or maybe just answers.

He doubted she would find them in the paranormal shadows cast by the mist. The thick stuff, infused with moonlight and energy, had rolled in off the lake shortly before sunset. It had flowed through the woods and flooded the small community, muffling sound. As far as he could see, it offered no answers.

"We've got new data," he said. "I'm not sure how far it will take us. I need time to think about it, and to be honest, I'm too tired to analyze the information now, at least not with the attention it requires."

"Not surprising. Neither of us got any sleep last night."

"No. We didn't get much sleep the night before, either."

The house was small but surprisingly cozy, considering no one had lived in it for almost a year. There was a rustic feel to the place. The large braided rug on the floor looked homemade. So did the curtains. A massive planter decorated with an abstract zigzag design sat on the floor next to the couch. It was empty.

"Mom painted the planter," Olivia said.

He nodded and continued his survey. The furniture was old, the coverings faded and worn, but the sofa and reading chairs had been built to last—built for a family. The coffee table and the dining table bore the patina that could only come from years of use in a household. Earlier he had lit the fire that Harmony had laid on the hearth. The aroma of the homemade cheddar-and-broccoli soup warming on the stove and the spicy polenta cakes in the oven filled the kitchen.

He could live in a house like this, he thought, just as he could live in Olivia's apartment. But neither was home for him. He was a guest, and not a particularly welcome one.

He thought he had learned to be at peace with the knowledge that he was doomed to be a traveler in life. After meeting Olivia he knew that was not true.

Great. Now he was making himself moody. Time to compartmentalize. Time to focus.

He shoved the emotions into a mental filing cabinet labeled *Not*

Useful and considered the painting that hung over the sofa. Time to focus.

"This is the painting you told me about," he said. "The one that illustrates the camera."

Olivia came to stand beside him. "Mom painted it when I was thirteen. I was just coming into my aura-reading talent."

The image was that of a girl on the cusp of womanhood gazing into a full-length mirror as if trying to see her future, trying to visualize the person she would become. The edges of the mirror were an intense blue, the same color as the dress Olivia had worn for the speed date event. The center of the mirror reflected the young Olivia and a portion of the room behind her. In the painting there was a massive vibrantly green fern cascading out of the planter.

The mirror also reflected the vintage camera. It was positioned on the floor in front of the planter.

"Are you sure you don't remember seeing the actual camera?" Harlan said.

"Positive." Olivia drank some wine and lowered the glass. Her eyes were drenched in shadows. "It wasn't part of the original composition. She added it later. She said she did it from memory. I asked her why. She told me it was a family heirloom from my grandmother and that I should think of her whenever I looked at the painting."

"Your mother definitely had it with her the day she was killed. She couldn't have taken the holographic image of the man with the recorder otherwise. Where do you think she hid it during the years you were growing up?"

"She had a safe-deposit box," Olivia said. "After her death I opened it, but it was empty. The bank had a record of her accessing the box a few days before her death. I suppose she could have stored the camera in the box all these years."

"And removed it when she made plans to meet the killer," Harlan said.

"Yes, but if she kept it hidden for so long, why would she give it to a stranger?"

He thought about that. "Maybe she never told you about it because you showed no signs of developing your grandmother's talent. It might have been her way of trying to protect you from the dangers involved with Vortex."

"But sHe left me the clue in the painting in case I someday discovered that I was the granddaughter of the Vortex oracle?"

"Maybe."

"Why not tell me the truth about my grandmother?"

"A lot of people function under the illusion that it's better to hide dangerous truths," Harlan said. "A case of need-to-know. You didn't have the oracle talent, so you had no need to know what it might mean. As for giving the camera to a stranger, he must have said something to convince her that it would be safer to get rid of it."

"So she gave it to a man who promised safety?"

Harlan swirled the wine in his glass, thinking. "He may have used the recorder to hypnotize her. Or maybe he simply told her he was from the Foundation and that she and her daughter would be safer if she gave up the camera."

Olivia's fingers tightened around her own glass. "You sound very sure of that."

"I'm pretty good at figuring out how the monsters think, Olivia."

She stopped in front of the fireplace and gazed into the flames. "The man in the hologram killed my mother for the camera. Presumably he got what he wanted. So how did it end up in Gwendolyn Swan's shop?"

He was on steadier ground now. She was asking for logical answers. He could handle that. "Here's what I'm seeing—"

"Seeing?"

He waved that off. "Visualizing. Whatever. Here's the scenario that is taking shape. The killer murders your mother, grabs the camera and then realizes he can't access it. And he has just murdered a woman who could unlock the artifact."

"He must be a strong talent," Olivia said. "I almost killed a much younger man with the camera. Mom managed to take that hologram of the monster, but he evidently survived."

"We can assume we're dealing with a high-end talent," Harlan said, "one who was able to resist the full force of the energy in the camera."

"Where does Blake Sefton fit into this?"

"Sefton must have been one of the few survivors of the Vortex project. It was a small team working in close proximity. He would have been acquainted with everyone involved. He may have managed to keep track of some of the others who escaped the assassin."

"Including my grandmother?"

"Yes. If he knew her real identity, he probably knew she died in that house fire. If he knew that much, there's a high probability that he was aware of your mother. He may have known she was living in Fogg Lake."

Olivia mulled that over for a moment. "You think the killer learned about my mother from Blake Sefton?"

"It fits," Harlan said. "After he got the information he needed from Sefton, he murdered him. There must have been a fortune in artifacts in that house, so the killer arranged to take possession of it with the offshore trust. He never found the Vortex relics in Sefton's vault, but he sold off the items in the gallery over the course of the past year."

"Assassins probably need cash like everyone else," Olivia said. "But he murdered my mother almost a year ago. Why wait so long to come after me?"

"He must have known about you but it was obvious you were an aura reader, not an oracle. He probably decided to try to find another oracle who could operate the camera. Or maybe he tried to tune the camera to his vibe. Eventually he gave up and pinned his hopes on you. But by then you were involved with the Foundation. That made things very dangerous for him."

"How did the camera end up in Gwendolyn Swan's shop?"

"I can think of one possibility that would explain it," Harlan said.

Olivia's eyes widened. "Gwendolyn Swan is involved in this thing?"

"At the moment, I am assigning a high probability to that scenario."

Olivia stilled. "She called me."

"Who called you?"

"Gwendolyn Swan. She hired me to verify the provenance of some artifacts she had acquired. She said she was worried they might have been stolen. I walked into her shop and saw the camera. I was drawn to it immediately. Swan sold it to me for less than a hundred dollars."

"And then she and the killer waited to see if you could resonate with it. They needed proof this time, and they had to be very careful. They were playing with fire."

"The Foundation," Olivia whispered.

"Lark and LeClair's biggest client. Arganbright and Pine know you personally. If you disappeared they would be sure to investigate."

"So there was no point taking the risk of grabbing me unless they were confident I could resonate with the camera. They were waiting and watching me and then you showed up."

"They realized I was after you, too," Harlan said. "Whoever is behind this must be in a full-blown panic by now."

"They are willing to risk everything just to get into the old Vortex lab? I'm sure it's worth a fortune, but there are other ways to make money, much safer ways."

"Some things are infinitely more valuable than money," Harlan said.

Olivia's mouth tightened. "Power?"

Harlan nodded.

Olivia finished her wine and lowered the glass. "It's just so hard to believe Gwendolyn Swan might know the man who murdered my mother."

"What do you know about Swan?"

Olivia released the mantel and began to prowl the room. "Not much, really. We've never socialized. We're not personal friends. She's been in business in Seattle for a few years. Caters to the paranormal trade. She obviously has a talent for picking up the psychic vibe in artifacts and relics. Collectors and other dealers respect her. The Foundation does business with her. If you want more information, ask Victor and Lucas."

"I will. Do you happen to know when she opened her business?"

Olivia stopped. "No. I didn't pay much attention to the paranormal artifacts market until Catalina and I opened Lark and LeClair a few months ago. We realized right away that the psychic antiques world was a potential business opportunity for us. Swan was one of our first customers. Do you think your father might have been aware of her?"

"I checked the Rancourt files on my phone the day we went to see her. There's no record of her, at least not under the name of Swan. I didn't do an exhaustive search, though. There wasn't time. It would be interesting to know more about her."

"If she murdered my mother for that damned camera—"

"Stop right there," Harlan said. "We don't know that she had anything to do with your mother's death. She may be an opportunist. Or simply a small business owner who got caught up in something dangerous that she doesn't understand."

"She's involved, Harlan. No coincidences, remember?"

"I agree the probability is high but I think we've done enough speculating for tonight. We're running on empty. Let's eat dinner and go to bed."

Olivia wrapped her arms around her midsection and went back to the window. "You're right. We need sleep. You can have my old bedroom."

Her edgy vibe was getting stronger. Stress, no doubt. Under-standable. She had been through a lot lately. But his gut told him there was something else going on.

A thought struck him. They had been generating a lot of heat in the back of the SUV last night. If they hadn't been interrupted by the damned recorder music there would have been some very intense sex.

She was probably regretting the whole incident, maybe worried he was expecting them to share a bed tonight.

Maybe he had been hoping to do exactly that.

Social skills.

"There are two bedrooms, right?" he asked.

"Yes." Her tone was very curt now. She did not meet his eyes.

"That makes it easy, then."

She glanced at him, frowning. "Easy?"

"Sure. I'll take one and you can take the other, no problem." He paused a beat, pleased with his performance. "Unless you would pre-fer to use your old bedroom and you'd rather I didn't use the other one. I'm good with the sofa."

"No, no, that's fine. You're welcome to use my old room." She unwrapped her arms. "I'm going to sleep in the car."

"What? Why?"

"I haven't been able to sleep in this house since my mother died," Olivia said. She waved a hand in a helpless, despairing gesture. "I can't explain it. I just know that I won't be able to stay here tonight. Don't worry about me. I'll be fine in the car."

"Okay, works for me. Can we grab a couple of pillows? And maybe some blankets?"

Tears glittered in her eyes. "Don't be ridiculous. There's abso-lutely no reason why you can't sleep in the house. I don't have an is-sue with that. You're more than welcome to stay inside. It will be warmer and a lot more comfortable."

"I'll take the front seat. But first we eat."

CHAPTER 34

can't believe you're doing this." Olivia pulled the down comforter
up to her chin and contemplated the window in the roof of the
SUV. "There's no need to worry about me. I would have been fine
out here on my own."

"I know," Harlan said.

He spoke from the passenger seat, which was reclined as far as
possible. Unfortunately that meant he was trying to sleep at an angle.
Like her, he was still fully clothed.

He had to be uncomfortable. *His choice,* she reminded herself.

"I should have asked Harmony if we could sleep in the library
basement," she said.

"This works for me," Harlan said. "I've slept in much more uncomfortable places."

"Such as?"

"Let me think. There was an abandoned temple on an island
somewhere in the Pacific. I was told I had to stay awake all night in
order to experience the paranormal effects. I remember a cave that

was hot with energy. I didn't sleep that night, either, because according to the legend, I would have slipped into a dream and never awakened. There was an old house in the UK that was supposed to be haunted, but it turned out an artifact infused with a lot of dangerous energy had been stashed in a Roman sarcophagus in the basement. I spent a few nights in a jungle drinking an interesting herbal tea. Didn't sleep at all for a few days. Worst crash ever. And then there were the ruins of an alchemist's library. Talk about weird dreams. Also, I think I remember an enlightening experience with some mushrooms, but it's a bit vague—"

"Okay, I get the picture. That's what you've been doing for the past five years? Studying paranormal legends and traditions around the world?"

"You could call it research. Sounds better than 'drifting.'"

"And you financed your research trips by doing odd jobs for that small psychic investigation agency you mentioned? Jones and Jones?"

"Serious drifting costs money."

"For what it's worth, I don't think you were born to hunt monsters," she said.

"No? What should I be hunting?"

"It sounds like you've been searching for answers during the past five years. Maybe you should keep doing that. It might be your calling."

"Are you speaking as an oracle?"

"No, as your partner."

"Thanks for the advice, partner. I'll think about it after we find Vortex."

She groaned. "And just like that we're back to Vortex."

"And identifying your mother's killer."

"Okay, we're both obsessed," Olivia said.

"For now. What will you do after we've finished obsessing?"

"Go back to my day job as a private investigator. I like the work.

Most of the time. Cases don't always have happy endings, but they can deliver answers. I find that satisfying."

"My turn to play therapist." Harlan shifted a little in the seat. "Let's see if we can analyze why you might be attracted to investigation work. You were raised in a small town infused with paranormal secrets and you possess the ability to read auras. There are unsolved mysteries in your past. You need some sense of resolution or closure, so you take on other people's questions and try to get answers because doing so gives you a temporary—"

"Stop right there. I get it."

"Are you really going to go to Vegas to sign up with that new psychic matchmaking agency you mentioned?"

"Maybe. What about you?"

Harlan didn't answer immediately. She heard him change position again and sat up to see what he was doing. He had turned so that he could look at her around the edge of the passenger seat. His eyes burned.

"I'm thinking there might be something to the speed date thing. I met you at my first-ever event."

She caught her breath. "Yes, you did."

"You asked me a question."

"You gave me the right answer. For the wrong reason, but still, it was the right answer."

"You were the woman I was looking for. A disinterested observer could call it a win-win."

"You're saying we're a good match?"

"All the available evidence indicates that, yes."

"For now," she said, feeling her way into what had suddenly become a very fraught conversation.

"For now," Harlan said.

"This is probably one of those be-careful-what-you-wish-for situations."

"Probably, but we won't know the outcome until we run some experiments."

"In the back of my car?"

"I'm told it's an old tradition that was popular in the twentieth century," Harlan said.

"I am not opposed to honoring certain traditions."

"Good to know, but a little enthusiasm would be nice."

She smiled. "Consider me enthusiastic."

He was suddenly there with her in the cargo compartment of the SUV, having forged a path over the console that separated the two front seats. He unbuckled the holster and put it within reach. And then he was sliding under the comforter, leaning over her, bracing himself with a forearm on either side of her head.

"I've been looking for you for a very long time, Olivia LeClair," he said. "You change everything."

His mouth closed over hers before she could decipher the meaning of his words. The temperature shot up several degrees and she stopped thinking about words and their implications. The intense physical intimacy was reinforced a thousand times over by the sense of resonance in their flaring energy fields.

She shoved aside all thoughts of the future. She wanted a time-out to explore and experience the currents of desire that flooded the confines of the vehicle.

Harlan deepened the kiss and moved one hand up under her pullover. The feel of his palm on her bare skin aroused and thrilled her. The sensation was similar to the vibe she got when she watched the approach of a storm. The energy crossed the spectrum, eliciting frissons of intoxicating excitement. She had never felt so powerful, so certain of what she wanted.

She struggled with the buttons of his shirt. When she got them undone she started to peel off the garment. Her hand brushed against an object strapped to his right arm. Leather.

"What?" she whispered, confused. "A wrist brace? Did you injure your wrist?

"Not exactly. Sorry, I forgot about it."

He turned away from her. She heard the sound of leather straps being unbuckled and then he was back and her palm was on the sleekly muscled skin of his bare chest. She forgot about the wrist brace. Everything about him was taut and hard. In that moment she knew she had his full attention. He was focused on her, only her.

Harlan stroked her breast. Tension coalesced in her lower body. She tugged at his belt. Got it undone. He lowered the zipper of her trousers.

Heat washed through her when she felt his hand on her belly. He moved his palm lower still and cupped the sensitive place between her thighs. She was suddenly drenched. A fierce urgency tightened her insides.

"You're soaking wet for me," he said. "I want you so badly I could come right now just thinking about what it's going to feel like to be inside you. Tell me you want me."

She reached into the opening of his briefs and gripped his rock-hard erection. "I want you, Harlan Rancourt. I never knew I could want anyone as much as I want you tonight."

"*Olivia.*"

He shoved her trousers down to her ankles. She kicked one foot free. He got his pants off, paused to sheath himself in a condom and then rolled back to settle between her thighs. He pushed slowly, deliberately into her, easing his way past the resistance of her clenching and unclenching muscles.

With a long, relentless move he lodged himself deep inside her, filling her completely. When he began to withdraw, she tightened herself around him, trying to hold on to him. Her fingers bit into his back.

He groaned. She opened her eyes and saw the blazing waves of his aura. It enveloped her, and once again she experienced a profound sense of knowing, an uncanny recognition that defied explanation.

He began to move, setting a maddeningly deliberate rhythm that tightened everything inside her until she could hardly catch her breath. The need for release became overwhelming.

Her climax, when it struck, was deep and powerful and thrilling.

Harlan thrust into her one last time, back arched, muscles taut. He fastened his mouth against the skin of her throat to muffle a primal howl of exultation and release. She thought she felt the edge of his teeth.

When it was over he collapsed onto his side, pulled her close and anchored her with one leg on top of her thigh. *As if she had any thought of escape.*

The glowing fog drifted around the SUV.

CHAPTER 35

Olivia awoke to the sound of someone rapping on one of the windows of the SUV. She opened her eyes and saw Harmony peering through the glass. The dissipating fog was infused with the light of early morning.

"I've got some ancestry information," Harmony said, her voice muffled by the window.

"Shit," Olivia yelped. She untangled herself from Harlan's arms, grabbed the comforter and pulled it up to her chin. "Could we do this later, Harmony?"

Beside her, Harlan stirred and stretched. "Is it morning?"

"Yes," Olivia hissed.

"Best night's sleep I've had in a long time."

"How nice for you," Olivia said. "In case you haven't noticed, we've got an audience."

Harlan saw Harmony and waved.

"Stop that," Olivia said. She raised her voice. "Go away, Harmony. I'll come find you as soon as I get showered and dressed."

"Okay," Harmony said. "I'll get the tea going."

Someone else knocked on the opposite side of the vehicle. Olivia turned her head and saw Dexter Rose.

"Lucas Pine just phoned with an update," he called through the glass.

"On my way," Harlan said. He sat up and started to push the comforter aside.

"Do. Not. Move," Olivia ordered. "You're in your underwear, in case you hadn't noticed, and you don't even have all of it on."

"But Pine phoned—"

"Stop."

"We can't stay here all morning."

"I am aware of that," she said through her teeth.

Several more curious faces appeared.

Euclid Oaks, the big, burly owner of the general store and the town mayor for as long as Olivia could remember, surveyed the scene through the rear window. His eyes sparked with amusement.

"None of my business," he said, "but wasn't it a little chilly out here last night?"

More faces appeared.

"Go away," Olivia shouted. "Everyone, go away. I mean it."

There was a lot of chuckling and several grins but, mercifully, the faces disappeared.

Olivia rounded on Harlan. "Get your pants on and get into the house."

"Yes, ma'am," Harlan said.

He tugged on his pants, picked up his shirt and grabbed the wrist brace. Except now, in the morning light, she could see it was not a wrist brace. It was a knife sheath. She decided she would inquire about it some other time.

"Go," she ordered.

Harlan maneuvered himself into the front seat and cracked open the passenger side door. "What about you?"

She ran through her options. There was no knowing when someone else would decide to peek through a window. The prospect of
trying to struggle into her clothes in front of an audience did not
appeal.

She wrapped the comforter around herself, gathered up her things
and got ready to throw open the rear door.

"Get the front door of the house open," she said. "I'll make a run
for it."

"Sure." Harlan got out of the vehicle and went up the walk to the
house. He opened the door and raised a hand to signal he was ready.

Clutching her clothes and shoes in one hand, securing the comforter around herself with the other, Olivia scrambled awkwardly
out of the back of the SUV and hustled, barefoot, to the front door
of the house. She was pretty sure she heard some giggling in the fog,
but she ignored it.

"You know, viewed from a certain perspective, one could say this
situation is sort of humorous," Harlan said as she zipped past him
into the hall.

"Only a dumbass would risk saying something really stupid like
that."

"Right."

CHAPTER 36

Fifteen minutes later, his hair still damp from the shower, Harlan was in the trailer that served as the headquarters for the Fogg Lake Foundation crew. At Olivia's insistence he had found a fresh set of clothes in his duffel bag, but he had not taken the time to shave. Thankfully, someone had placed a cup of coffee in his hand.

He put the landline phone on speaker so that Dexter Rose and some of his team could listen. Victor Arganbright and Lucas Pine were on the other end of the connection.

"What have you got?" Harlan asked.

"Not everything you need," Lucas said. "Not by a long shot. But there's been some progress on this end. North Chastain was able to stabilize Ash's aura. The kid's no longer in a deep trance, but he's not fully awake. He keeps sliding in and out of a dreamstate. North thinks he'll recover in a few hours."

"Who is North Chastain?" Harlan asked.

"Long story," Victor said. "All you need to know is that he has an artifact that can be used to stabilize psychic trauma in some cases."

"When Ash is awake he's in a state of near panic," Lucas said. "He says he'll die if he doesn't get a dose of the serum. When he's not fretting about that, he's panicked about being separated from the rest of the team. Says if he's not there when Barrow arrives, he'll die."

"Who is Barrow?" Harlan asked.

"We're not sure yet," Victor said. "But I think we can assume he's the one who is supposed to pick up the team and take them back to the island."

"Where does the team meet Barrow?" Harlan asked. "Ash must know that much."

"Good question," Lucas said. "We're working on that angle, too, but Ash's pals will have been picked up by now. They'll be back on the island."

"Maybe not," Harlan said.

"Why would they be sitting around at the pickup point?" Victor asked. There was no sarcasm in his tone. He was intrigued.

"Because they failed," Harlan said. "Got a feeling that is not an option for them. They're young, they're kept on a tight leash with the serum, they're disposable. We need to find the rest of Ash's crew before it's too late."

"Before it's too late for what?" Lucas asked.

"Before they're all dead. One of them will know something. As soon as we end this call I'll be on my way to Seattle. I want to be sure I'm on the ground there so that I can move quickly once we have the information we need."

"If you do find them in time, you'll need North and his aura-stabilizing gadget," Lucas said. "I'll put him and a team on the Foundation jet as soon as possible. They will be in Seattle about the same time you get there."

"What about Olivia?" Victor said.

"She stays here until we locate the island and have control over it," Harlan said. He glanced at Dexter Rose.

Dexter nodded. "This is the safest place for Olivia for now. Fogg Lake is a fortress."

———————

Twenty minutes later Harlan and one member of the Fogg Lake security team were standing outside a Foundation SUV. Olivia and Harmony were there to say goodbye. They were not alone. Euclid Oaks, Dexter Rose and several local residents were present.

It was the biggest send-off of his career, Harlan thought. For a man who had always worked alone, it was a little disorienting.

It dawned on him that this would be the first time he had been separated from Olivia since he had met her. She was going to spend the night in the library with Harmony, so he didn't have to worry about her sleeping in the back of her vehicle. The town was a fortress. She was safe.

He finally realized that his reluctance to leave had something to do with the fact that he was not sure how to say goodbye. Sure, they had become lovers during the night, but the circumstances were not exactly normal. On the other hand, what did he know about normal relationships? He had never actually had one.

This morning Olivia had been mortified by the fact that her neighbors had seen her wrapped in his arms in the back of her SUV. Would she be embarrassed if he kissed her goodbye in front of everyone now? What was she expecting him to do? Wave? *Social skills, dumbass.*

But whatever he had in the way of social skills deserted him in his moment of need. He froze.

Olivia walked toward him. Stood on tiptoe and brushed her mouth against his. Before he could unfreeze and return the kiss she was already stepping back out of reach.

"Be careful," she said.

He jerked his head once in a nod that was supposed to acknowledge her words, yanked open the passenger side door and got into the SUV. The security agent assigned to accompany him got behind the wheel. His name was Andrews. He fired up the big engine and put the vehicle in gear.

Harlan focused on the side mirror, watching Olivia until she and the others disappeared around a curve in the road.

He could not remember the last time someone had told him to be careful.

"Don't worry about Ms. LeClair," Andrews said. "That town is like a fortress."

CHAPTER 37

T he name Goodwin isn't in any of the Fogg Lake ancestry files, and it doesn't appear in the Foundation records that Victor and Lucas have at headquarters," Harmony said. "But I contacted a relative of mine—a distant cousin—who has access to the ancestry files of the Arcane Society."

Olivia looked at her across the workbench. "Harlan mentioned Arcane. He told me it's an organization that is much older than the Foundation. Apparently it has a long history of paranormal research. Very secretive."

Harmony gave her an amused smile. "He's right. An alchemist named Sylvester Jones founded the Society back in the seventeenth century. The story is long and complicated and much of it has been lost, but suffice it to say the ancestry records are interesting."

She and Harmony were in the basement of the library. Agnes the cat had joined them and was now observing from the far end of the long workbench. The table was littered with yellowed file folders, notebooks and leather-bound volumes.

"Does my grandmother's family name appear in the Arcane records?" Harmony asked.

"There are several Goodwin families in the files but one in particular looks promising," Harmony said. "My cousin told me there is a long line of Goodwin women who appear to have had various versions of a talent that made it possible for them to resonate with crystals. Several were also artists who worked in a wide variety of mediums."

Olivia leaned forward. "Were any of them oracles?"

"Doesn't look like it," Harmony said, "at least not as we usually define the talent."

"Hah." Olivia sat back. "I knew it."

"The thing is, the oracle talent takes several different forms. Crystals are frequently involved."

"I've never had a thing for crystals."

"But you can work the camera. It's crystal-based technology."

"I really don't want to be an oracle, Harmony."

"Neither did I. Shit happens."

"What were you before you got stuck with the talent?"

"A librarian. I was also a fairly strong dream reader. I'm good at interpreting dreams."

"Harlan says he thinks the oracle talent is linked to the dream-state."

"He's probably right," Harmony said.

"So what was the shit that happened that made you realize you were also an oracle?"

"Someone tried to kill me."

"What happened?"

"He's dead. I'm alive and stuck with the oracle gig. For now."

"You mean it might not last indefinitely?"

"It's a weird talent, Olivia. It can vanish as suddenly as it appears."

CHAPTER 38

"We're dead," Trev muttered. He huddled on the floor of the cheap motel room, arms wrapped around his knees. trying to stop the shivering. "We screwed up. We lost Ash and now the Piper is going to let us die."

Ink just shook his head. "We're fucked."

He should know. He was the strongest of the three, but he could feel himself going down. He leaned against the wall because he no longer trusted his balance. The weird sensation of starting to separate from his body was crawling through him. It was getting harder to coordinate his senses.

A moment ago he had experienced a terrifying panic when he realized he did not know where his left foot was. He knew he still *had* a left foot—he could feel it—but he could not figure out where it was in relation to the rest of him. He'd had to look down to locate it.

"Maybe Barrow is just late," Ox said. He was sitting on the edge of the bed, rocking back and forth. "Caught in traffic or something.

He'll be here. The Piper can't afford to let us get picked up by the Foundation. We know too much."

"By the time anyone finds us, we'll be dead," Ink said. "We won't be doing any talking."

"We have to call nine-one-one," Trev said. "We don't have a choice."

"What good will that do?" Ink closed his eyes. "You know what the Piper said. The only thing that can stop the deterioration is the serum. The ER medics will assume we OD'd on some street drug and shoot us full of some shit that will kill us even faster."

"It's our only chance," Trev insisted.

"We've got some time left," Ox rasped. "A few hours, maybe. I'm telling you the Piper won't let us die. He needs us. We're valuable because we can handle the enhancement treatments. He can't afford to lose us. Barrow will be here soon."

Ink didn't argue. He desperately wanted to believe the Piper hadn't abandoned them, but hope was draining away very quickly. Reality was setting in, and it was horrifying.

"The Piper lied to us," he said. "He lied about everything. Know what I think? I think he knew from the start that we were going to have a short shelf life. He planned to let us expire."

"What about him?" Trev said. "And Barrow? They take the same treatments. Been doing it for decades."

"Think about it," Ink said. "The Piper makes the serum. He controls the machine. How do we know that he and Barrow inject the same stuff they give us? How do we know the machine is broken? Maybe they're still getting the full enhancement treatments."

Ox shook his head. "I don't think so. The Piper and Barrow both look like they're getting sick, if you ask me."

"Any way you look at it, they used us," Ink said. "We screwed up. Now we've become a problem, because we screwed up and we know too much. They're going to let us die."

The sudden, impatient rap on the door sent a jolt of adrenaline through his veins. He drew his pistol and staggered across the room. Trev and Ox watched, auras sparking and flashing with desperate hope.

Ink looked out through the peephole, pistol shaking in his hand. Overwhelming relief soared through him when he saw the man on the doorstep.

"It's Barrow," he announced.

"I told you he would come," Trev gasped.

Ink opened the door. Barrow walked into the room.

"Sorry I'm late," he said. "Got held up in traffic."

Ink closed the door. "You cut it damn close."

"I know, but I'm here now." Barrow slipped off his small pack. "And I've got just what you three need."

CHAPTER 39

*T*he dreamer stands in front of the glass-walled chamber and watches the wild storm of paranormal energy inside. She knows she is dreaming. She does not try to write the script. She is open to whatever her intuition can tell her.

The forces at work inside the glass room are fearsome, but the more serious threat is the crystal pyramid in the center of the tempest. It seethes with a dangerous heat.

The dreamer understands she must enter the chamber and go inside the pyramid, but a blue mirror guards the heart of Vortex. She thinks she hears her grandmother's voice—or maybe it is her mother speaking. "When the time comes you will know how to go through the mirror."

The music slithers into the nightmare. Pure and piercing and powerful. It summons and compels, promising release from the disturbing dream. Promising answers.

The music grows stronger, more insistent. Perhaps it holds the key. All she has to do is follow it.

There is a weight on her chest. It is suddenly hard to breathe. Anxiety flashes into a rush of panic . . .

Olivia struggled to make the transition from the lucid dreamstate to the fully awake state. Emerging from the nightmare did nothing to alleviate the pressure on her rib cage. *Breathe.*

She opened her eyes and saw Agnes standing on top of her chest. The cat stared down at her.

"Agnes, you scared the living daylights out of me. Just so you know, you're a lot heavier than you look."

Agnes made the demanding whine that cats make when they are impatient with a human and bounded down to the floor. She padded to the partially open door of the apartment, stopped and waited. Her tail slashed back and forth.

The door should not be open. Before going to bed Harmony had closed and locked it.

Olivia pushed aside the covers and got to her feet. Automatically she reached for the camera.

"What's wrong?" she said to the cat.

Agnes made another soft, impatient noise and slipped through the doorway.

A draft of fog-laced air whispered into the apartment. It carried the music of the recorder. Olivia suppressed the panic that threatened to choke her. She went out onto the landing and looked down the stairs, studying the library with her senses at full throttle. There was no sign of any human auras but the front door of the library stood ajar.

The clear, sharp, compelling notes drifted through the opening and up the staircase. Agnes whipped her tail against Olivia's ankle, urging action. Now.

"I understand that something is wrong, Agnes," Olivia whispered. "But this looks like another one of those don't-go-down-the-stairs situations. The last one did not end well. We need backup. I'll wake Harmony and call Foundation security. They'll handle this."

She rushed back into the apartment, shut the door and slammed the security bolt home. She hurried across the living room and pounded on the bedroom door.

"Harmony, wake up. The guy with the recorder is in town. Can you hear the music? We need to call Foundation security."

There was no response from the bedroom. Olivia wrapped her hand around the antique glass knob and opened the door.

The glowing fog illuminating the room through the uncovered window revealed the empty bed.

"Harmony." Olivia hit the light switch.

The light did not come on. It was common to lose power during storms and high winds in the mountains but the atmosphere outside was calm and still. The only sound that pierced the muffled silence was the music of the recorder.

Understanding struck with the force of lightning. The piper had summoned a real oracle. The wrong oracle.

CHAPTER 40

Olivia flew back into the other room and went to the window overlooking the town square. Kneeling on the cushioned window seat, she pulled the curtain aside. Down below a cloaked figure moved slowly through the glowing fog. Harmony.

Olivia opened the window and leaned out.

"Harmony," she shouted. "Come back. It's the piper. Don't listen to the music."

Harmony did not pause. Olivia tried again, screaming now.

"*Security.* The piper is in town."

There was no response from the darkened trailer that housed Foundation security.

The only phone in the library was the landline on the librarian's desk downstairs. She would have to unbolt the apartment door to get to it. She had no choice. Harmony was walking toward disaster, summoned by the hypnotic effects of the recorder.

Olivia tugged on her low boots, pulled her down jacket over her long nightgown and gripped the camera. Cautiously, senses heightened, she unbolted the door.

Agnes was waiting on the other side. The cat whined, as if to say, *It's about time*, and started down the staircase. Olivia stood at the railing and surveyed the first floor of the library again. There were still no auras blazing in the shadows.

The recorder music permeated the night. It was everywhere. Whoever was playing the instrument was much stronger than Ink. Tonight the piper seemed to know how to use the currents of paranormal energy in the fog to enhance the power of the artifact.

Olivia went down the stairs. With each step it became harder to suppress the disturbing summons of the recorder.

She reached the librarian's desk and grabbed the phone. It was dead. That did not come as a huge surprise. *Call me psychic,* she thought.

Agnes was silhouetted in the doorway at the bottom of the stairs. She made another impatient sound.

Olivia crossed to the entrance, camera gripped in both hands. She could barely make out the cloaked figure near the fountain in the center of the square. Harmony had come to a stop, but there was something wrong with her aura. It was strong, but certain wavelengths appeared to be frozen.

Agnes trotted out into the fog. Olivia did another check for auras, concluded that there was no one except Harmony in the immediate vicinity and hurried after the cat.

She reached Harmony and stopped, uncertain how to proceed.

"Harmony, can you hear me?" she said. "You must listen to me. You're in terrible danger. I'm going to take you back to the library."

Harmony shuddered and raised her head with a sudden, wild move. The hood of her cloak fell back. Her mane of silver hair spilled around her shoulders. She stared at Olivia with dream-struck eyes and fell into her oracle voice.

"You are the key. Only you can stop the lightning in the mirrors."

The words shuddered with power.

Olivia shivered. "You must come with me, Harmony."

Harmony collapsed in on herself and crumpled to the ground.

"No," Olivia whispered. "Harmony, wake up. Please."

The cat made another annoyed sound.

"You're not a lot of help, Agnes."

Olivia crouched at Harmony's head, got a grip on the hood of the cloak and tried to use it as a sled. Harmony was built on statuesque lines. She was no lightweight. Olivia managed to drag the unconscious woman a couple of feet before she was forced to stop to get a better grip.

With the next attempt she succeeded in hauling Harmony to within a few yards of the door.

"Almost there," Olivia said to Agnes.

Agnes lashed her tail again.

The recorder music grew louder, more intense.

Utterly focused on the struggle to drag Harmony back into the comparative safety of the library, Olivia was unaware of the figures moving up fast behind her until Agnes hissed a warning. By then it was too late.

She felt the sharp jab of a needle in her upper shoulder and tried to turn to confront her attacker. She caught a glimpse of an aura; she had time enough to realize it was not the energy field of the young man who had been playing the recorder the night before, and then she registered the truth.

She was looking at the man who had murdered her mother.

The night closed in around her.

CHAPTER 41

Harlan crushed the phone to his ear. "Do we have a last name for Ash?"

"He says it was Talbot back when he was living on the streets," Lucas said. "After he became a student on the island he dropped it. None of the Piper's students use last names, apparently. Typical cult indoctrination tactic. A symbol of leaving the past behind."

"Looks like the Piper recruited his so-called students from the streets," Victor said. "Ash tells us they all had some natural talent—aura readers for the most part. Once on the island they went through an enhancement process that involves a combination of paranormal radiation and a serum. Something, however, has gone wrong with the machine that delivers the radiation, so the Piper and his students are getting by on the serum."

"Tell me about the serum."

"Aside from the fact that the formula is based on paranormal-charged botanicals, we don't have much information," Lucas explained. "The lab people are working on it now. Ash tells us that, once started, you have to continue the injections on a regular basis. He says the Piper concocts the serum in a small lab in the old monastery building. Uses plants grown in a maze. Each student gets one auto-injector every day."

"Olivia and I used Ash's last auto-injector on him two nights ago," Harlan said.

"Ash is amazed he isn't dead," Victor said. "He's convinced he still might die. North says he thinks the kid will be okay but that only time will tell."

"Talk to me about the machine that delivers the radiation that is part of the enhancement process," Harlan said.

"Lucas and I think it's the original Vortex," Victor said. "You were right. Someone called the Piper has been using it for decades, possibly since the Bluestone Project was shut down. The current Piper is the second one, not the first. The radiation is essential for the enhancement treatments. Ash tells us the machine is failing and only the oracle can fix it."

"You still haven't located the island?"

"No," Lucas said. "But we now know it's within an hour's boat ride from a private dock somewhere north of Seattle."

"*Somewhere* north of Seattle?" Harlan said. "Doesn't Ash know where the dock is located?"

"No," Victor said, his tone even more grim than usual. "Evidently the students are given another injection when Barrow picks them up to take them back to the island. It induces a selective amnesia."

"Who is Barrow?" Harlan asked.

"He appears to be the Piper's confidant," Victor said. "Among other things, he operates the boat and is the only one, aside from the Piper, who has the coordinates for the island."

"Barrow uses a drug to make the students forget the location of the dock?"

"North thinks it reinforces a hypnotic suggestion," Victor said.

"Judging by Ash's description, I think Barrow has a psychic talent for hypnotism."

"You need to break through the hypnotic suggestion," Harlan said. "We have to locate that damned island."

Victor grunted. "Believe it or not, we know what we're doing here, Rancourt. I've got the whole Halcyon team working on this."

CHAPTER 42

The shivering was getting worse. Ink did not have a thermometer, but he didn't need one to know that the fever was climbing. Ox and Trev were huddled on the floor of the cheap motel room. Trev had his arms wrapped around his knees. He rocked back and forth, moaning. Ox had already slipped into unconsciousness. Ash was the lucky one, Ink thought. He was probably dead already. Or maybe not. Maybe Ash was locked in a coma populated by nightmares.

Barrow had murdered them. The process was just taking time. When he had finally arrived at the motel he had given each of them a fresh auto-injector. But instead of another dose of the serum, the auto-injectors had contained poison.

When the drug had begun to take hold on all three of them, Barrow had quietly walked out the door, leaving Ink and the others to die in the shabby motel room. Ink knew that when their bodies were found the cops would conclude he and Trev and Ox were three addicts who had gotten hold of some bad shit. That was too fucking close to the truth.

They had all fallen for the Piper's promise, he thought. Who could turn down an offer of genuine psychic powers? But it was more than that. The Piper had made them feel special. Important. Destined for greatness instead of a short life span in prison or on the streets. He had told them his mission was to take them to the next level of human evolution with the serum and the Vortex machine. They would become an elite special forces team, warriors. They would fight bad guys around the world. Fucking heroes.

Ink knew the only reason he was not deteriorating as fast as the others was because he was the strongest. He had been the first student and he had received more treatments in the Vortex chamber. He was the one with the high-grade talent it took to use the recorder. Trev and Ox were still in training. Sure, they had some talent, but he was the team leader because he was the only one aside from the Piper who was able to handle the recorder.

He was fucking special.

So much for the Piper's promises. Ink knew he might live a few hours longer than the others, but in the end he would be as dead as Trev and Ox and Ash.

The door of the motel room opened. Two men appeared, silhouetted in the doorway. Ink squinted against the sudden glare of light. A faint flicker of hope shot through him. Maybe Barrow had changed his mind. Maybe the Piper had decided he could not afford to lose three loyal students. Maybe . . .

Each of the men in the doorway had a gun. Hope died as swiftly and as mercilessly as it had sprung to life. So much for hoping Barrow had come back for them. Ink knew he and the others were about to die at the hands of dealers looking for their stash. At least a bullet would be a faster way to check out.

"If you're looking for drugs, you're too late," Ink mumbled. "They're gone and we're dead."

"Not quite," the first man said. He moved into the room. "Maybe not for a few decades, if you're smart."

The second man was in the room now, his powerful aura flaring. He made his gun disappear inside his leather jacket and crouched in front of Trev, checking for a pulse.

"This one's still alive," he announced. "Barely."

The first man slipped his weapon into a shoulder holster and stopped in front of Ink. "This is the one who played the recorder. Goes by the name of Ink. He's conscious and able to make eye contact."

Ink tried to get a close look at the man looming over him. He wasn't nearly as scary as the other guy. Everything about him was less threatening—well, except for the gun.

"Who are you?" Ink rasped.

"As we used to say in the old days, we're from the Foundation and we're here to help."

"Did you really say that?" the man examining Trev asked, not looking up.

"For some reason, it always made the bad guys nervous," the first man said.

A jolt of recognition slammed through Ink. "You're Harlan Rancourt, the guy who grabbed the oracle. The Piper told us your family used to run some kind of mob operation called the Foundation."

Rancourt crouched down in front of Ink. "We liked to think of it as the family business. Are you three dying because you need the serum?"

"Bastard poisoned us. Said it would be quicker than the serum."

"Who poisoned you?"

"Barrow. He's the Piper's friend. Had a feeling we couldn't trust him if things went wrong. I was right."

"Where's Barrow?"

"Gone. Left us here to die."

"Did Barrow take the recorder after he poisoned you?" Harlan asked.

Ink snorted. "He searched for it after he murdered us with the poison. When he realized I didn't have it on me he wanted to know where it was. I lied. Told him you stole it when you took Ash. Turns out I'm pretty good when it comes to lying."

"Probably a side effect of your talent for the recorder," Rancourt said. "I'm a pretty good liar, too. So Barrow believed you?"

"Yeah. He didn't think much of me or the others. He didn't like any of us. Figured we were all weak compared to him and the Piper."

"Just assets to be used and discarded."

"I guess," Ink muttered.

"Where is the recorder?" Rancourt asked.

"When things went wrong in the mountains I got a real bad feeling. I knew the recorder was valuable to the Piper and, like I said, I didn't trust Barrow. So after we made it here I buried the recorder out back. Barrow believed me when I told him you had it. He was pissed, but we were dead as far as he was concerned, so he left." Ink looked across the room. "What's your friend doing to Ox? I told you, you don't have to murder him. He's already gone. Just a matter of time."

"My friend's name is North Chastain," Rancourt said. "He saved Ash, and he thinks he can probably stabilize you and your pals."

"Whatever Barrow injected these kids with is complicating things," Chastain warned from the other side of the room.

Ink tried to process what was happening. "Ash is alive?"

"And talking," Rancourt said. "That's how we found you. The doctors at Halcyon were able to break through the hypnotic suggestion. That's how we got the location of this motel."

"Huh?" Ink stopped because Chastain was aiming a clear crystal object shaped like a flashlight at Ox.

Energy suddenly illuminated the room. Ink could have sworn he was seeing auroras. Hallucinating. Maybe he was imagining everything that was happening.

Ox sucked in a hoarse breath. His eyes opened. He stared at Chastain.

"What the fuck?" Ox said.

"You're stable," Chastain said. "You'll live. But the instability was in the psychic wavelengths. They were artificially enhanced by the treatments you were receiving. You didn't have the control or the power to handle them. The result was that you were slowly going insane. Eventually you would have died. Whatever was in the poison accelerated the process. It was sending you straight into a coma."

"I don't understand," Ox muttered.

"Here's the short version," Chastain said. "From now on you'll have whatever talent you had before the Piper started enhancing you."

"Seriously? I'm not going to die?"

"Not today," Chastain said.

He moved on to Trev and repeated the process. Trev convulsed and gasped like a drowning man who has reached the surface just in time. He gazed, dumbfounded, at Chastain.

"Your pal here will explain it," Chastain said.

He crossed the room and stopped in front of Ink. "You're not as far gone as the others. Probably because you had some strong talent to begin with. Also, you're awake and coherent, so I'm asking you if you want me to stabilize your energy field. You heard what I told your pals. If I do it you'll lose whatever talent you acquired after the Piper started enhancing you."

"What is that thing?" Ink rasped.

"It's called a night gun, but it's really a medical device," Chastain said. "It works on human auras. I can use it to locate the unstable or frozen waves and try to undo the damage."

"Do it," Ink said. He was shivering so badly now he could barely get the words out. "I know what's going to happen if you don't." He looked at Harlan Rancourt. "But I'll tell you right now none of us knows how to locate the island. The only way in is by boat. Dock is inside a flooded cave. Barrow is the only one who has the coordinates."

"How long ago did Barrow leave?" Harlan said.

"I dunno. A few hours ago, I guess. Probably back on the island by now."

Rancourt's phone rang. He stood and looked at Chastain. "He's all yours."

Rancourt moved to the doorway and took the call.

Ink didn't hear what was said next because Chastain was doing something with the crystal gun, something amazing. Ink could feel his fried senses settling down. His breathing steadied. The icy shivers faded. He was no longer on fire.

He could not figure out exactly how he felt now. The only word that came to mind was *normal*. It wasn't just the shaking and the fever that were fading. The deep, dark fear that had been gnawing at the edges of his mind—the feeling that if he did not keep swimming he would sink to the bottom of a very cold sea—was retreating.

No more dreams of being a super psychic special forces agent, but that was okay. No more treatments in the radiation chamber. No more night sweats. No more worrying about being only one injection away from insanity and death.

His breathing was steady and his pulse was no longer racing at the speed of light. Maybe he would live after all.

Rancourt ended the call and looked at Chastain.

"He has her," Rancourt said. "He grabbed her sometime during the night."

That was all he said. He sounded cold and calm. But Ink nearly stopped breathing again, because a storm of energy was suddenly swirling in the small motel room.

Rancourt looked at him, eyes burning with a cold fire. "Your pals are going to Las Vegas. You'll be coming with me."

Ink swallowed hard. "Are you going to kill me?"

"Not yet," Rancourt said. "I need information from someone who has been on the ground on that island."

"I told you, I don't know how to find the island."

"That's my problem. Looks like you've got some natural talent. Think you can still play the recorder?"

"The Piper said it was tuned to my vibe," Ink said. "I won't be able to play it the way I did before Mr. Chastain used that night gun on me, but I'm pretty sure I can do it at least as well as I did back at the start, before I got the treatments."

"How well did you play it at the beginning?"

"Better than any of the others." In spite of all that had happened, Ink got a small rush of pride. "That's why the Piper made me the team leader."

CHAPTER 43

Ｈow did they get inside Fogg Lake?" Harlan said into the phone. "That town was supposed to be a fortress. *Who let the monsters grab Olivia?*"

He was standing beside one of the Foundation SUVs parked in the motel lot. He had his phone in one hand. He was using the other to grip the top edge of the driver's side door so fiercely he was vaguely surprised that he did not dent it.

He was pulling on everything he had to control his rage and fear while he talked to Dexter Rose. Yelling at the man was pointless. He understood that, but the need to howl his fury to the skies was almost overwhelming.

Almost. He had not spent the past five years learning to tame his talent only to lose control now. He could handle his emotions. He had to, because unless he did, he had no chance at all of finding Olivia.

It was early morning. The motel where they had discovered the Piper's dying students was located outside a small town north of

Seattle. The vehicle transporting Trev and Ox had left a short time ago, headed for the airport. The two kids and their security escort were on their way to Las Vegas. Ink had been left behind and was currently slumped in the rear seat of the SUV that Harlan would be driving as soon as he knew where the hell he was going.

North Chastain and several members of the Foundation security team were waiting, armed and ready. All they needed was a destination. Harlan knew it was up to him to produce the coordinates of the island with no name. But first he needed more information, and that meant he had to stop scaring Dexter Rose.

He forced himself to loosen his death grip on the door of the vehicle and reminded himself he had data now that he had not possessed a few hours ago.

"Tell me what happened," he said. "Walk me through it."

"Sir, we are still investigating, but there is no indication that anyone on the Foundation staff or here in town assisted the kidnappers," Dexter said. "It looks like they entered through the caves."

"They knew how to navigate the Fogg Lake caves?"

"Evidently they were aware of a route through them that took them into town. Once inside the caves they were somehow able to use the energy in there and in the fog to amplify that damned recorder music to the point where it was powerful enough to put everyone in Fogg Lake into a deep sleep."

"Everyone except Harmony and Olivia. The Piper knows what he's doing. How did he and his men get into the tunnels?"

"We know they didn't just drive into town," Dexter said. "They must have accessed an entrance to the cave system that we haven't discovered. Maybe the original one that was used when the Bluestone Project built the lab. We've known for quite a while there had to be a main entrance somewhere well outside of town, because the people who lived in Fogg Lake at the time had no knowledge of the lab. The construction crews and the staff did not come and go through the town. They used another entry point, but we haven't located it. Figured it was buried in a rockfall when the explosion occurred."

"The Piper knew about that entrance and managed to reopen it. He cut the library phone once he and his team were in town."

Dexter grunted. "If the Piper was able to lead his people through the heavy energy inside those caves, he's got some serious talent."

"And a compass." Harlan thought about the paranormal tracking device that had been used to follow Olivia's vehicle into the mountains. "He's got a direct connection to the history of Bluestone and to Vortex. No telling what he has in the way of artifacts. I'm going to end this call, Rose. I need to talk to Harmony."

"She's in the library. Said something earlier about expecting to hear from you. Let me know if there is anything else I can do. Everyone here in town wants to help."

"Thanks."

Harlan ended the call. He was about to contact Harmony, but he got a mental ping that made him pause. There was something he had missed.

He walked back into the motel room, shut the door and looked at his reflection in the grimy mirror. Everything was connected. No coincidences. He had so much information, but the most important piece of the puzzle was missing. Why?

All the data was locked in images—paintings and holograms. The location of the island had to be in one. If it was in one of the two paintings that had disappeared, he was screwed.

But there was still one picture available.

Only one image contained both the oracle and the camera.

He took out his phone and called the number of the landline in the Fogg Lake library.

Harmony answered halfway through the first ring.

"What can I do, Harlan?"

"Go to Olivia's old house. I think the information I need is in the picture hanging on the wall of the living room, the one that shows Olivia as a young teen."

"I know it. I never said anything to Olivia or her mother, but that picture always gave me chills."

"Probably because you're an oracle."

"Probably. All right, what do you want me to do?"

"I want you to look into a mirror."

CHAPTER 44

Olivia fought her way out of a nightmare featuring a maze of burning mirrors, opened her eyes and saw the monster who had murdered her mother.

Instinctively she froze, the way a child did when she realized she was in the same room as a predator. She reminded herself that she had been dreaming.

I accidentally activated the camera. It's just a hologram.

But the monster spoke from the doorway, and she knew he was real.

"Sorry about the hallucinations," he said. "Over the years the plants in my garden have developed powerful properties. These days when I use them to make up the sedative I gave you, they produce side effects that can be unpleasant and unpredictable—especially if the individual has a strong psychic talent."

Rage infused her with adrenaline. She summoned every ounce of will she possessed to control her aura-reading talent and got a wobbly fix on the hot energy field of the man who lounged in the doorway.

There were enough pale wavelengths to mark him as a blank—a sociopath. That was not a surprise. Neither was the fierce radiation that identified him as a very powerful talent.

The most disturbing aspects of his aura were the signs of instability. In her experience, no one possessed a completely stable energy field. Everyone had some distortions and weaknesses. But the man in the doorway was one of the human monsters, and the erratic spikes and shivering oscillations indicated he was barely hanging on to his control—to his sanity. Physically he did not look healthy, either. It had been nearly a year since her mother had taken the holographic image. It was obvious that the man in front of her had deteriorated. Her mother's words whispered in her head. *"Dead man walking in a dying garden."*

She remembered what Harlan had said when she asked him how he managed his human chameleon trick: *The old saying that people see what they expect to see is true, but it goes deeper—they see what they want to see, what they need to see.*

The monster in the doorway not only expected to see an oracle; he *wanted* to see one. He was desperate to see one.

It was all about meeting expectations. People expected oracles to be fragile, unpredictable—at the mercy of their own talent. Time to act like an oracle.

Deciding to take inspiration from her nightmare, she shot to a sitting position and threw her head back in what she hoped was a dramatic pose.

"He who dares to enter the maze of burning mirrors without the key is doomed."

The monster's eyes heated with unwholesome excitement. He did not appear to be alarmed by the words of warning. If anything, he looked gratified.

Maybe she had chosen the wrong course of action. On the other hand, her options were extremely limited. Real oracles got treated with respect, because they had some serious powers. She had to act like a woman of power.

She took a moment to orient herself. She was on a narrow cot in a small, austere white-walled room. There was no religious paraphernalia, but the space looked like it had once served as the cell of a cloistered nun or monk. There was a single window. The monastery in the hologram.

She wondered how long she had been unconscious.

She swung her legs over the side of the cot. Relief washed through her when she realized she was still wearing everything she'd had on when she left the library to try to rescue Harmony. Long flannel nightgown. Down jacket. Low boots.

She looked around for the camera. She'd had it with her when she ran out into the night.

"It's over there," the monster said, as if he had read her mind. He gestured toward a table across the room.

She turned her head much too quickly and had to swallow a wave of nausea before her senses steadied enough to allow her to focus. The camera was on the table.

"Let's hope you can use it," the monster said. "It's the reason why I've gone to so much trouble to obtain your services."

"My services?"

"Allow me to introduce myself. They call me the Piper. In another life I had a more conventional name—Jake Spode."

"You think the camera holds the key to Vortex," she said.

This time she used her normal voice. She could not continue to toss out one-liners in the dreamstate voice, even if she was creative enough to come up with a string of fake prophecies. Spode would know she was faking it. Real oracles did not deliver their messages nonstop. They uttered their warnings only when they experienced an overwhelming need to give voice to an inner vision.

This fake oracle business was tricky.

"I'm certain the camera is the machine that is needed to access the pyramid and reset Vortex," Spode said. "But you are the key. Unfortunately, the damn thing is locked with your grandmother's signature. You are the only one who can operate it."

Words screamed in her head, acid hot—not the urgent, compulsive proclamation of an oracle; rather a cry of rage and vengeance. *You discovered that truth after you murdered my mother.* But she managed to swallow the accusation. Harlan would be searching for her. She had to buy time. That meant she had to maintain control.

"How did you find me?" she said instead.

"It wasn't easy. I found Blake Sefton first. He was an old man by the time I located him. Sinking into dementia. He was one of the engineers involved in Vortex. His specialty was the paranormal physics of mirrors. He went into hiding when the word came down to destroy the lab and everyone connected to it. He was one of the few who survived the layoff process."

Olivia's stomach knotted. "Layoff?"

"When the order was given to destroy Vortex, it included all personnel closely affiliated with it. The explosives that were used to close the lab took care of several targets. The rest were tracked and removed within a few months. But there were a few who escaped detection for decades. Sefton was one of those. Got to hand it to him—he was well on his way to dying of old age when I found him."

"Why?" Olivia asked, shocked. "Why murder all those people?"

"Because they knew the truth about what Vortex could do," Spode said. "That made them a threat to the man in DC who was in charge of the project."

Harlan had been right. The individual in charge of Vortex had tried to get rid of all the witnesses.

"Who is he?" Olivia whispered. "Who is the monster in DC who gave the orders?"

"No need to worry about him," Spode said. "He's been dead for a very long time."

"I'm assuming it wasn't natural causes."

Spode chuckled. "Depends on your definition of 'natural causes.' The assassin who was selected to track down and eliminate the personnel associated with Vortex learned his identity and terminated him."

"One of the monsters turned on his creator. Who could have seen that coming? Guess the guy back in DC didn't learn anything from the Frankenstein story."

"The assassin understood that once he had gotten rid of the Vortex team, he would become a liability as far as the man in DC was concerned," Spode said. "He decided to be proactive."

"Was that assassin the one who murdered my grandmother?"

"Unfortunately, at the time, he did not realize that Grace Goodwin was the only one who could tune the heart of Vortex."

"What happened to him?"

"The assassin? He died when he was about my age."

"In a lives-by-the-sword kind of way?"

"No. Suicide. He knew he was slowly going insane. He was losing his talent and his control. Looking back, I have concluded that was when the serum started to become a problem. The plants used in the formula had been mutating for years because of the radiation from the Vortex machine. Initially my father thought that the increasing potency was a good thing. Yes, we had to take the injections more often. Yes, more treatments inside the chamber were required. But the trade-off was increased talent. But in the past couple of years deterioration has set in. No amount of serum can stop it. And then Vortex went into meltdown. That's when I knew I had to find the camera."

"You used Sefton to find Grace Goodwin's daughter—my mother."

"Sefton had kept track of a few close friends who had survived the layoffs," Spode said. "He knew your grandmother had a daughter and that there was a possibility she had inherited the camera. His dementia made it difficult to question him but I eventually got the facts I needed to find your mother."

"You contacted her, told her you were from the Foundation. That the camera was dangerous. She mentioned my grandmother's paintings. You conned her into giving everything to you, and then you murdered her."

"A costly miscalculation on my part," Spode admitted.

It was all she could do to keep from flying at him, fingers flexed to claw out his eyes. But the reality was that, even though he looked ill, he was physically a lot stronger than she was. She was buying time.

"How long did it take you to realize you couldn't work the camera?" she asked.

"I wasted months trying to use Vortex to tune the vibe to my signature. A few weeks ago I gave up."

"You decided to see if I could resonate with the camera. You got Gwendolyn Swan involved. How much does she know about Vortex and you?"

"Enough."

That wasn't much of an answer, but this wasn't the time to push for more.

"Who was your father?" she asked.

"He was the greatest success of the Vortex machine, the first Piper."

"He was the monster who murdered my grandparents and everyone else he could find who was associated with Vortex."

Spode's eyes heated with sudden rage. "My father was the future."

"And your mother?"

"My father had an affair with her. He never brought her to the island. As far as she knew he was a consultant for an international firm. I didn't see much of him when I was young, but when I started to come into my talent, he realized I was his heir. My mother died when I was thirteen. My father brought me here."

"Convenient."

Spode frowned. "What?"

"Your mother's death just as you came into your other senses."

Fury blazed in Spode's eyes. "It was an accident."

"Right. If Vortex and this serum you're talking about were such terrific scientific advances, why were the Bluestone labs, including Vortex, shut down?"

Spode exhaled slowly. "My father explained that there were problems, hurdles to be overcome, just as there are at the start of any world-changing technology. Unfortunately, there was a lack of vision at the time when it was most needed."

"Tell me about this lack of vision."

"It's easier to start with the people who actually had the vision. Aurora Winston was a research scientist at Vortex. She worked with her husband, Alexander Winston, to develop a method for unleashing the full potential of latent psychic talent. Alexander Winston died in a lab accident, but Aurora carried on. I won't waste time on the details. All you need to know is that she solved the last major problem and came up with an enhancement technique that works. My father was living proof. So am I."

"You're telling me this Aurora Winston figured out how to create monsters?"

Fury sparked again in Spode's eyes. It vanished in an instant, but the shiver of it iced the atmosphere in the small space.

"Those who are capable of surviving the process become psychically enhanced human beings, not monsters," he said.

She thought he sounded as if he was trying to convince himself but resisted the urge to ask him that question. It didn't seem to be a smart time to pick a fight with an unstable killer.

"Whatever," she said. "How does this treatment work?"

"There are two basic steps in the process," Spode said in a voice that was unnaturally even. "First, Aurora Winston's serum is administered to a suitable subject."

"Define 'suitable subject.'"

"Someone with a measurable amount of natural talent. If the se-rum is successful, the subject is then exposed to certain wavelengths of paranormal radiation for a period of time. Once that has been done, the subject's talent is enhanced and strengthened to a remark-able degree. In a particularly strong subject, a second powerful talent sometimes appears."

"What sort of talents are we talking about?"

"It depends on the individual." Spode began to pace the cell. "I'm sure you're aware that no two talents are precisely the same. Blue-stone was a government project, so you won't be surprised to learn that the goal of the Vortex lab was to create psychics whose talents would be useful to the military and to the nation's intelligence op-erations. The enhancement treatments were fine-tuned to optimize that objective."

"In other words, they were designed to create killers with para-normal talents."

Anger glinted again in Spode's eyes. "It's true that the original intention was to create government assets that could be deployed strategically, but in the long run the potential of the serum and the machine was incalculable. Think of what can be accomplished if we take full advantage of our latent psychic abilities. There will be sci-entific breakthroughs in every field of human endeavor. Medicine. Space exploration."

"Apparently the only thing it's accomplished so far is to create a couple of assassins and get a lot of people killed. I am unimpressed. Speaking of me, what, exactly, am I doing here?"

"I'll show you." Spode snapped his fingers. Two young men ap-peared from the hallway. "Put the hood on her and take her to the entrance of the maze. I'll bring the camera. We can't risk waiting any longer."

The two men moved toward the bed. One of them had a fabric hood. Panic shot through Olivia.

"No," she said. "Don't put that thing on me."

The hood was pulled down over her head. The claustrophobia slammed through her. She started to shake. Frantically she tried to reach up and yank off the cloth covering. The two men restrained her.

She kicked out wildly and managed to connect with a leg.

"Take it off," she screamed. In desperation she went into her oracle voice. *"Take it off or all will die today."*

She thrashed about, twisting violently in an attempt to get rid of the hood.

"Shit," one of the men said. "She's losing it, sir. It's like she's on drugs or something."

"Take off the hood," Spode said. He sounded weary. "It doesn't matter what she sees."

One of the men yanked off the hood. Olivia gasped for breath, a toxic brew of fury and panic flooding her veins. Her mother's words stormed into her head. She raised her voice.

"Dead man walking in a dying garden."

"I know," Spode said. "We're all dying. That's why you're here, you see. You are the only one who can fix the problem."

CHAPTER 45

Five steps into the topiary maze, Olivia realized she was already so disoriented she might not be able to find her way back to the entrance.

It was difficult to focus because the waves of paranormal energy were coming at her with the force of a river in flood. The vibes churned all her senses. She found it took concentration just to stay on her feet. If it hadn't been for Spode's bruising grip on her arm she would have stumbled and gone down.

He yanked her around another corner. Up ahead she saw a wall of impenetrable green foliage studded with needle-sharp thorns. Another intersection. Spode paused briefly. She realized he was using an object that looked like a small penlight to chart a course through the maze. The device emitted a narrow beam of energy. He started to turn right. The light abruptly disappeared. He turned in the opposite direction. The light grew strong again.

"What is this place?" she said.

"Welcome to my memorial garden," Spode said, steering her

around another corner. "My father started it. When he died I took over."

Olivia took a closer look at the topiaries. "These plants have been shaped to look like crypts and funeral vaults."

"It's my art."

"Who, exactly, are you memorializing here?"

"Each of these vaults represents a successful mission," Spode said. "The earliest topiaries mark my father's work. The rest are all mine."

She looked around, horrified. "Do you even know how many people you've murdered?"

"They were missions, not murders," Spode snapped. "I do not kill for sport; neither did my father."

"Money?"

"My father was a professional. So am I."

"Right. So it's the money."

Spode steered her through another intersection. She tried to focus on the glowing green corridor. It was like moving through a multi-dimensional kaleidoscope. The greens were violently green. Each leaf sparked with the acid-and-neon-light characteristic of the paranormal. Mushrooms of all shapes and sizes illuminated the shadows of the vaults and crypts in ominous colors. Orchids twisted amid the foliage, the blooms resembling the open jaws of snakes.

She knew how to handle heavy energy, thanks to growing up in Fogg Lake, but she had never dealt with anything as disturbing and disorienting as the fierce storm of hot psi that swirled within the towering green walls of the maze.

"You do realize you're a serial killer," she said. "So was your father."

To her surprise, Spode seemed to find that amusing. "Tell that to the intelligence agencies, global corporations and heads of state around the world who were my father's clients and are now mine."

"Okay, you're a serial killer who bills for his services. That makes such a difference."

He used his grip on her arm to give her a short, rough shake.

"Bitch. If I didn't need you . . ."

"You'd kill me free of charge. I get it. You still haven't told me what I'm supposed to do with the camera."

"You have two missions. First you must shut down the Vortex machine. It's in a meltdown."

"What are you talking about?"

"The machine has become unstable. It's in a runaway mode."

"And if I don't stop it, you and your monster wannabes will die?"

"So will you. Everyone on this island will die, and there's a high probability that's just the beginning."

"*What?*"

"The forces that will be unleashed may trigger an earthquake and a tsunami massive enough to inundate Seattle and every other city, town and island in the region. And then there's the volcano."

She tried to read his aura to see if he had slipped from unstable into full-on insanity. It wasn't easy because of the rivers of paranormal currents in the atmosphere, but she saw enough to be fairly certain he was telling the truth, or at least what he was convinced was the truth. Delusional people, by definition, believed in their visions.

"Why will there be so much damage?" she asked.

"Because this island sits at the center of a major geographical vortex," Spode said. "It's the reason for the code name of the old lab. The site was chosen because of the powerful forces in this area. There's an ancient undersea volcano nearby. A major tectonic plate fault line runs through here. Add to that the heavy currents of the waters of Puget Sound and you've got all the ingredients you need to generate an explosion of energy across the spectrum. If the machine melts down, there is a chance it will light the fuse of a very big bomb."

She took a deep breath. "You're sure of that?"

"Technically it's still a theory, but I don't think it would be a good idea to put it to the test, do you?"

"Vortex was supposed to have been destroyed when the Bluestone Project was halted."

"Here's the dirty little secret of Vortex: Aurora Winston could not bear to see her life's work destroyed. Instead, she shut it down— she didn't destroy it. She was sure that in the future researchers would want to restart the machine and explore its potential to change the destiny of humanity. Scientists have surprisingly large egos."

Olivia eyed the foot-long needles of a nearby plant. "Even if I'm able to stop the meltdown, that won't help with the serum problem."

"I have an answer for that, but it won't do me any good unless you reboot the lightning crystal."

"What is that?"

"The heart of Vortex. Trust me, you'll know it when you see it." Spode came to a halt in front of a looming topiary structure.

"This is the center of the maze," he said. "The door to the Vortex machine is inside."

He pushed her through the shadowed entrance, reached into the foliage and pressed a series of buttons. Crystals glowed amid the leaves. Olivia heard the sound of gears moving inside a steel wall. A door slid aside to reveal an entryway lined in glowing green tiles.

Psi-hot currents of paranormal energy wafted out of the opening.

"Do your job, Oracle," Spode said. "Stop the meltdown. Bring me the lightning crystal. Once I have it I can escape this damned island forever."

He planted a hand against Olivia's back and shoved her through the entrance. She stumbled forward, struggling to adjust to the eerie lighting and the vibe of the currents.

"You'll need this," Spode said.

She turned around in time to see him toss the camera through the doorway. She managed to catch the artifact before it clattered on the green tile floor.

The door started to slide shut.

"How am I supposed to find Vortex?" she called.

"That won't be a problem," Spode said as the door closed. "I'll wait out here for you. I can't handle the heat inside anymore. Tune the crystal and bring it to me."

"And then you'll kill me."

"No." Spode gave her a twisted smile. "I won't kill you. I need you, at least until I figure out how to use the camera myself. No telling when the crystal will have to be tuned again."

The heavy steel door closed. There was a nerve-jarring clang when it locked.

Olivia stood still, allowing her senses to adjust to the new vibe in the atmosphere. The energy in the maze had felt like the swirling currents of a river. Now she was in the midst of a storm. Her hair lifted and floated around her face. Adrenaline generated by the fight-or-flight response surged through her. She gripped the camera, seeking comfort from the one familiar object in the space.

Her grandmother's warning crashed through her and spilled out. *"Here there be monsters."*

"No shit," Gwendolyn Swan said. She sounded weak, exhausted. "The question is, what are you going to do about it?"

CHAPTER 46

Gwendolyn was sitting on the tile floor, her back propped against the wall. Her hair hung in limp strands around her shoulders, and her jeans and shirt looked as if she had slept in them. But it was the desperation in her eyes and the air of fatigue that marked her as a woman who was barely hanging on.

She was not alone. Another woman slumped beside her, clearly fighting to stay conscious. It took Olivia a couple of beats to recognize her because the hair that had once been caught up in a flirty twist was now tangled and snarled, she was no longer wearing the chic, sexy little red dress and there were no statement earrings. Instead, she was in trousers and a sweater. A stylish backpack was slung over one shoulder. She had a leather-bound notebook in her hand.

"You're the woman who sat behind me at the speed date event," Olivia said. "The one who told me I was scaring off all the good prospects."

"I fucked up there, didn't I? When you left with Mr. Nobody-in-Particular I figured you just didn't have good taste in men. Imagine my surprise when I found out you took off with Harlan Rancourt. Some days it just doesn't pay to be psychic."

"Who are you?" Olivia asked.

"Meet my sister," Gwendolyn said. "Eloisa. The reason we've been stuck here waiting for you is because my crazy client kidnapped us."

"Spode is your client?" Olivia said.

"Showed up one day with the camera and a good story. Look, we don't have time for a chat. If you think you can stop the meltdown, you'd better get to it. Spode is right about one thing—there is no telling what will happen if Vortex explodes."

Olivia looked around and saw three branching tunnels. "Where is the machine?"

"Chamber at the end of that corridor." Eloisa made a vague gesture with one hand. "Trust me, you can't miss it."

There was nothing else to do except make the trek along the corridor. Clutching the camera in both hands, Olivia went forward into the tiled hallway. The paranormal energy grew increasingly powerful with each step.

The currents howled, whined and shrieked from one end of the spectrum to the other. Auroras shimmered and flowed, ominous waves of light in colors that had no names. In spite of the effort of raw will required to make the journey, she knew that part of her was thrilled. So much power. It was intoxicating even as it threatened to destroy her.

"I'm from Fogg Lake," she said to the storm. "Takes more than this to scare me."

Halfway along the hall she realized the camera was glowing with its unique silver energy. She had activated it intuitively. Unable to think of anything else to do, she pulled up the holograms. The Speed Date Killer appeared first, lunging at her with his knife.

She heard a startled scream behind her.

"No," Gwendolyn shouted. "Wait. Don't kill her. She's all we've got."

"Nice to feel needed," Olivia said.

She dismissed the Speed Date Killer. Spode popped up next. Hot excitement glittering in his eyes as he reached out to grab the camera.

"What the fuck?" Eloisa screamed.

Olivia dismissed the Spode hologram.

"What's going on?" Gwendolyn said. Her voice echoed down the hallway. "It's the energy. It's driving us over the edge."

Olivia pulled up the next image. The camouflaged vintage trailers appeared. She dumped it and went on to the image of the flooded cave. Useless. She ditched it.

Intuitively she knew she needed the last hologram, the one still locked inside the camera.

At the end of the hallway there was a chamber formed of thick, green-tinted glass. A paranormal hurricane raged inside. The energy was so hot, so brilliant, she could not look straight into it.

On a hunch, she raised the camera and peered through the crystal lens. It was as if she had put on a pair of sunglasses. Now she could see a crystal pyramid inside the chamber. It was large enough to accommodate a person. There was a door—a cobalt blue mirror.

"Oh, joy. My favorite color."

Now what?

She lowered the glowing camera. Out of nowhere, Harlan's explanation of how his chaos talent worked whispered at the edge of her consciousness: *I look for the places where the circles overlap. Connections.*

She raised the camera again and examined the storm of energy that swirled around the pyramid the same way she studied an aura.

"What am I looking at, Grandma?"

The answer was obvious. Out-of-control currents of energy were slamming back and forth. The oscillating waves were growing increasingly wild, out of sync. At the center of it all was the pyramid.

She had to calm the raging currents. She needed the last image on the camera.

"I need a little help here, Grandma."

She gathered her senses, focused on the artifact and pressed the crystal button that brought up the holograms.

An image flashed into existence, one she had not viewed previously. Somehow she knew it was the final hologram. At first she did not recognize the scene of slanting walls lined with mirrors. A heartbeat later she realized the picture had been taken from inside the pyramid. In the center of the scene was a crystal the size of a man's two fists. The stone was cut in the shape of a pyramid.

The heart of Vortex.

Words crashed through her head and she fell into her other voice.

"To stop the monsters you must quench the lightning in the mirrors."

To get to the crystal she would have to enter the storm-filled chamber. If she survived the energies inside, she would be faced with the cobalt blue mirror that guarded the interior of the pyramid.

Before she could give herself any more time to think about it, she went to the glass door of the chamber and turned the handle. She was vaguely amazed when the heavy door swung slowly inward.

She stepped into the storm . . .

. . . and was amazed again when she did not immediately lose consciousness. She looked down at the camera. It was glowing much more strongly now. *She* was glowing. No, not exactly. She was enveloped in the energy field of the camera. It was acting like a shield, protecting her from the paranormal storm.

No, not a shield; a *cloak* of energy. She was wearing the paranormal version of the cloak her grandmother had worn in the paintings.

She walked through the storm and stopped in front of the blue mirror that sealed the pyramid. Now that she was close she could see the reflective effect was an optical illusion. Instead of a solid sheet of glass, she was confronting a gate of shimmering energy. All she had to do was go through it.

Right.

She reminded herself that she and her mother had escaped through a similar gate in her grandmother's safe room.

When the time comes you will know how to go through the mirror.

"Thanks, Grandma. I hope you know what I'm doing here."

She gripped the camera, closed her eyes and stepped forward. She heard and felt the crackle of energy around her, but there was no resistance. It was like walking through a sparkling waterfall without getting wet.

She opened her eyes and found herself inside the pyramid.

Lightning flashed and burned in the mirrors that lined the interior walls of the pyramid. The sense of violently oscillating energy was everywhere. She was intensely aware of it but unaffected by it. The energy field of the camera continued to protect her.

The heart of Vortex, a crystal ablaze with lightning, sat on the mirrored floor. Dazzling bolts of energy leaped from it, striking the mirrors and rebounding.

To stop the monsters you must quench the lightning in the mirrors.

How did you go about quenching lightning in a crystal that you didn't dare touch? If only there was a sledgehammer or some other object heavy enough to shatter the crystal.

You could use fire to fight fire. Maybe the theory worked with paranormal lightning, too. A small, strategically aimed bolt might fracture the crystal.

She gripped the camera in both hands and focused energy through the lens and straight into the Vortex stone. At first she thought nothing was happening. If anything, the crystal seemed to grow hotter. She pulled harder on her talent and sent another blast through the lens.

This time she heard a startling *crack*. The Vortex crystal fractured and exploded into countless shards. The lightning ceased abruptly.

So much for giving Spode the heart of Vortex.

The fire in the mirrors vanished. The once-dazzling surfaces faded into sheets of dull gray glass. Twilight fell inside the pyramid.

Gasping for breath, heart racing, Olivia turned toward the entrance. The blue energy gate was weakening. A moment later it vanished. The storm in the glass-walled chamber disintegrated rapidly.

She moved out of the pyramid, crossed the chamber and opened the glass door. She discovered she was light-headed. A strange exhaustion was tugging at her, but a giddy, adrenaline-enhanced euphoria was warding it off, at least for now.

She started down the tiled hallway. Each step seemed to require an enormous amount of effort and concentration. Gwendolyn and Eloisa met her halfway down the corridor.

"You did it," Gwendolyn said. "I didn't think it was possible. I thought we were all going to die in here."

"You used the camera, didn't you?" Eloisa said. "It was the secret. I knew it."

"What are you two doing here?" Olivia said. "How are you involved in this mess?"

"We started looking for Vortex a couple of years ago, right after we found our grandmother's journal," Gwendolyn said.

"Who was your grandmother?" Olivia asked.

"Aurora Winston," Eloisa said. "She was the genius behind the machine and the serum that makes the enhancement effects stable."

"Stable?" Olivia said. "Have you met Jake Spode and company?"

"Yes, well, Aurora didn't have time to tweak the serum," Eloisa said. "Some fool back in DC shut down the whole Bluestone Project just as she made her final breakthrough."

"What happened to Aurora Winston?" Olivia asked.

"She died in an asylum for the insane," Gwendolyn said. "At least, that's the official story. After we learned about the Bluestone Project, Eloisa and I wondered if she had been murdered by whoever erased almost everyone else associated with Vortex. I guess we'll never know."

"Spode said his father was the assassin assigned to track down and murder the Vortex staff," Olivia said.

"That explains a lot," Eloisa muttered. "Spode and his father knew where Vortex was all along. They kept its secret until things started to go wrong. Then Spode had to go out into the world and start looking for the camera and the oracle."

"He's the one responsible for firing up the recent rumors in the artifacts market," Gwendolyn said.

"You two were also looking for Vortex," Olivia pointed out.

"True," Eloisa admitted.

They reached the entrance, stopped and contemplated the vault-like steel door.

"I don't suppose there's another exit," Olivia said.

"No," Gwendolyn said. "Trust me, we looked. If there was another way out of here, it was blocked when they detonated the explosives that were supposed to destroy Vortex."

"Spode's bound to open the door soon, because he'll realize the machine has been shut down," Olivia said.

"You're right," Eloisa said. "The energy level is dropping rapidly. He'll sense that."

"I'm afraid he's going to be very unhappy when he finds out what happened to the crystal," Olivia said.

Eloisa glanced at her. "What did happen to it?"

"Shattered," Olivia said. "Literally. A gazillion pieces."

"Shit," Gwendolyn said. "Once he discovers that, he'll kill all of us."

"He can't just shoot us," Olivia said. "Guns won't work in that maze or in here. Too much heat."

"All he has to do is leave us in the maze," Eloisa said. "We'll never find our way out."

"Spode has a compass that he uses to navigate the maze," Olivia said. "We have to get it. We need weapons."

"There's an old supply closet around the corner," Gwendolyn said. "There may be some things inside we can use."

The closet yielded a treasure trove of janitorial supplies and equipment. A short time later, armed with a rusty metal bucket, a couple of sturdy broomsticks and a vintage wrench, they went back to the entrance.

"You do realize that any one of these things would be worth a fortune to a collector?" Gwendolyn muttered.

Olivia and Eloisa ignored her because the door was open. For a moment the three of them stared out into the maze, uncertain what to do next.

There was no sign of Spode. The thick, disorienting currents of the topiaries swirled and sloshed through the entrance, mingling with the waves of paranormal energy infused into the walls of the lab.

"Where is he?" Gwendolyn said. "This is some kind of trap."

Olivia gripped the wrench and moved cautiously through the doorway. She stepped outside into the topiary crypt. Eloisa and Gwendolyn followed her, makeshift weapons in hand. Spode did not appear.

"He said he would be here." Olivia studied the green corridor outside the crypt. "He was desperate to get his hands on the crystal."

"And us," Gwendolyn said. "He needs Eloisa and me because we have two of Aurora Winston's journals. One of them has the original formula for the serum and the other describes Aurora's last breakthrough with the radiation. Both are in code. I'm the only one who can decipher the journals, and Eloisa is the only one who has Grandma's talent for creating the formula. Why leave us here?"

Gears rumbled, startling all three of them. Olivia turned around in time to watch the steel door slam shut. The bolt slid into place. There was no one around.

"Probably some sort of automatic security feature," Gwendolyn said.

"Listen," Eloisa said.

Gunfire cracked in the distance. It was muffled and distorted because of the hot paranormal atmosphere inside the maze, but there was no mistaking the sound.

"I smell smoke," Gwendolyn said. "What is going on?"

A sudden sense of knowing soared through Olivia.

"Harlan figured out where the island is," she said. "I think Foundation security is invading. No wonder Spode disappeared. He'll be running for his life by now."

"He must have been surprised right after he got the door open," Gwendolyn said. "He took off, and that means we've got a serious problem. We're stuck here in this damned maze."

"The Foundation team or whoever is out there will find us eventually," Eloisa said. "Our best bet is to stay right where we are."

Olivia started to agree but the smell of smoke was getting stronger. It drifted through the atmosphere, mingling with the scents of the foliage.

"The maze is burning," she said. "I'll bet the gunfire ignited it. This garden was already a tinderbox."

"These plants are very lush and green," Gwendolyn said. She looked around. "They won't burn easily."

"You're wrong," Eloisa said. "Fire is one of the elemental forces. It runs the full spectrum, from the normal straight through the paranormal. The intense energy in here will act like oxygen on the flames. This maze will burn, all right. We're standing at the heart of what will become an inferno. We have to get out of this place. We don't have a choice."

"She's right," Olivia said. "But I think we've got a chance if we pay attention. This maze feels like the caves in Fogg Lake. Every kid who grows up there knows that if you get lost your best bet is to find the strongest current and follow it. Cave divers use the same principle."

"It's up to you, then," Gwendolyn said. "Eloisa and I don't have any experience with caves."

"Give me a minute," Olivia said.

She heightened her senses, searching for a vibe that felt right. Before she could settle on one she heard the sharp, pure notes of a recorder. The music rolled through the maze, piercing the thick atmosphere, providing exactly the strong current they needed.

"Shit," Gwendolyn whispered. "Be careful what you wish for. Spode is hunting us with his damned recorder."

"No," Olivia said. "There is no hypnotic effect in the music. No compulsion. Just a clear vibe. I think someone with the Foundation team is playing the recorder."

"Who would be playing a recorder in the middle of a Foundation takedown?" Gwendolyn demanded.

Olivia smiled. "Someone who knows we're trapped in here and is throwing us a lifeline. If we follow the music, we'll find an exit."

"And maybe walk straight into Spode's hands," Eloisa said.

"No," Olivia said. "We're going to assume the Foundation is in charge of this island now."

Eloisa narrowed her eyes. "Why?"

"Two reasons. The first is that we don't have much choice. The smoke is getting stronger, in case you haven't noticed. The second is that Harlan is very good at what he does, and what he's been doing since he found out I disappeared from Fogg Lake is searching for me."

Gwendolyn's eyes narrowed. "You sound certain of that."

"Yes," Olivia said, "I am. Very certain."

"You're right," Eloisa said. "It's not like we've got options. Let's go."

She started down the corridor formed by the towering green walls. Gwendolyn followed. Olivia fell into step behind the sisters. The prospect of dying in the maze had a remarkably fortifying effect;

nevertheless, she was pulling on the last of her reserves. You couldn't burn through both physical and paranormal energy resources without paying a price. She was going to crash soon. Just a matter of time. For now, though, she was on her feet and moving. She had to stay that way until she was out of the maze.

The recorder music brought them to yet another intersection. Eloisa turned a corner, took a few steps and stopped so quickly that Gwendolyn bumped into her.

"No," Eloisa said. "The music is fainter in this corridor. We have to turn the other way."

Gwendolyn swung around and hurriedly backtracked. This time she was in front. Eloisa followed her. The sisters rushed past Olivia and disappeared into another corridor.

Olivia took a few deep breaths and listened intently for the music. There it was, piercing the smoky vibe that flooded the maze. She started forward. She was turning another sharp corner when she realized that at some point she had dropped the wrench. There was no going back to find it. She still had the camera. *Better than a wrench,* she thought.

She was just so exhausted. Maybe she could risk a short pause to catch her breath. She glanced down at the vibrant green grass, saw the ominous-looking mushrooms and changed her mind.

The recorder led her around another corner.

A massive hand slapped across her mouth and nose, cutting off her breath. She was hauled back off her feet.

"You're not going anywhere, bitch," Spode said. "You murdered me. You and your mother and your grandmother. I may be dying, but I'll watch you bleed out first."

Desperate to catch her breath, she clawed at Spode's arm and then went after his hand. She managed to pry two big fingers free. She gasped for breath.

Spode appeared oblivious to her struggles.

He talked to himself as he dragged her down another corridor.

"Fucking Foundation," he hissed. "The garden is going to go up in flames. Everything my father and I built will be destroyed. Rancourt will pay. They'll all pay. I'm not dead yet."

He was right about one thing, Olivia thought. The garden was about to explode in flames. She could feel the heat in the maze rising. Out of the corner of her eye she saw an emerald green leaf ignite. The ultraviolet orchid next to it flared, the snakelike bloom now a torch.

The recorder music faded as Spode dragged her in the wrong direction. She had to get free before she lost the vibe.

She clutched the camera in one hand, but in her current position there was no way she could focus energy through the lens to aim it at Spode. She reminded herself she did not need the lens to summon the holographic images.

She concentrated fiercely even as Spode dragged her around another corner. The life-sized hologram of the Speed Date Killer snapped into view inches away from Spode. He jolted to a stop.

"*What the fuck?*" he rasped.

Olivia fell to the ground and realized somewhat vaguely that he had dropped her so that he could grab the recorder off his belt. She rolled to her knees and looked up.

The Speed Date Killer blocked Spode's path, mouth twisted in rage, knife extended. Motionless.

"Shit," Spode said. He rounded on Olivia. "This is one of your tricks, LeClair. That picture is from the camera, isn't it?"

She had one chance. She focused through the lens, found the wavelengths she needed to identify with his aura for maximum effect and pressed the button.

Nothing happened.

She realized she must have shattered the crystal lens when she used it to stop the Vortex meltdown. There was no choice now but to run. The smoke was stronger. More topiary vaults were catching fire. The recorder music was still floating through the air, but it came from the same direction as the smoke. If she followed the notes she would run straight into the fire.

Spode reached for her, his face twisted with madness and fury. She needed another distraction. Holding her breath, her heart pounding, she reached for another image on the camera.

The hologram of Spode stretching out his hands to push her mother off the cliff sprang to life. Spode stumbled to a halt, shock spiking in his aura.

Olivia heard her mother's voice thundering in her head. The words spilled out, reverberating in the hot atmosphere.

"Dead man walking in a dying garden."

Spode stared, transfixed, at the image.

"Fucking bitch," he screamed.

Olivia no longer had the energy to maintain the holograms. She let them evaporate. She whirled around and fled into the maze, frantically seeking the recorder music with her exhausted senses.

Spode lunged after her.

"I'll kill you like I did your mother," he shrieked.

He was close—so close. It was true that his energy field was weakening, but he was still powerful, still strong. She knew she could never outrun him.

She made it around a corner and staggered to a halt when she saw Harlan running toward her. He had a gun in one hand. She started to tell him that Spode was right behind her, but there was no need.

Spode whipped around the corner and stopped when he saw Harlan. Then he laughed, a shrill shout of triumph.

"Fucking idiot," he said, raising the recorder to his lips. "Guns don't work in here."

"I know," Harlan said. "That's why I brought a knife."

The blade was in his hand before Olivia could begin to comprehend what was happening.

But Harlan did not throw the knife. There was no need. Spode was screaming in terror. He stared, stricken. It was as if Harlan had metamorphosed into a monster.

Which, Olivia realized, was technically true. Senses-searing energy straight from the heart of a nightmare iced the atmosphere. It was coming from Harlan's unveiled aura. Panic. Horror. The feeling of drowning in a bottomless lake. Going down, down . . .

With a shriek, Spode hurled his navigation device over the top of the nearest wall of green.

"You'll never find your way out," he said. "The entrance is in flames by now. You'll die in here, with me."

He whirled and ran blindly into one of the intersecting corridors of the maze.

Seconds later he screamed again. This time the cry was abruptly cut off.

Harlan holstered the gun, took Olivia's hand and went forward, knife at the ready.

Spode was only steps away, sprawled on a bed of neon-orange mushrooms inside a topiary crypt. Olivia could still see his aura, but it was rapidly fading.

"He's alive, but not for long," she said quietly.

Harlan released her hand. "Don't move. I can't risk losing sight of you. The fire is moving fast."

She nodded her understanding and watched him go into the crypt. Cautiously he leaned down and turned Spode onto his back. Spode swallowed a mouthful of neon-orange mushroom and peered up at Harlan with eyes that were already glazing over.

"The oracle was right," he whispered. "She said I was a dead man walking in a dying garden."

"My mother," Olivia said.

"She did something with the camera right before I grabbed it. It was as if she took my picture, but I felt a shock. I realized later that's when she murdered me. Just took a year to finish the job."

"Anything you want to tell me for the Foundation archives?"

Harlan asked. "I can already promise you that you're going to be famous. You'll become part of the legend of Vortex."

Spode grunted. "So will you and LeClair. You're my last two kills."

"Is that right?" Harlan asked.

"You'll never find your way out of here, not without the nav-flash. The fire will get to you long before a search party. Just a couple of dead people walking through my dying garden."

"Oh, right," Harlan said. "About your navigation device." He reached into his jacket and pulled out an artifact that looked identical to the one Spode had tossed over the burning topiaries. "Your friend, Barrow, gave me his. He also told me there is more than one way out of the maze."

"Barrow." Spode closed his eyes. "Can't trust anyone these days, can you?"

The last of Spode's aura winked out. Olivia knew he was gone.

Harlan picked up the recorder, dropped it into the pocket of his jacket and walked out of the crypt. "Ready to leave?"

Olivia looked at the body of the man who had murdered her mother. She turned back to Harlan.

"Yes," she said. "But how?"

He activated the small navigation artifact. A beam of light appeared. "I used this to find the path through the maze. It will guide us to the nearest emergency exit."

"There really is more than one way out?"

"Yes."

He aimed the navigation device down an aisle of hot greenery. They started forward.

"Why the gun?" Olivia said. "You knew it wouldn't work in here."

"Distraction. People see what they expect to see, and they usually go with it."

"Spode saw the pistol and concluded that a man who carried a gun into this maze wasn't going to be much of a problem."

"Something like that."

"And the knife?"

"My talent isn't good for much except hiding in plain sight and scaring the shit out of people. I like to have backup."

"I'm crashing, Harlan."

"I know. We're almost out of here. Just a few more steps."

"You're supposed to be an illusion talent," she said. "But you're not."

"No?"

"You're exactly who you said you were the first time I met you— the man who would walk into hell to find me."

He said something, but she could no longer concentrate enough to understand the words. The dark night of a total psychic crash descended. The last thing she remembered was Harlan picking her up in his arms. He carried her out of the dying garden.

CHAPTER 47

The first time she woke up, it was dark outside. It took her a moment to realize she was in her own bedroom. A familiar voice spoke to her from the shadows.

"How are you feeling?" Catalina asked.

Olivia yawned and turned onto her back. Catalina was sitting in a chair near the window reading a book on her e-reader. Keeping watch. In the shadows Olivia could see that her childhood friend was wearing her signature black—black trousers, black pullover. Her dark hair was clipped back in a stern knot.

"I'm okay," Olivia said. "I need more sleep, but I'm okay. When did you get into town?"

"I'm not sure. It's all a bit of a blur. At some point Lucas Pine called us to tell us what was going on. We caught the first flight home, but it's a long haul from Australia. By the time we landed at SeaTac most of the excitement was over. Harlan delivered you here to your apartment. I told him I'd keep an eye on you while he and Victor and Lucas figure out what happened to Gwendolyn and Eloisa Swan."

"I don't understand. I thought they were all right. The last time I saw them they were following the recorder music out of the maze."

"They made it out of the maze. In the confusion they managed to grab the boat Spode and Barrow used. The Swans have since disappeared."

"*What?*" Olivia tried to absorb the implications. "You mean deliberately?"

"Yep."

"Well, that is interesting."

"Very," Catalina said. "Got some ideas?"

"Turns out Gwendolyn and Eloisa Swan are the granddaughters of Aurora Winston, the woman who was responsible for overcoming the last technological hurdles involved with the development of Vortex. They told me they had two of Winston's private journals. Gwendolyn said something about the original formula for the serum that made the enhancement process fairly stable."

"The Vortex machine was destroyed when you somehow shattered the crystal that was the power source," Catalina said. "But the serum is a big mystery as far as everyone can tell. Barrow talked before he went into the maze."

"Barrow got away?"

"No. He's dead. The consensus of opinion is that he planned to eat some of those mushrooms that Spode ingested, but he didn't last that long. Before he went into the maze he told the Foundation team that Spode had been making the serum based on Aurora Winston's formula but that the plants had changed because of the intense radiation leaking out of Vortex all these years. The serum had become too strong. On top of that, the Vortex machine had become unstable. The enhancement treatments that had kept Spode and Barrow alive were slowly killing them, but they couldn't stop because they would have died even more quickly. They were two very desperate men."

"They had so much information to work with because Spode was the son of the assassin who had been assigned to murder everyone connected to Vortex."

"It's amazing that he was able to keep the location of Vortex a secret as long as he did," Catalina said.

"Hiding in plain sight." Olivia shifted position. "I was exposed to a lot of radiation when I went into that chamber, Cat. I think the camera protected me but I can't be sure—"

"Relax. North checked your aura vitals. You're fine."

"Good to know." Olivia hesitated a moment. "Spode murdered my mother."

"Yes. And now he's dead."

"I think I understand how some of our clients feel when we get answers for them even though the answers aren't happy."

"Closure?" Catalina asked.

"I'm not sure what to call it. Feels like an ending of some kind. Time to move on in a different direction."

"That's what smart people do," Catalina said. "And you're a very smart woman."

Olivia was quiet for a while, letting it all sink in.

"I found him, Cat."

"Who?"

"The man who is willing to walk into hell to find me."

Catalina smiled. "I know."

CHAPTER 48

Harlan studied the body on the basement floor. "The first raider didn't make it, but the ones who came after him cleaned out the place."

He turned away from the dead thief and examined the space. There was still a lot of residual energy shivering in the downstairs salesroom of Swan Antiques, but the display cases had been emptied.

"It's amazing how fast the rumors of a hot collection of artifacts left unprotected spread in the underground market," he said. "Makes you wonder if the raiders have some version of a psychic Internet."

Lucas Pine studied the empty basement and shook his head. "I'm still trying to figure out how we screwed up so badly. The Foundation has been dealing with Swan Antiques for years. Never had a clue that Gwendolyn Swan and her sister were searching for Vortex, let alone that they had a family connection to that lab."

Victor examined the mechanical figure of the nurse. "It's a clockwork mechanism. Probably has to be reset after every injection. The syringe is empty. The first raider out of the tunnel accidentally cleared the path for the others."

Harlan tried the door of the vault. "Locked. The raiders didn't get inside."

"Let me take a look," Lucas said. "I think I've got a lock pick that can handle it." He removed a small gadget from the pocket of his jacket. "It's the latest toy out of the Foundation labs."

He went to work. A short time later there was a sharp click and the sound of a bolt sliding aside.

"Stand back," he said. "There's always a chance Swan set another trap for anyone who got this far."

Harlan did not argue. Neither did Victor. Dealing with safecracking and booby traps was one of Lucas's skills, courtesy of his years in the CIA and a strong talent for finding that which was hidden.

The big vault door swung open. Currents of paranormal-infused air wafted out. So did the smell of death. They all looked at the body on the floor.

"One of the raiders actually made it this far," Victor marveled. "Amazing."

"No," Lucas said. "I don't think it went down that way. He's been dead longer than the other raider."

"I agree," Harlan said. "No visible wound. Looks like the nurse got him. The Swans probably dragged him in here to hide the body but didn't get a chance to dispose of it before Spode grabbed them."

Victor contemplated the partially emptied shelves and then looked at the door that sealed the rear of the vault. "The Swans went through here on their way out of town. They packed up several pieces—probably the most valuable artifacts—and escaped through a tunnel on the other side of that door."

Lucas examined one of the artifacts, a vintage typewriter. "Hotter than a two-dollar pistol, as they used to say. Must have hurt to leave these relics behind. Everything in here is worth a fortune."

"Imagine the value of what they took with them," Harlan said.

Lucas glanced at Victor. "I assume the Foundation will be claiming what's left in this vault?"

"We're taking control of the whole damn shop," Victor said. "And the condo upstairs. Gwendolyn Swan owned both. I want a security team set up here immediately. I'll also bring in forensics. Swan was in business for several years. She took off in one hell of a hurry. She will have left something interesting behind. They always do."

Lucas looked at Harlan. "Back in the day, people in the Foundation said the bad guys never saw you coming. Evidently you aren't the only one who's got a talent for hiding in plain sight."

CHAPTER 49

The next time Olivia woke up she was greeted by the aroma of freshly brewed coffee. Wispy dream fragments faded even as she tried to grasp them. Lightning sparking in mirrors, a fiery maze, the piercing notes of a recorder. Harlan.

She opened her eyes and saw him standing in the doorway of her bedroom, a mug of coffee in his hand. He was wearing trousers and a T-shirt. There was no sign of the pistol or the knife sheath. She felt the familiar whisper of awareness and automatically went into her other senses. His compelling aura blazed.

"Good morning," he said. "Catalina left when I got back from Swan's shop. It's about time you surfaced. How are you feeling?"

The last vestiges of the dream vanished. She was in her bedroom and Harlan was there. She was in the right place.

"Good," she said. "Surprisingly normal, whatever that is." She levered herself to a sitting position against the pillows. "That coffee smells great."

He moved to the bed and gave her the mug. She drank some, exhaled with pleasure and took another sip.

"Catalina filled me in on most of what happened after I crashed," she said. "I hear the Swan sisters disappeared. I'll bet Victor and Lucas are exceedingly embarrassed. They hate it when they don't look too smart."

"I'm not feeling especially bright, either." Harlan sat down on the bed. "But you're a heroine, as far as Victor and Lucas and everyone else are concerned. You shattered the Vortex crystal and stopped the meltdown. The Foundation is now in control of the invisible island with no name. It would have been good to interrogate Spode and Barrow, but North Chastain says that given their long history with the drug, they were both so unstable he couldn't have saved them."

"What about the students?"

"All under observation at Halcyon, but Chastain says they will be okay. We found what was left of a small lab in the monastery, but we didn't find the formula for the serum. Spode must have committed it to memory. After all, he had been making the stuff for decades."

"His father made it before him. Apparently it worked fairly well until the plants began to change because of the radiation."

"Arganbright and Pine are not so sure about that. Spode was dying, and so was Barrow. The formula apparently has a destabilizing effect on the aura."

Olivia shuddered. "So much for Spode's conviction that it could accelerate human evolution."

"Victor has a research team on the island," Harlan said. "The plan is to get the lab secured once things cool down. They're hoping to find some answers and artifacts inside. It would be good to turn up some old logbooks."

"*Logbooks.*" Olivia had been about to swallow more coffee. She paused, the mug halfway to her mouth. "Oh, shit."

"What?"

"Did you happen to notice if Eloisa Swan was carrying anything when she came out of the maze?"

"I think she had a broomstick and I seem to recall that she had a small leather backpack, too. I wasn't paying much attention to her or Gwendolyn. I was looking for you. Why?"

"When Spode locked me inside the lab I saw Eloisa holding what looked like a black, leather-bound logbook. I didn't notice it later when we escaped but I wasn't thinking clearly because I had just shut down Vortex and I knew I was going to crash. There was a lot going on."

"I noticed."

"Gwendolyn mentioned that she and Eloisa had two of Aurora Winston's logbooks."

Harlan's expression was utterly neutral but his eyes got cold. "Two logbooks?"

"I think so, yes."

"That is probably not good news."

"Probably not." Olivia set the empty mug on the table, swung her legs over the side of the bed and stood. "But before you start worrying about it, I need a shower. And then I need food."

Harlan got to his feet. "I'm not a great cook, but I can do a few things with eggs. I'll have breakfast waiting when you get out of the shower."

She smiled. "That sounds lovely."

She started into the bathroom but stopped when she saw the vintage camera sitting on the table. She changed course and crossed the room. Tentatively she touched the camera.

The familiar vibe was still there. She would always recognize it. But the obsessive need to keep it close and discover its secrets had faded. She had done what needed to be done. *Rest in peace, Grandma. Rest in peace, Mom. Love you both. I won't ever forget you. You'll always be a part of me.*

"Olivia?" Harlan said quietly.

"I'm all right." She went into the bathroom and partially closed the door. She looked at him through the narrowed opening. "Thanks to you."

"We were a team. A damn good one."

"Yes, we were." She paused. "Are we talking past tense?"

"That depends on you."

"I thought I made it clear you're the man I've been waiting for."

"That was hours ago when you were crashing. There was a lot of hot energy in the atmosphere. You had been through a traumatic experience. I thought you might need time to think."

"About what?"

"It's one thing to want justice for your mother. It's something else entirely to see a man killed in front of you."

"You didn't kill Spode."

"I know what my talent can do, Olivia. I used it to drive Spode over the edge."

"He was already over the edge. You're a powerful talent, and you've done some serious monster-hunting, but just because you can think like the monsters doesn't mean you are one."

"You're sure?"

"I've met monsters," she said. "Spode, for example. Did you know that each of the topiary funeral vaults in that horrible maze marked one of his murders or one of his father's? He was a serial killer. So was his father. Spode told himself he wasn't because he did it for the money. But he was one of the real monsters."

"I didn't know about the topiaries." Harlan paused. "Can I assume we are not talking about us in the past tense?"

"Unless you run very far, very fast, I'm going to marry you."

He smiled a slow smile that was so hot it could have ignited a fire. "What happens if I run?"

"I'll walk into hell to find you."

"Right answer." His eyes burned. "No one has ever offered to do that for me."

"It's not an offer, it's a promise," she said.

"I love you, Olivia."

"I love you, Harlan." She started to close the bathroom door but paused. "Wait. You never told me how you found the island."

"People keep asking me that question."

"Gee, I wonder why."

"I'll tell you at breakfast, and then I'll have to go through it again later this morning when we meet with Arganbright and Pine and the others."

CHAPTER 50

They gathered in the reception area of the offices of Lark & LeClair. Daniel Naylor, the administrative assistant, was ensconced behind his desk, looking cool and effortlessly trendy, as usual. Victor and Lucas were seated in the two chairs intended for clients. Additional chairs had been hauled out of the inner offices to provide seating for Olivia and Catalina. North Chastain and Catalina's husband, Slater Arganbright, were propped up against one of the walls.

Harlan was standing at the window. Olivia knew the position was strategic. It allowed him a view of the street as well as the door of the office. He was back in his nothing-to-see-here mode. *Old habits die hard,* she thought. Or maybe he wasn't ready to risk a few new habits.

She did not need her aura-reading talent to pick up the vibe of relief that flooded the small space.

"We discovered early on that the old Vortex lab was on an island in the San Juans," Harlan said. "Given time we could have searched each one, but time was the one thing we didn't have. We had a lot of other data, however."

"The paintings, the camera and our very own oracle," Victor said.

Olivia was tempted to interrupt with another denial of her so-called oracle status but decided that, under the circumstances, she would exercise some restraint.

Harlan folded his arms. "We had a lot of information, but the one piece of the puzzle we needed the most was missing. It just didn't make sense that Olivia's grandmother would leave so many clues but not the most important one. Turns out it was available all along. I finally realized it was in one of the paintings."

"Which one?" Victor demanded.

"The one involving a mirror, of course," Harlan said. "Olivia's mother painted it. It's hanging on the wall of their Fogg Lake home. It's the only painting that includes the camera, a blue mirror and Olivia. The one picture where all the circles overlap. Where all the connections are visible. It's the only painting that points to the future instead of the past."

"It was a future that my mother hoped would never come about," Olivia explained. "As I grew up and showed no signs of becoming an oracle, she concluded that maybe I would never have to locate Vortex. And then one day a man telling her he was from the Foundation found her and offered to take the burden of the camera off her hands. I think she gave him two of my grandmother's paintings, too. She hoped she wouldn't have to worry about them anymore. She thought she and her daughter would be safe."

"I remember that picture of you in front of a mirror," Catalina said. "I saw it every time I went over to your house. I always thought there was something weird about it."

"You were right," Olivia said.

Catalina looked at Harlan. "Where in that painting are the coordinates of the island?"

"In the picture, Olivia is standing in front of a mirror," Harlan said. "The mirror reflects a small portion of the room behind her, including the camera and a large ceramic planter that sits on the floor beside a couch. The planter is painted with what looks like an abstract zigzag design. Lightning bolts. I asked Harmony to examine the planter. The coordinates were scratched on the bottom."

"Mom bought the planter from a local potter in Fogg Lake," Olivia said. "It was unpainted. She did the abstract decoration and evidently etched the coordinates on the bottom."

Slater Arganbright got a thoughtful expression. "Your mother had the coordinates the night you and she escaped the fire that killed your grandmother."

"Yes," Olivia said. "My mother had the camera and the coordinates in case she needed them, but she knew everything about Vortex was dangerous. As the years went by she began to relax. I grew into my aura talent but I showed no indication that I had an affinity for crystals."

"Crystals?" Victor asked.

"I've been telling everyone who will listen that I'm not an oracle talent," Olivia said patiently. "But according to Harmony there is a long history of crystal talents in my family. I got the ability, but it remained latent until the camera came into my hands."

"Huh." Victor's brows scrunched together. He was clearly not convinced, but he didn't argue. "Spode initially assumed he could work the camera. He discovered eventually that he could not break the psychic signature. He had to find someone who could unlock the device. He assumed he needed a true oracle. You were the obvious choice, but you showed no signs of having that sort of talent."

"He spent months trying to tune the camera to his own vibe before he gave up and turned to Gwendolyn Swan and her sister," Lucas said. "He knew they were the granddaughters of Aurora Winston, and he had already realized he was going to need their help with the formula, because the serum was failing. In the end they concluded

Olivia was their only hope. It was obvious she responded to the psychic signature of the camera. They all decided she must have inherited her grandmother's talent."

"I'm not an oracle," Olivia said, "and neither was my grandmother or my mother."

Everyone in the room looked at her. Victor cleared his throat, but no one spoke.

"I can prove it," Olivia said.

Victor's eyes narrowed. "How?"

"Think about it," she said. "I only do the oracle thing when I am in close proximity to the camera. It's true I recognize and resonate with my grandmother's signature, so I can summon the images and pick up the warnings attached to them. I can also sense the words my mother recorded. But I'm seeing and hearing what they locked into the camera. I have never once experienced the compulsion to proclaim a new prophecy. I rest my case."

"Huh." Victor rubbed his jaw, looking thoughtful. "We could probably test that hypothesis in one of the Foundation labs. What do you think, Lucas?"

Lucas raised a shoulder in an elegant shrug. "Doesn't sound too difficult. We could set up a series of experiments—"

"Forget it," Olivia said. "I know the truth, and that's all the proof I need. I am not going to let you conduct experiments on me."

Harlan looked at her. "The ability to resonate with crystals is linked to the dreamstate. So is the oracle talent. The two can look very similar, but they are different."

Victor glared. "You sure about that, Rancourt?"

"Yes," Harlan said.

"What about the oracle imagery in the paintings?" Victor said.

"The oracle appears only in the pictures that Olivia's grandmother did," Harlan said. "It's not in the one Olivia's mother painted. Grace Goodwin probably used that particular iconic figure because she knew it would get the attention of anyone connected to Bluestone and the Foundation. The oracle talent has been embedded in the my-thology of the lost labs since the beginning."

Lucas looked at Olivia. "I understand you did a very good job of convincing Spode and his students that you were a genuine oracle."

Olivia touched the camera.

"In real life I'm a private investigator," she said. "A talent for act-ing is a job requirement."

CHAPTER 51

Y ou're telling us Stenson Rancourt died because he got involved in a *love triangle*?" Victor said. He looked and sounded dumbfounded.

The bar was lightly crowded, because the happy hour crowd was fading and the evening dinner hour was not yet in full swing. Olivia had chosen the location because it was an easy walk from her apartment building. Victor and Lucas were staying at a nearby hotel. They had arrived on foot, too.

Lucas was the one who had requested the meeting, but now that the four of them were gathered in the booth it was clear Victor intended to interrogate Harlan. His determined expression would have been amusing if not for the energy in the atmosphere. He wanted answers.

Harlan appeared unfazed. He was back in camouflage mode, once again playing the role of Average Guy, Seattle Tech Engineer Edition. Olivia had been aware that some people had glanced at her when she had walked into the bar. She could tell that several had taken a second look at Victor and Lucas, too, even though they didn't realize they were intuitively reacting to the presence of a couple of strong talents.

But, as usual, no one looked twice at Harlan.

Olivia took a sip of her wine and picked up the bar menu. The steamed edamame sounded interesting. So did the antipasto platter. And the cheese and olive plate. Did you need both an antipasto platter and a cheese plate? What about the artisanal thin crust pizza? You could never go wrong with pizza when you were feeding men.

She circled her choices and handed the menu to the waiter as he went past.

"Victor and I have had two theories about the explosion," Lucas said. "The first was that your father caused it with the intention of killing us but something went wrong with the timing. Stenson died instead."

"I assume theory number two was that I had planned the lab disaster intending to take out both of you but that things went wrong and I accidentally killed my father," Harlan said.

Olivia glanced at him. His voice sounded a little too even. Nothing to see here. Just speculating.

"That was theory number two," Lucas said. "Figured you blamed us for your own miscalculation. We were certain that, if you were alive, you would be out for revenge. Instead, you just vanished."

"That's one of the few things my talent is good for," Harlan said.

"Not true," Olivia murmured.

The men paid no attention. They were focused on settling the great mysteries of the past.

"You figured we would try to eliminate you," Victor said. He nodded a couple of times. "Logical assumption."

"Certainly seemed that way to me," Harlan said. "I was supposed to be the heir apparent to the Foundation throne. Figured you'd want me out of the picture."

"What the hell have you been doing for the past five years?" Victor demanded.

"Drifting. Odd jobs."

Victor and Lucas looked skeptical. Olivia decided it was time to speak up.

"And research," she said. "By the way, he's telling the truth."

Victor, Lucas and Harlan finally remembered that she was at the table. They all looked at her.

"You're certain?" Victor asked.

She gave him a dazzling smile. "Absolutely certain. I'm supposed to be an oracle, remember? We know stuff like that." She saw the waiter approaching and straightened in anticipation. "Oh, good. Here comes the food."

The waiter arranged the dishes on the table. Harlan, Victor and Lucas were immediately distracted.

"Can I get you anything else?" the waiter asked.

"Another round of drinks should do it," she said. "Thank you."

The waiter nodded and departed. Harlan, Victor and Lucas descended on the food. Olivia managed to commandeer the bowl of edamame. The men either didn't notice or didn't care. They were preoccupied with the pizza.

Victor contemplated Olivia with a reflective air while he munched a bite of pizza. "What makes you so sure Rancourt is telling the truth?"

"Elementary, my dear Victor." She picked up one of the steamed soybean pods. "When you have eliminated the impossible—"

"Yeah, yeah, get to your point," Victor growled.

She put the pod between her lips and used her teeth to slide the beans out directly into her mouth. She tossed the empty pod aside, munched and swallowed. She smiled at Victor.

"I'm sure Harlan is telling you the truth because he has no reason to lie. He was forced to sacrifice his goal of avenging his father because the man who murdered Stenson Rancourt took his own life. He stayed away from the Foundation all these years because he did not want any part of it. The only reason he showed up at your front door a few days ago was because he realized Vortex had become a serious problem for all of us."

Victor and Lucas exchanged looks. Harlan ate some pizza.

Victor turned back to Olivia. "Huh."

Lucas nodded, satisfied. "A moment ago you said there were other uses for Harlan's talent besides hiding in plain sight. What did you have in mind?"

"Thank you. I didn't think anyone was listening." Olivia picked up another edamame pod and waved it at Victor and Lucas. "For the past five years the Foundation has relied on the two of you to keep a lid on the monsters and other threats arising within the paranormal community. But that's a full-time job in itself. You both have a lot of responsibilities. It strikes me that the Foundation needs a separate department that can focus exclusively on collecting and analyzing data from around the nation and the world."

Victor's eyes narrowed. "With Rancourt at the helm?"

"Who better?" She popped the pod between her lips, removed the beans and tossed the empty pod into a bowl. "Harlan spent the past five years exploring various paranormal traditions and identifying other organizations that are engaged in psychic research—"

"*What* other organizations?" Victor yelped.

Olivia ignored the interruption. "He established connections outside the closed world of the Foundation. As he has pointed out to me on more than one occasion, Bluestone and the Foundation are not the first or the only organizations that have investigated the paranormal. They are not the only ones dealing with monsters."

"Hang on," Victor sputtered. "I want to know exactly what other organizations we're talking about. Intelligence agencies? Academic institutions? Foreign governments?"

"All of the above," Harlan said. He munched on an olive. "And others. The Foundation does not have a monopoly when it comes to investigating the paranormal. The interesting thing is that every agency, society or group I've come across is intense when it comes to maintaining secrecy. Reminds me of the Foundation. Something to do with the concept of power, I guess."

Victor sent him a withering glare.

"You have to admit Harlan is uniquely qualified to establish an intelligence-gathering and data-analysis operation to help guide the Foundation in the future," Olivia said.

"Huh." Victor ate some cheese. "Huh."

Lucas studied Harlan. "What about it, Rancourt? Interested in the job?"

Harlan ate another bite of cauliflower. "I'll think about it."

He looked and sounded cool but Olivia felt energy shift in the atmosphere. He was intrigued by the offer. She smiled.

"One of the convenient things about the job," she said, "is that you could set up your headquarters anywhere you like. No need to work out of the other Washington or Las Vegas. You could run the whole show right here in Seattle, for example."

Harlan's eyes burned. He picked up his whiskey and smiled at her over the rim of the glass.

"Okay, I've thought about it," he said. "As the director of the Agency for the Investigation of Atypical Phenomena, I hereby announce the establishment of the Division of Intelligence Analysis. It will be overseen by the director of the Agency for the Investigation of Atypical Phenomena."

"You," Victor said.

Harlan drank some whiskey and lowered the glass. "Me."

"Where do you plan to set up your headquarters?" Lucas asked.

"Seattle is the ideal location," Harlan said.

Olivia smiled. "Perfect."

CHAPTER 52

Gwendolyn Swan gripped the balcony railing with both hands. She looked out at the white sand beach and the sparkling ocean beyond. "Perfect weather. Perfect island. And the local government encourages small businesses like money laundering and private pharmaceutical labs."

"Stop trying to cheer me up," Eloisa said. She walked out of the cottage, crossed the wide balcony and stopped at the railing. "The project was a disaster. After all our planning. All our work. I still can't believe it ended the way it did."

"We have the most important thing: Aurora Winston's logbooks. We've also got a fortune in artifacts. I know that market and I know the players in that world. We'll soon have the cash we need to set up your lab. Thanks to Grandmother, we have enough data to make it possible for us to create some basic paranormal weapons and we have the original enhancement formula."

"We have what Aurora Winston believed is the original enhancement formula," Eloisa said. "But she notes it came from an old herbal, and the herbalist said it was copied from an alchemist's journal. Even if it works we're going to have to figure out how to re-create the Vortex crystal. There's a lot of work ahead."

"Think of it as our life's work," Gwendolyn said. "We're going to create Vortex 2.0."

"Starting over." Eloisa sighed. "Well, at least I'm no longer working for a big corporation that has its own agenda."

"And I'm no longer dusting artifacts and trapping rats in a basement," Gwendolyn said. "This sun is amazing, isn't it? So very un-Seattle." She put on her new designer sunglasses and smiled. "Know what?"

"What?"

"I think Aurora Winston would be proud of us."

CHAPTER 53

They stood in the hallway outside the locked room on the locked floor of Halcyon.

"You don't have to do this," Olivia said.

Harlan looked at the door of Room 5. "Yes. I do."

"I understand," Olivia said. "I'll wait out here."

The orderly unlocked the door of the hospital room.

"Miss Whittier is in a nonresponsive state," he said. "She appears to be awake, but she isn't. The doctors aren't sure what's going on."

"I understand," Harlan said.

He walked into the room and stopped. Low classical music was playing from concealed speakers. Larissa was sitting in a chair, facing the window and a view of the gardens. Even dressed in the uniform worn by all the patients on the locked ward—blue scrubs—she was a striking woman. She was only a few years younger, the product of one of Stenson's early affairs.

"I'll be right here outside the door if you need me," the orderly said.

"Thank you."

Harlan waited until the door closed and then he went toward the window. He came to a stop a few feet away from the chair and studied Larissa's profile. She gave no indication she was aware he was in the room.

"Hello, Larissa," he said. "My name is Harlan Rancourt. I'm your half brother."

Larissa did not respond.

"I'm sorry Stenson Rancourt never acknowledged you. I don't think he was aware of your existence. That's not an excuse. It's who he was. I'm also sorry you felt you were cheated out of your inheritance. You had a right to be angry, but you tried to murder the innocent because you could not make the guilty pay for what was done to you. There is a line between justice and revenge. That's the line you crossed. I know what it feels like, because I've come close to that line, too."

Larissa continued to gaze, unseeing, out the window.

He stood quietly for a while, letting the silence lengthen. Larissa did not move.

"Believe it or not, I didn't come here to deliver a lecture. I'm here because I'm your brother and you are my sister. Nothing and no one can change that fact. I wanted you to know that as Stenson Rancourt's son, I acknowledge you as his daughter. That may not mean anything to you, but it means something to me. I have a responsibility toward you. I will make sure you get the best of care here at Halcyon."

Another silence.

"I won't disturb you any longer, but if you wake up and decide you want to talk to me, the hospital staff has instructions to make it happen. I will check in on you from time to time to say hello. Goodbye, Larissa."

He turned and signaled the orderly, who was watching through the narrow, shatterproof window.

The orderly opened the door. Olivia was waiting. Harlan started to walk out of the room, but a frisson of energy on the back of his neck made him turn his head.

Larissa was staring at him. For an instant he thought he saw emotion flash in her eyes. It vanished in a heartbeat, but he knew what he had seen.

Rage.

CHAPTER 54

Victor stood at the window wall of the office and looked down. It was one o'clock in the morning and the Strip was on fire. The aura of glamour, the heat of gambling fever and the excitement that came from taking risks and stepping over the line sent waves of heat into the starry desert night. He could feel the vibe all the way up here in his office.

"Hard to believe it's over," he said. "After all these years, we finally found Vortex."

"What's hard to believe is that we needed the help of a Rancourt to do it," Lucas said. He crossed the room to the window. "But you always knew that might be the case, didn't you? It's why we did not spend a whole lot of time, money and energy looking for him. You knew that when the time came he would show up."

"It was a hunch, that's all. Harlan Rancourt was a black box mystery. That's why we didn't focus on him. It wasn't at all clear how he fit into the picture. But one thing was obvious—if he had wanted to regain control of the Foundation or take revenge against us, we would have heard from him long ago. He would not have waited five years to come calling."

"Think he might be a problem in the future?"

Victor was surprised to find himself smiling. He had not smiled a lot in the past few years. "Probably, but not in the way you mean. He's smart, he's a high-grade talent and he's got strong opinions. I think it's safe to say we will be hearing from him on a regular basis. But Olivia was right; he's not out to avenge the past. He's got another agenda, one that aligns with ours."

"I agree we need to expand our intelligence gathering and analysis. We've been living within the cocoon of the Foundation and its secrets since the beginning because we were focused on the fallout from the Bluestone Project."

"Which is still going on," Victor said. "We've just scratched the surface. We found Vortex, but who knows what other threats will turn up? The excavation and research on the Fogg Lake lab has barely begun. We haven't even started on what's left of the Vortex facility. And now we have to worry about the Swan sisters. Meanwhile, we have almost no idea of what else is happening out there in the paranormal underworld."

"We need an organization that can deal with whatever comes at us. That means we need information."

"It occurs to me that we really ought to have seen Harlan Rancourt coming," Victor said. "It shouldn't have been such a surprise when he knocked on our door."

"We were looking too hard in another direction," Lucas said. "That's often how it is when it comes to the important things."

"Is that so?"

"Case in point—I never saw you coming until I sat down at that poker table all those years ago."

Victor snorted. "I saw you coming when you walked through the door of the casino. Watched you cross the room. By the time you got to the table I already knew you were the one."

Startled, Lucas turned his head. "Seriously?"

"When it comes to game changers, I'm always serious. You were a game changer."

Lucas glanced down. Their matching gold rings gleamed in the shadows.

"Always knew you had a romantic streak buried under all those gruff layers," he said.

"I wasn't talking romance. I was stating facts."

"Right." Lucas smiled. "Speaking of romance, it occurs to me that you and I have not had a real vacation in five years. What do you say we book a week or two in Hawaii?"

The notion of a vacation was such a novel one that Victor had to take a moment to adjust his focus.

"Huh," he said. "Now that you mention it—"

The ringing of the telephone stopped him in mid-sentence. He turned to look at the device on his desk. It rang again. Frissons of awareness went down his spine.

Lucas exhaled. "No one calls at this time of night unless there's a problem."

Victor crossed to his desk and picked up the phone. "Argan-bright."

"This is Fallon Jones. I operate a small investigation agency for an organization called the Arcane Society. Harlan Rancourt contacted me."

Chills electrified the back of Victor's neck. "How do you know Rancourt?"

"He did some odd jobs for me in the past. That talent of his is scary as hell, but it makes him useful in certain situations. The monsters never—"

"See him coming. I've heard that. Are you telling me you're in the monster-hunting business?"

"Among other interests. You know what they say. It takes a psychic—"

"To catch a psychic. I've heard that, too." Victor angled himself on the side of the desk. "Why are you calling me in the middle of the night, Mr. Jones?"

"Rancourt says we should talk. Seems to think your Foundation and the Arcane Society have a number of mutual interests."

"He may be right." Victor looked at Lucas, who was watching him with an intense expression. "Why don't we set up a meeting here in Vegas?"

"When?"

"Two weeks from now," Victor said. He did not take his eyes off Lucas. "My husband and I are on our way to Hawaii in the morning."

Lucas smiled.

Jones fell silent for a beat. "Isabella has been telling me we need a vacation."

"Who is Isabella?"

"My wife. Great plan, Arganbright. Two birds and so on. We'll meet you in the islands."

"What? Wait—"

Victor realized he was talking to himself. He looked at Lucas. "Some guy named Jones just hung up on me."

Lucas's eyes lit with amusement. "Sounds like the two of you have a few things in common. Let's go pack for Hawaii."

CHAPTER 55

Olivia was using a pair of kitchen shears to snip the sharp points off the tips of the leaves of two plump artichokes when she heard the front door open. She put the implement aside, wiped her hands on a dish towel and went down the hall.

Harlan walked through the door. He was in casual-day-at-the-office mode. Olivia doubted that anyone on the street or in the lobby of the apartment tower had bothered to give him a second glance, but when she went into her other senses, she was aware of the heat and power of his aura flooding the small space.

"I got your message saying you would be late," she said. "Is everything okay?"

"Everything is great. I hope."

He had a sack in one hand. In his other hand he gripped a cat carrier. A pair of glittering eyes surveyed her through the mesh screen. The cat made a cat sound. Olivia couldn't tell if the beast was viewing her with approval or disapproval.

"Okay," she said. "I did not see this coming."

"And you call yourself a psychic." Harlan kissed her soundly. When he raised his head, anticipation whispered in the atmosphere, but there was also a hint of anxiety. "This is Joe."

"Joe." Olivia looked down at the carrier. "The cat I was thinking of adopting the night you found me at the speed date event?"

"I hope it's the right Joe. I only got a glimpse of him on your phone that evening. When I went to the agency to see if he was still available, the staff told me that a cat named Joe seemed to be waiting for someone. He didn't have any objection to coming with me, but it turns out there's a lot of paperwork involved in this sort of thing. Also, I had to pick up cat food and kitty litter. The whole process turned out to be time-consuming. That's why I'm late."

He handed the cat carrier to Olivia. She took it in both hands, carried it into the living room and set it on the floor. She went into the kitchen and opened a can of expensive, line-caught, sashimi-grade albacore tuna and put it on a plate. She put the plate on the floor outside the carrier.

Joe watched the process with great attention. When everything was ready Olivia unlatched the screen.

"Hello, Joe," she said softly.

Joe stepped out of the carrier and gave her a long, considering look. Apparently satisfied, he butted his head against her hand.

"It's the right Joe," Olivia said.

Harlan smiled. "Joe the junkyard cat?"

"Joe the excellent cat."

"You're sure?" Harlan asked.

"Positive."

She reached out to stroke Joe. He tolerated her for a moment, sampled some of the food and then set out on an exploration of the living room. When he reached the collection of cat paraphernalia lined up under the window, he checked each item with great care.

Olivia smiled at Harlan. "I think he likes it here."

"I like it here, too," Harlan said.

Joe vaulted up onto the back of the cobalt blue sofa and stretched out in a regal pose.

"There's going to be cat hair on your sofa," Harlan warned.

"Who cares?" Olivia got to her feet. "We're all home. That's the most important thing."

"Yes," Harlan said. He opened his arms. "It is."

Olivia went to him with joy in her heart.

If she ever went missing, she had a man who would walk through hell to find her, and she had an excellent cat.

Home.

I hope you enjoyed *Lightning in a Mirror*. I absolutely loved writing it. I never set out to create a Jayneverse, but as my wonderful, insightful editor, Cindy Hwang, recently pointed out to me, it seems to have come into existence. When I look back I can see that I have been exploring it for a while now. I hope you will join me.

Readers who are familiar with the Jayneverse know that I write romantic suspense in three different fictional landscapes under three different names: contemporaries as Jayne Ann Krentz, historicals as Amanda Quick and futuristics as Jayne Castle.

If you are interested in the history and mystery of Fogg Lake, be sure to catch up with the first two books in the trilogy: *The Vanishing* and *All the Colors of Night*. Both are under my Jayne Ann Krentz name.

Those who read across my three worlds will have recognized some references to the Arcane Society in *Lightning in a Mirror*. To learn more about Fallon Jones and his psychic detective agency, try *In Too Deep*, written under my Jayne Ann Krentz name. As for

Vortex, it's been a problem for Arcane as well as the Foundation for quite a while. If you're interested to see what that crowd is up to in the future, try *Guild Boss*; I wrote that one under my Jayne Castle name.

As usual, for a complete list of my titles sorted by series and worlds, be sure to check out my website: jayneannkrentz.com.

Discover a breathtaking romantic suspense series by Jayne Ann Krentz ...

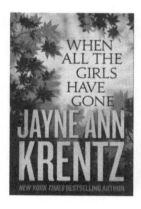 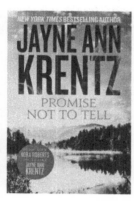 

Praise for the Cutler, Sutter & Salinas series:

'Jayne Ann Krentz is one of my favourite romantic suspense writers. I love her **feisty heroines, her sharp wit and humour**, family loyalty, and all the unexpected twists and turns. *When All the Girls Have Gone* has all of this and more and **will keep you guessing right until the end**'
—Meg Tilly on *When All The Girls Have Gone*

'**The master of romantic suspense** ... Krentz dives into sociopathic psychology and complex characterization to great effect in this twisty story, whose plot clips along at a **terrific pace**'
—*BookPage* on *Promise Not To Tell*

'A couple to root for, a tiny hint of the supernatural, **a page-burning plot** ... a **sexy, heart-warming romance**'
—*Kirkus Reviews* on *Untouchable*